BREAKING HEARTS

BOOK 7 OF THE
SEAL TEAM HEARTBREAKERS SERIES

Teresa J. Reasor

This is a work of fiction. Names, characters, places, and incidents are the product of the author's imagination or are used fictitiously, and any resemblance to actual persons, living or dead, business establishments, events, or locales is entirely coincidental.

BREAKING HEARTS
A SEAL TEAM HEARTBREAKER NOVEL

COPYRIGHT © 2018 by Teresa J. Reasor

Contact Information: teresareasor@msn.com

Cover Art by Tracy Stewart
Edited by Faith Freewoman

Teresa J. Reasor
PO Box 124
Corbin, KY 40702

Publishing History: First Edition 2017

ISBN-13: 978-1-940047-14-0
ISBN-10: 1-940047-14-5
Print Edition

TABLE OF CONTENTS

PROLOGUE

Iraq 2011

Ensign Daniel Rivera, aka Bowie, gripped the edge of the truck bed and held on as the vehicle spun around the corner. Derrick Armstrong shouted out directions to Greenback, their driver, as he read the GPS. The engine revved and the transmission ground with every shift. Steam shot out from under the hood.

The Iraqi insurgents driving this hunk of junk had borne down on them, spraying gunfire, so his SEAL team took steps to *commandeer* the vehicle. It wasn't like the assholes were going to miss it. And damaged as it was, it still beat the hell out of the hide-and-seek drill they'd been doing with the Talaban on foot.

A small pickup just like the one they were riding in fell in behind them. The tango in the passenger seat fired from the cab while two more popped up from the bed to fire over the top.

Bowie dove behind the tailgate for cover and Hawk grunted as he banged his injured knee, now swollen the size of a soccer ball. Doc, their medic, covered Brett Weaver with his body. Weaver, unconscious for nearly two hours, didn't look like he was going to wake anytime soon—if ever.

Bowie raised his Mk5 submachine gun and opened fire in the direction of the truck without aiming, the gun bucking in his hands. Then he darted up to see if he'd hit anything. Bullet holes pockmarked the windshield, and a spiderweb of cracks frosted the passenger side. The tango in the passenger seat wasn't firing anymore.

Greenback weaved the pickup back and forth, somehow dodging the hail of bullets. Bowie had never been seasick, but Greenback's driving was making his stomach churn. But still better that than bullet holes.

He waited for the tangos to fire again. A head popped up. Flash, the sniper of their team, fired from beside him before Bowie could take aim, and the insurgent fell back out of sight. Bowie opened fire again. He and Flash got a tag team thing going, keeping the guys in the truck behind them pinned down.

Another truck skidded around the corner in pursuit. Hawk opened fire on that one from Bowie's other side, hitting the hood and the windshield. The Toyota swerved back and forth across the road, on the point of wiping out, but by some perverse miracle the driver regained control and fell in behind the first truck, using it for cover.

Hawk's voice carried from beside him, warning the chopper it would be a hot extract and reciting the coordinates of their extraction point.

Bullets pinged against the back of the truck, and the smell of gasoline intensified.

"We're losing gas," Greenback yelled out the shattered back window at the back of the cab.

Armstrong yelled back, "We're only a hundred yards from the extraction point."

"Flash, guard our back door. Bowie, I'm going to need help. Doc…" Hawk shouted above the wind tearing at his words.

"I've got Brett covered," Doc yelled back.

"Everybody hold on," Greenback shouted over his shoulder. "We're going off-road."

Doc threw himself over Brett again and braced an arm under his head to cushion it on the makeshift stretcher. They hit the rough terrain of the desert, driving over scrub brush and rock-packed areas with bone-bruising jerks and lurches.

The truck's engine died, and Flash jumped out to lower the

tailgate. Doc and Bowie dragged Brett out of the truck bed, and Doc tossed him over his shoulders in a fireman's carry and ran toward the extraction point.

While Hawk maneuvered his softball-sized knee out of the truck, Bowie turned his Mk-5 on the truck barreling down on them. He cut loose on it, and the vehicle rolled to a stop, the driver as motionless as his dead passenger.

Four tangos bailed out of the bed and sprayed bullets helter-skelter, hitting the truck the team had abandoned with hollow plunks of punctured metal.

"Get a move on, guys. I've left a little surprise behind for the ones on our ass," Strongman said into his com. Bowie slung Hawk's arm over his shoulder and they double-timed it in a zig-zag out into the desert.

Strongman, Greenback, and Flash leapfrogged behind Hawk and Bowie, taking turns protecting their back door. Three more trucks pulled up, loaded with men.

Bowie tensed, waiting for the baseball-bat impact of a bullet between his shoulder blades while more bullets whizzed by. To give him credit, Hawk somehow kept up with him, though his teeth were bared in a grimace, and he huffed as he breathed through the pain.

An explosion rumbled behind them, and Bowie turned to see the truck they vacated leap into the air and fly apart, slinging shrapnel in all directions. Several men lay motionless on the ground.

Doc waved an arm, urging them toward him, and a depression in the ground opened in front of them like the answer to a prayer. Bowie leaped down and tried to offer some support while Hawk did the same. The two of them lay down covering fire while Flash, Greenback, and Strongman double-timed it toward them. The three leaped into the depression and spread out to defend their location.

Brett's unconscious form lay in the center, reminding every-one of what could happen to any of them, at any time.

Bowie watched Brett's still form for two beats before turning back to the thirty or more armed tangoes making their way across the dry-packed earth and thick scrub. Every few seconds a shot whipped by and pinged into the ground.

Bowie kept his eyes on the quarter of space he was defending. Tangos crept closer across the open field.

"Hold your fire until they're close enough to drop them," Hawk whispered into his com. "Every shot counts." They were all running low on ammo.

Bowie pulled four grenades out of his vest and set them on the ground in front of him while he took cover behind a spindly plant.

The stray shots were slowing as the group continued to grow by two more truckloads of men. The Taliban fuckers were spreading out, searching for them. Bowie's stomach tightened, but he continued to breathe evenly to calm the sudden rush of anxiety. It was going to get hairy. He counted a ten-to-one ratio.

Bowie set his trigger to do three-round bursts and focused in on the lead tango closest to him, blocking off everything else.

"Fire when ready," Hawk's voice remained dead calm.

The leader was twenty-five feet to the left when Bowie fired. The tango dropped to his knees and did a face-plant. Shots went off all around him as the rest of the team got in on the action. Return fire hit the dirt ten feet to his right as he took out two more. He inched farther right and hit another.

Silence settled in as the tangos took cover and crawled forward. Brush nearby waved and Bowie fired. Everything went still again.

Hawk was on the radio requesting air support when the attack started. Bowie switched the trigger setting to full auto. Bullets whizzed by his head so many times he thought only God could be diverting them.

Five minutes crawled by. Hawk popped smoke at the last minute and yelled into the com, "Take cover." Bowie dove as close to the center of the depression as he could to help cover Brett. All six of his teammates joined him.

He slapped his night vision goggles up and covered his ears.

The ground shook, and the world went bright for what seemed like minutes, though it couldn't have been more than a second or two. The first two explosions were followed by several bursts of machine-gun fire, then more explosions so close he'd swear he could feel the heat off the ordnance.

Silence followed, and each one of them eased back from the pile. Doc checked Brett's pulse. It was then Bowie realized Cutter wasn't coming back from this. If the explosions couldn't snap him out of it, nothing would. And what the fuck had happened to him? He reached out to touch Brett's shoulder. He had the head injury before Hawk went in to get him.

Which meant someone tried to kill him, and it wasn't a tango.

"This is Alpha-bravo-four-niner. Remaining targets are bugging out. We're ready for extract, but this will be a hot extract." Hawk said into the radio, his voice calm and all business, but Bowie could read the relief on his face.

Five minutes later a Chinook came over the rise and landed. They hustled across the field, with Strongman hefting Brett and wasted no time getting aboard.

Once aboard, Bowie leaned back in the hard, unyielding seat, taking the time to study each of his teammates, one after the other. Not Flash or Greenback, they never entered the building. Not Hawk, he'd gone back into the building to get Brett. Not Doc, he'd worked like hell to keep Cutter going.

And it sure as hell wasn't him.

His gaze settled on Strongman Derrick Armstrong. He didn't want to go there. Derrick had saved his life more than once and covered his back every mission. As Bowie did his. And Derrick carted Cutter's unconscious body from the mission site to here. They were a team. All of them.

Or were they?

CHAPTER 1

THERE WAS NOTHING worse than running into one of the women he'd dated and not being able to remember her name. He hated the look of disappointment and hurt they shot him when he slipped up and couldn't remember where he met them or the small details of their dates. It made him feel guilty and defensive, which pissed him off. Not at them, but at himself.

One woman blended into the next between deployments. He hadn't slept with them all...not that he could ever convince his teammates that he hadn't. Their eagerness to believe in his legend was a thorn in his side at times.

So what if he enjoyed women? He was a red-blooded, hetero-sexual male. What did they expect?

He was getting all worked up, and the woman in question had yet to turn around so he could get a look at her.

She might not be one of the many. But there was something distinctly familiar about her. The way she stood, the perky way her ass filled out her black slacks—the way her sun-streaked, light brown hair hung between her shoulder blades with just enough curl to look like a neat row of upside down question marks—niggled at the edge of his brain like a word that just wouldn't come.

The bank teller at the window beckoned for her to step forward. Since he was standing four people behind her, he couldn't hear her voice or what was said, but the way her back and shoulders stiffened didn't bode well.

"I want to speak with the bank manager."

He heard that clearly, but with an added note of stress in her voice, it didn't help. But she was just so damned familiar.

The teller stepped to the phone. In just a few seconds a tall, well-dressed, balding man appeared. "Please come into my office, Mrs. Harper."

Mrs. Harper. No, he'd never dated a married woman. Maybe she got married after they dated. Good. If she was already hitched, she wouldn't be interested in renewing their acquaintance. Relief relaxed the muscles in his neck and shoulders.

Two minutes later the young, attractive brunette teller beckoned to him. "I'm so sorry we're having trouble with our drive-through, Mr. Rivera." She smiled at him.

Mister instead of Lieutenant sounded strange. "No problem." He laid the two pieces of paper he held on the counter. "I just need to cash these two checks."

"I'll take care of that right now."

She was back in less than a minute with the money, counting the bills out for him, placing them in the envelope and sliding it across to him. When she tapped the top, he noticed the writing on the flap and picked it up. "Call me. I'd like to get to know you," was written on it with a number and the name Melissa.

He smiled. "I'm only on leave for a few days, and I'm on my way out of town, but maybe when I get back..." He left it hanging.

Her smile tipped over into a grin. "I'll be here."

"Thanks, Melissa."

He strode to the exit and pushed through the first door. Sensing someone behind him, he paused to hold the door open for the woman.

Recognition zapped him like a bolt of lightning.

Alayna Wieland. He never thought to see her again. Never thought he'd want to see her again. He automatically reached for her, and his palm skimmed her shoulder as, head down, she rushed past him and hit the exterior door with both hands. He caught it as it swung back and took two paces out to follow her. She paused at the top of the sidewalk, her body stiff, her hands fisted. Things had obviously not gone well in the bank.

"Alayna."

She turned, and shock bolted across her face, her lips parted, eyes wide, and her brows shot up. "Bowie..." She sounded as breathless as he felt.

Ten years had passed since he last saw her, but she hadn't changed much. Her hair still lay wavy and thick across her shoulders, her pale green eyes looked bright as peridots. The need to touch her rose, hungry and insistent. He fisted his hands at his sides to fight the urge. Moments ticked by as they stared at each other.

A kaleidoscope of memories raced through his mind. Alayna naked beneath him, her body moving in response to his. Alayna basking in the sun, her skin a beautiful gold against his duskier tone. Holding her as close as another layer of skin while they slow danced on the dock at the pond on her father's ranch. Lying together on an air mattress in the bed of his rusty truck and talking about their future. Her tearstained face when their families clashed and she'd broken it off.

She drew a deep breath. "Bowie..." She seemed at a loss about what to say. "I-I need to go and pick up my children."

"Children." Of course, she had moved on with her life. Just as he had. "How many?"

"I have three. All girls. Six, four, and two."

At least she hadn't moved on as soon as he was gone. "That's incredible. You always said you wanted a big family." Those could have been his children. Emotion churned in his belly.

"Bowie..." There was a catch in her voice and a look of uncertainty in her eyes. "You're okay?" She seemed distressed.

Right now he wasn't so sure. "I'm in the Navy. Six years. A Lieutenant." He looked her directly in the eyes. "No wife, no kids." She left him emotionally stranded, but he'd survived. Thank God for his rage. It kept him motivated for a year, and by then he stayed focused because he had to. Some of the pain bubbled up inside him now. Ten years, and he still hadn't gotten over it.

"That's…that's good. Wonderful."

He raised a brow.

"It suits you. You're fit and tan, and you have the air of someone who's extremely focused."

He ducked his head. "I learned that long before I enlisted." A note of bitterness came through he couldn't control. He cleared his throat. "I won't keep you. You have kids to pick up, and I have friends waiting for me." Not true. Doc bailed at the last minute due to a scheduling snafu on post. And the rest were deployed.

Cut loose from his team, he felt at sea while he waited for re-assignment. And working BUD/S training at Coronado was getting old.

He nodded. "Goodbye, Alayna."

She looked stricken at his abrupt tone, but murmured, "'Bye."

Though it was the last thing he wanted to do, he brushed past her and walked away.

ALAYNA FOLLOWED BOWIE'S progress as he strode down the sidewalk to his car. He was still angry. And she didn't have the energy to defend herself. Didn't have a clue how she'd defend herself. She purposely hurt him to keep him safe, but at this point he probably wouldn't care why she broke things off with him. He'd moved on with his life.

She had tried to move on too, but failed miserably. Three children and a broken marriage later, she was right back where she was after graduating from high school. Alone, broke, and still longing for something she lost ten years ago.

Would she have contacted Bowie if she'd known he lived here? Probably. She wouldn't have been able to resist. But she'd done enough damage ten years ago. Her family did enough damage to them both. Damage she had plenty of time to regret. Ten years of grief, regret and longing. She made so many mistakes, and never figured out a way to fight her father *and* protect Bowie. Her father had the law on his side, and Bowie's life would have been over if she hadn't walked away from him.

Even that hadn't saved her from one of the most painful episodes of her life. Seeing him brought it all rushing back.

She glanced at him as he paused next to his car. He was still gorgeous. Even more gorgeous than in high school, which she never would have believed possible.

He was older, of course, and more muscular, his shoulders broader. It was hard not to stare at him and just drink him in. The well-defined muscles were delineated by the gray T-shirt hugging every one of them. He still had those compelling, chocolate brown eyes with a striking rim of gold around the iris, and a manly face that could cause angels to weep. But he hadn't smiled, so she didn't get to see those dimples.

She was close to weeping as she trudged down the sidewalk to her car.

She couldn't believe the police had frozen her bank account because of an investigation into her ex-husband's real estate dealings, dealings she never had any part in.

How she was supposed to pay her bills and feed her girls? She needed to go to the police station and talk to someone. If she couldn't provide a home for her children, even if it was because of something Aaron did, he'd go to court to take the girls away from her. He didn't want them, of course. He just wanted her to suffer.

She hit the key fob, unlocked her car, and reached for the door handle. Her attention was drawn back to Bowie. She'd probably never see him again. He turned and looked toward her over the tops of the cars.

For a moment their eyes met. Her heart rose up to choke her. She'd loved him since she was fifteen. Wanted to marry him, have his children. They had such plans for after graduation—college, a home, a family. "I'm sorry." The words came out a whisper.

An engine revved behind her, and gravel shot across the asphalt when the vehicle braked. Alayna turned and eyed the van blocking her car. The side door opened, and two men leaped out, their faces covered by stocking masks. When they both rushed toward her, she stumbled back and turned to run.

The two men swooped down on her and grabbed her arms. She screamed, twisted and turned in their grasp, then attempted to dig in her heels. They lifted her off her feet. She squirmed and kicked, hitting the calf of the guy on her right. He stumbled.

A another man leapt from the side, slid across the trunk of her car, and hit the attacker on her left mid-body. They all went down sideways, hard. The only thing that saved her from being hurt was the cushion provided by the guy on her right. She planted an elbow in his gut as she struggled to jerk away and get up.

Bowie rolled onto his knees. The kidnapper beneath him struck out, hitting him in the jaw and rocking his head back. Bowie punched the guy in the face, reared up, and grabbed her arm, his fingers digging in as the man on her right held onto her arm at the same time. She was a rag doll between the two men, their fingers bruising her. She kicked the guy at her feet in the balls, and her skin burned as she was wrenched from his grip. Though he was groaning, he grabbed her ankle, and she pulled her foot free, losing a shoe, and scrambled to get her legs moving.

Bowie half-dragged, half-carried her away from the van and the men. The two kidnappers ran after them toward the bank until a security guard rushed out the front door, his weapon drawn.

The two turned tail and ran to the van, jumped inside, and the vehicle peeled off and shot away.

Alayna bent at the waist and braced a hand on one knee to catch her breath. There'd been little time to feel scared until now. Now she was shaking with adrenaline and shock. All the possibilities raced through her head. White slavery, rape, murder. Dear God.

"Alayna." Bowie's voice dragged her thoughts away from what could have happened and back to what was. "You okay?"

"Yes." She straightened, and the world tilted, going grayish-black for a moment, then righted itself. Bowie grabbed her elbow to steady her until everything came back into focus.

The security guard looked like a boy scout with a gun. "Come inside the building, ma'am, until the police get here. I've already called them."

"I have to pick up my children."

"Is there someone you can call, Alayna?" Bowie asked.

"No." Who had time to make friends when you worked fifty hours a week and cared for three children? "They're at my ex-husband's house, and if I'm five minutes late…" He didn't need to hear about the state of her relationship with her ex. Why would he care? After what she'd done to him, after what her father planned to do, and her brother had done, he'd probably think she deserved whatever she got.

"Call him." He handed her his phone. "I think an attempted kidnapping is a good enough reason for being late."

Her hands shook as she trailed a finger across the screen to open it and dialed the number. The phone rang several times, and no one answered. "They must be outside in the backyard." Which didn't ease her anxiety. She hoped someone was out watching the children. The pool was right there, just waiting for an accident to happen. And Rosa couldn't swim without her floaties.

"I'll call Aaron's cell." She'd hear about that later, too. She dialed the number. The muscles in her shoulders and back tightened as she braced to defend herself. The phone went to voice mail after only three rings. If Aaron was playing at his passive-aggressive bullshit, she'd lose it when she saw him. She'd lose it even worse if something happened to her children while they were at his house.

"No one's answering."

"They're probably outside grilling burgers. As soon as the police have taken your statement, you can go get them."

If only he knew. It was never that easy.

CHAPTER 2

THESE TWO DETECTIVES needed training in victim advocacy. They were more interested in extracting as much information about her ex-husband than the two men who'd attempted to drag her into the van.

"Has your husband ever asked you to sign paperwork for him?"

"Ex-husband, Detective Gray. We've been divorced for three years. You do realize he's married to someone else now?" The detective suited his name so well. With his gray hair, brows, suit, and gray-blue eyes, how could his name be anything else? His well-worn features settled into a bulldog scowl.

"Yes. We are aware of that."

"Then why are you purposely calling him my husband? He is the father of my children, but absolutely nothing else to me anymore. And if you've looked up our history in court, you know I've had to take him before a judge several times just to get the court-ordered child support payments. Knowing that I'm determined to make sure he follows the letter of the law, and I keep forcing him to support his children, do you really think he'd want me to have any part in his business dealings?"

"When you were married to him…"

"No. *Never.* Aaron *never* gave me access to any money other than grocery money. He had his thumb on everything. Including my paycheck."

She changed the subject back to the earlier attack. "The two men who tried to drag me into the van wore stocking masks over their faces, but they were Caucasian, had dark hair, and were wearing coveralls and gloves. I didn't see the driver. The van was white and opened on both sides, but they only opened one door. There was an emblem of some kind on the side. I'd be happy to look through a database to identify it if you have one."

"We've already recovered the van, Mrs. Harper," Gray's partner, Detective Stansberry, said. "It was discovered four blocks from here in an apartment complex parking lot."

Stansberry had been in and out several times when his phone buzzed. At least he'd been doing some investigating into the attempted kidnapping.

"I no longer go by that name. I've gone back to my maiden name of Wieland. And thank you very much for letting me know. What are you going to do about the three men who tried to abduct me? Or isn't that important enough to even discuss?" Her composure started to crumble, but she beat back every emotion but anger.

Detective Stansberry continued. "We're processing the van, and we're checking traffic cameras in the area to see which direction the men fled. We think they probably changed vehicles."

Duh. She looked first at one then the other. "Neither of you really give a damn, do you? This is all about Aaron, isn't it?"

Detective Gray persisted. "Has Mr. Harper ever threatened you?"

"He's threatened to take my children away from me. He's threatened to take me to court and attempt to prove I'm an unfit mother, though I don't drink, smoke, take drugs, gamble, or even date. He's threatened to get me fired from my job. My boss finally had to file a restraining order against him so he can't come onto the property to harass me, him, or his clients. He's threatened to torch my car.

"And yes, he's threatened me with bodily harm. But he's never done any of that in front of witnesses other than the girls, so it's my word against his. I do have one rant recorded on my phone where he calls me a whore and threatens to hire men to testify against me in court to prove I'm unfit. I recorded it last week. I can play it for you if you want to hear it."

The two partners exchanged a glance. "He's being investigated for several forms of real estate fraud and trust fund mismanagement. Four of his clients have come forward, and we think there may be more soon."

"And you froze my accounts, because...?" She raised her brows.

"We had to be sure he wasn't laundering some of the money through your accounts."

"The money that goes into my bank account is *mine*. I earn it working every day as a paralegal at the firm of Kappes, North, and Black. You can look through the records and see the money going into my account is direct-deposited from my office. I feed my children from that account. I keep a roof over their heads by paying my bills out of that account. I want it unfrozen. *Now*."

Detective Stansberry said, "But the money he gives you each month for the children isn't."

"That goes into a separate account. I only touch it if I have an emergency, like taking one of the children to the doctor." She was going to go off any minute. "Take the damn money out of that account and..." She caught back the words *ram it up your ass* with an effort. "...keep it. I don't give a damn. But I have to have access to my account to feed my children."

Detective Gray's scowl deepened. "Does your ex-husband have a life insurance policy on you or your children?"

Her mouth flew open. Tingles of shock ran over her scalp like a thousand needles. The sensation raced down the back of her neck. Dear God, the children were with him. "He took out a policy on me when we first got married. I don't know if he still has it."

"How well do you know Lieutenant Rivera?" Gray's partner asked.

"We were close friends back in high school. We dated. I haven't seen him in ten years. It was a fluke, our running into each other today."

"It's damn strange he was suddenly Johnny-on-the-spot on the day you're attacked."

She thought about it for a moment. She had hurt Bowie, badly. Rejected him. Her brother had hurt his family worse.

Though he was outnumbered, he'd still taken on the guys who had attacked her. "Unless Bowie Rivera has changed a hell of a lot in the last ten years, he's the last man on the planet who would hurt me."

"Why would you say that?"

"It isn't in him to hurt a woman. *Ever.* And I'm leaving now. You're wasting my time and yours, and I need to go get my children."

ALAYNA WAS A woman under siege. Through a narrow, vertical glass in the door, Bowie watched the interactions between her and the detectives who converged on the bank ten minutes after the attempted kidnapping. They were grilling her. He'd witnessed enough interrogations to know. But what were they after?

He'd seen a lot of ugliness in his line of work as a SEAL. He didn't want to imagine any of it directed at the people he knew or cared about. Had he not been there to intervene, the assholes would have muscled her into the van, and God knows what would have happened next. Rape, torture… Worse.

He homed in on Alayna's body language. At first she'd been anxious, shaken, then nervous. Now she was pissed. Her eyes were narrowed, and her jaw tensed. She rose, grabbed her purse, and stood nearly nose-to-nose with the older detective though he stood a head taller than she was. She stalked to the door and yanked it open.

"We're not finished here, Ms. Wieland," the older detective said.

"Yes, we are."

With her cheeks flushed and her eyes narrowed, she reminded him of the Texas girl she'd once been. Or the girl he'd believed her to be.

"If Aaron has done what you believe he has, arrest him. If he's a threat to me and my children, you have an obligation to arrest him. I've reported his behavior toward me to you. And right now my children are with him. And I need to go get them. Unless you want to go in and get them for me."

The detective hadn't expected that. "We're on the brink of an arrest. But we're still gathering evidence."

"So you're happy leaving my children in his custody while you keep me here asking questions?"

"Do you believe he's capable of hurting his children?"

"If Aaron Harper wants to hurt me, they're the one sure way to do it. And that's why I'm going after them."

She rushed out into the hall, her purse clutched against her because the strap broke during the struggle. Bowie stood, and she stopped in front of him. She trembled visibly as she dragged in hard, shaky breaths. She seemed to be holding onto her composure by a very thin thread.

"Bowie, thank you for everything you did. But I need to ask a huge favor. I know I have no right to ask anything of you, but…if you're willing to go to my ex-husband's house with me, I'd appreciate it."

He'd hung around to make certain she was okay because he felt guilty as hell about the short way he'd spoken to her. And now she was asking him to get involved.

Hell, he already was. He'd saved her from those assholes. And the cops didn't seem interested in the possibility that they might try again. *What the hell?*

He raised a brow at the two detectives. Were these assholes really more interested in a white-collar crime than the threat to a woman and her kids? What the fuck? "Sure. I'll go with you."

He followed her down the hall to the main bank lobby. Her gait was uneven because for some weird reason, even though one shoe had disappeared, she refused to take the other one off. It made him smile.

She seemed stronger, more stubborn than she was in high school. A divorce and raising three kids alone probably had a hand in that. This was a different woman from the one he knew ten years ago. But then he'd changed in too many ways to count, too.

She stormed out the front door and slowed as her bare foot met the concrete sidewalk. He touched her elbow lightly. "I think my car might be safer. If the guys who attempted to take you are targeting you specifically, they'll be on the lookout for your car, Alayna."

She hesitated, her brows drawn together in a frown. "Is that what the policeman who interviewed you said?"

"No, but this was an organized attack. Whether it was random or not, they had to have followed you here."

She seemed to take in what he said calmly enough, but her hand shook as she brushed her hair back from her face.

"I can't leave my car here in the parking lot indefinitely. They'll tow it."

"Let's get the kids first. Then we'll decide what to do about your car."

"Okay."

"Do you have car seats for the baby and other girls?"

"Yes, they're in my car."

"I'll move my SUV over to yours and we'll transfer them."

He walked beside her to his vehicle, but didn't attempt to touch her, even though he wanted to. She'd been manhandled, then intimidated by the cops. His experience with hostages told him she didn't need another man getting too close. Not yet.

It took a few minutes, but he got the car seats installed and transferred a couple of stuffed animals and a bag with clothes and pull-up diapers for her two-year-old. The normalcy of the whole thing seemed to calm her. She tried her ex-husband's number again, and once again it went to voice mail.

"There's something wrong. Aaron isn't picking up."

"We'll be there in a few minutes." He backed out of the parking space and pulled out into traffic. "I'm going to need directions."

"They live on Coronado island. On Glorietta Boulevard."

So the guy she'd married was rich. He had to be to live on the island.

"Are you going to tell me what's going on?" he asked.

"I think my ex is up to his neck in bad real estate deals, and they've frozen his bank accounts and mine. Because of this attempted kidnapping, they think he may have hired someone to…to…."

Jesus! He glanced in her direction. "And you walked out of there without protection?"

"They weren't going to offer me protection, Bowie. They're only interested in what I know about Aaron's business. They weren't even interested in the kidnapping. It was of secondary interest to them—at best. One was working one angle while the other one did bad cop to try and intimidate me."

She pushed the icon on her phone again. "Bliss isn't answering either."

"Bliss?"

"His new wife."

"Is that really her name?"

"Yes. As far as I know."

"Sounds like a hooker."

"I don't think she's ever done that. Or at least I hope not."

If the ex had hired these guys to kidnap and kill her, he might have taken the kids and his new wife and run for it. He glanced at Alayna again. She gripped the phone like it was a lifeline, and her focus remained ahead, as though every mile was a hundred. If he said out loud what he was thinking, she'd lose it.

He concentrated on weaving through the traffic. When they reached the bridge leading across the bay to Coronado, she seemed to relax some. He followed her directions through a hodgepodge of homes of different sizes, styles, and ages. Some looked modern and new while others looked like they'd been there for decades. They pulled up in front of a two-story white house with an upper floor balcony and a large two-car garage. Picture windows stretched across the second story, reflecting the cloudless blue sky overhead.

Bowie got out of the car and walked around to open her door. She slid down out of the car, took her remaining shoe off, and tossed it on the passenger floorboard.

Gripping her cell phone in one hand and her purse in the other, she marched down the sidewalk toward the front door.

"Is this where you lived before the divorce?" he asked.

"No. We had a small three-bedroom house in Linda Vista. He moved here as soon as he sold that house and married Bliss."

Bowie's stomach tensed as they climbed the two steps to the covered porch and reached the front door. She rang the bell, and he could hear it it peal through the house. When no one answered, she opened the storm door and knocked. Silence stretched, and she knocked again, harder.

She gripped the doorknob and twisted. The door opened easily. She hesitated then took a tentative step forward to stick her head in the door. "Bliss? Anybody home?"

Bowie wished for his Sig. There was too much room for something to go wrong if they entered the house without being invited.

"Bliss?" Alayna took two big steps into the foyer. "Emilia? Addison? Rosa?" The pitch of her voice rose. Brackets appeared around her mouth, along with two lines between her brows. "Em?"

A faint sound came from somewhere in the depths of the house. It was impossible to tell whether it was upstairs or down.

Bowie caught her by the shoulder as she started forward. "We stick together, Alayna. And you stay behind me."

She nodded.

They passed through an expansive, open living room with a white leather sectional and glass-topped tables. The furniture was big, comfortable, and expensive. An ottoman as big as his kitchen table stood in the center of the room.

"Emilia?" Alayna called out.

On the left was a dining room. The formal table and chairs

were just as expensive and proportional to the space. A china cabinet filled with glassware graced one wall, and a wet bar the other. Alayna moved to look behind the bar, then shook her head.

Bowie strode forward into the kitchen and froze. A woman lay beside the island that stretched horizontally across the open space. Blood and other tissue splattered across the counter of the island and some of the cabinets. Her blond hair was matted with it on one side. He knew from a glance that she was already gone. A high-velocity bullet had entered the side of her head and left an exit wound the size of a fist. Jesus!

He held up a hand. Alayna stopped.

"Don't come in here," he ordered. He was careful where he placed his feet as he backed away.

CHAPTER 3

ONE LOOK AT Bowie's face and Alayna's throat went dry as sunbaked sand. She tried to swallow and couldn't. "What is it?"

"There's a blond woman on the floor. She's dead. We need to dial 911 and get the police out here."

"It has to be Bliss," she whispered. "But who would have killed her? Not Aaron. She didn't want to think Aaron would have done something like that with the girls in the house. He was more about passive-aggressive manipulation and empty threats—until he wasn't. Where were her girls? To keep from screaming, she called for her daughters instead, her voice cracking with panic. "Emilia? Addison? Rosa?"

A dull thumping sounded from somewhere past the kitchen was followed by a faint, high-pitched mumble. "There's a mud-room and laundry just through that doorway. Please…"

"Come on." He beckoned for her to come forward, but positioned his body to block her view of the woman. He needn't have bothered. She couldn't bring herself to look. They reached the mudroom together, and Bowie opened the door and eased through. "It's clear."

Alayna rushed into the room. "Emilia?"

A dull thump came from the door to the left. It was the laundry room. "Mommy!" Her daughter's voice came through the solid wood door. Alayna rushed forward to move a heavy wooden bench out of the way, and Bowie helped her.

She opened the door to find Emilia standing there, her blond curls tangled about her shoulders and darkened at the neck with sweat. Her face glistened with it. She threw her arms around Alayna's legs.

Addison sat on the floor with Rosa next to her, Rosa clinging to her monkey while Addison held them both. Both rolled to their feet and scampered to her as fast as their chubby legs could carry them. Their hot, sticky, precious little bodies pressed against her wherever they could, and she held them tight, her breath hitching.

The room, stuffy with the afternoon heat, smelled rank. Probably a dirty diaper.

"Rosa had to go potty in the bucket, Momma. We helped her," Emilia said pointing at a small mop bucket. "Bliss told us we had to stay quiet. Not to make a sound. We didn't for a long time, but it was hot, and Rosa cried."

The ditzy blond Aaron married saved her children's lives. She regretted thinking even one unkind thought about the woman. Tears streamed down her face, and she brushed them away. "You did good, Sugar Pop. Real good."

Rosa clung to her arm, and she touched her baby's flushed face and clutched her close. The room was hot and smelled horrible. She hiked the toddler on her hip and brushed at the sweat-dampened curls clinging to Rosa's face and the back of her neck.

From her position half behind her right leg, Addison pointed at Bowie. "Who are you?"

He knelt on the floor in front of her and spoke just above a whisper. "I'm your mother's friend, Daniel, but you can call me Bowie. We came to get you and take you home."

"Okay." Addie plopped down on her bottom and started putting on her shoes, a skill she'd just mastered. Once she was finished, she raised her arms to Bowie, and he lifted her. "We need to get out of here and make that call," he urged.

"We can go out the back door and walk around to the front. The girls need water, and there's bottled water in the pool house."

Now she held her children, the horror of what happened here was sinking in, and her composure threatened to crumble. She had to keep it together for the children. She grabbed Emilia's hand.

Bowie led the way, then urged her forward in front of him. They exited the house onto a concrete patio surrounding the backyard pool.

She went directly to the pool house, which was more a large gazebo with a bathroom and bar, and got cold bottled water from the small fridge there, opening one for each of the girls and offering one to Bowie.

Emilia climbed into a cushioned rattan seat, and Addie soon joined her. She gave a bottle to each of them. She sat in a similar chair next to them and held Rosa on her lap, cupping her chin to keep the water she guided into her mouth from splashing her clothes. Rosa held her monkey up. "Bebe drink." Alayna pretended to give it a sip.

How long had they been locked inside that room? They could have become dehydrated.

She grabbed a towel hanging over the back of one of the chairs, wet it with some of the cold water and wiped Rosa's sweaty face and sticky hands. She needed a bath and a new pull-up, but for now Alayna took her into the bathroom to clean her up a little.

When they emerged, Bowie was standing outside the pool house while he talked on the phone. His eyes were never still as he scoped out the area. He climbed the two steps to the interior of the pool house, out of the sun, and leaned against the edge of the door, standing guard, his phone never leaving his hand.

She felt calmer for having him with her. Had she entered the house alone she'd have been terrified. "What do you do in the Navy, Bowie?"

He didn't glance in her direction, but kept his attention focused on the backyard gate and the house. "I'm a SEAL."

She'd read about them. Seen documentaries about them. They'd taken down Bin Laden.

He was trained to kill terrorists.

The way he put his body in front of hers as they went through the house. The way he blocked her view of Bliss on the floor. The easy way he picked up Addie and carried her to the pool house. He kept his body between them and the house the whole time. She pressed her cheek against Rosa's to hide the tears choking her.

"You okay?" he asked from the door.

"Yes. Just a little overwhelmed."

"The cops will be here soon."

A siren wailed in the distance, louder every second until it screamed from the front of the house and then died.

BOWIE LEANED BACK in the chair, crossed his arms over his chest, and closed his eyes. He might as well get in a nap, since it didn't look like he was going to the cabin tonight, and the cops were pulling a let's-sweat-the-guy-who-found-the-dead-body routine.

Of course they couldn't tie him to a murder when he'd been somewhere else when it happened. He'd fucking been with them. And why were they looking at him? Because he'd run into an old girlfriend five minutes before she was attacked? What possible part did they think he could have played in this?

The door opened at the same time a cell phone rang. The person paused to answer the phone, and Bowie semi-listened to Gray's conversation all about vomiting, temperatures, and calling the doctor. Sounded like a sick kid.

When the detective finally walked into the room, Bowie took his time about opening his eyes and acknowledging him. He raised a brow as Detective Gray sat down across the table from him.

"Lieutenant Rivera, I had a long talk with your CO, Lieutenant Commander Yazzie. He gave you a resounding alibi, as could a whole class of SEAL BUD/S trainees, so you've been cleared of any involvement in this."

Bowie remained silent.

"I need to ask you what you saw at the house when you and Ms. Wieland arrived?"

"We arrived at the house around eighteen-fifty. The house was quiet. The driveway empty. Nothing looked disturbed."

"Then?"

"Alayna rang the bell, and no one answered. She knocked twice. The same. Then she opened the door and called out. The place was quiet, and I heard a faint knocking sound from somewhere, but couldn't really tell where it was coming from."

"Did you go upstairs?"

"No. We walked through the living room. Nothing seemed out of place. She was behind me when we reached the kitchen, and I told her not to come into the room. There was a woman on the floor next to the island. She'd been shot in the head. There was a small amount of blood on the floor, but other matter sprayed across some of the cabinets and the countertop. I knew she was dead without checking for a pulse.

"Did you touch anything?"

"No. The knocking sound was louder, and we could hear a faint voice. I touched the doorknob to open the door to what she called the mudroom. Poked my head in to make certain it was clear, and we went in. A chest had been shoved in front of the laundry room door. We moved it.

"The kids were inside. We took them out the back door to the pool house. The girls were overheated, and Alayna got them water from a small refrigerator while I called 911. Nothing seemed disturbed out back either."

"Was the back door locked?"

"No. I stood guard while Alayna cooled the girls down with a wet towel in the pool house and we waited for you guys to arrive. The first patrol car arrived at nineteen-ten."

"Okay." Gray stood. "That's all I need. You can go."

Bowie shoved to his feet. "You're going to provide Alayna and the kids protection, aren't you?"

"I'd like to, but our budget doesn't stretch to that or a safe house."

Heat flared in Bowie's face. "What are you going to do? Use her and the kids for bait?"

Gray's face went rigid. "No. We're not. We'll send patrols by the apartment every hour, but short of putting Ms. Wieland in protective custody and putting her children in foster care... You can imagine her response when we suggested that. We've urged her to stay with a friend, but she said there wasn't anyone she'd feel comfortable asking to take the four of them."

"Jesus." Bowie shook his head in disgust. "What about the ex?"

"He's missing."

He had to be on the run because of the real estate deals. Or the person responsible for his wife's death had him, or he was dead. "So the dead woman was his wife?"

"Yes."

"She hid the children. So she must have realized the danger. I don't think she would have felt it was necessary if it had been the husband. But why wouldn't she hide too?"

Gray shrugged. "She might have thought she needed to distract whoever it was away from the children."

He'd had to make similar decisions, but luckily they'd turned out better than ending up dead. She'd had more balls than her name suggested. Good for her. If they'd found the kids...

Gray continued. "The ex has stolen money from some very rich, very bad people. Some who aren't going to take it lying down. The ex-wife and kids could be used as leverage." He let that hang between them for a moment. "Your CO said you were on leave for a couple of weeks."

Bowie remained silent, letting the detective's words hover there for a moment. It had been ten years. He and Alayna were strangers to each other. And the past stood between them, thick as a brick wall.

But the past meant nothing when he thought about those three little girls. And her.

Gray picked up the paperwork lying on the table. "I can't ask you to get involved. But she trusts you."

He met the detective's gaze. "It seems I'm already involved."

Gray nodded. "She's going to need a ride home. She's waiting for one of my patrol officers."

"I have the car seats in my SUV."

Gray raised a brow. "So I was told."

Bowie shook his head. "Are you going to be calling all the time to check on where she is?"

"I would of course like to be informed of Ms. Wieland's whereabouts."

He motioned for Gray to lead the way. If Gray thought he was going to use him as some kind of spy, he was wrong. Not gonna happen.

CHAPTER 4

A LAYNA SHOT GLANCES toward Bowie as he drove. The girls, whiny and restless, wiggled in their car seats. Rosa, positioned between her two sisters, pulled at the straps of her seat as she worked toward a tantrum. It was hard to reason with a two-year-old when she was tired and hungry.

Bowie turned the car into a Denny's and parked. "Let's eat."

Alayna nearly wept with gratitude. "Thank you." She was hungry herself, and feeling a little nauseous.

He looked over the back of the seat at the girls as he un-hooked his seatbelt. "Who likes mac and cheese?"

"Me!" Emilia and Addison shouted together, distracting Rosa. Miraculously, she stopped crying.

"We're going to get some." He exited the car and opened the back door. He unhooked Addison while she got Emilia, and tilted Addie's chin up with one finger to look her in the face. "Do not move from that spot," he said in a voice that brooked no disobedience.

Next he worked the release between Rosa's legs, and lifted her free from the seat like a pro.

"Are you sure you don't have children?" Alayna commented as they walked toward the restaurant, her borrowed flip-flops, loaned to her by a female police officer at the station, living up to their name.

He seemed very at ease carrying Rosa and holding Addie's hand.

"I have several teammates who have kids. When we're together, we all keep an eye on them." Bowie released Addie's hand to hold the door open for them. She urged Addie forward with the tips of her fingers.

The hostess, a slender redhead with dark brown eyes approached them, her gaze homing in on Bowie, her smile conveying more than a little warmth. "Bowie, how have you been?"

"Good, Sheryl. What about you?"

"Great. It's good to see you." The warmth tripped over into flirtation.

Alayna bit her lip and attempted to ignore the sinking sensation in the pit of her stomach.

"I hope you have mac and cheese," Bowie said.

The hostess laughed. "Yes, we do."

"Hear that, girls?"

Addie jumped up and down. "And nuggets?"

"Yes, and nuggets." The hostess smiled. She got two menus and some coloring sheets from the counter. "Please come this way, and we'll get you settled."

Once seated, Alayna said, "Could we have a few crackers while we wait for the food? Rosa's a little fussy."

In fact, she wasn't. She laid her head on Bowie's shoulder and cuddled against him, her thumb in her mouth while he rubbed her back.

He stopped long enough to accept the packet of crayons Emilia handed him, tore them open with his teeth, and poured the four crayons out on the table beside her. Emilia shot him a sweet smile.

Any female within charming distance gravitated to him like a planet to the sun. She remembered that being an issue between them for a time. It was hard to believe he'd remain faithful when so many girls were throwing themselves at him. Even her best friend in high school had admitted she fantasized about him.

A waitress brought the crackers, and Alayna rose to take Rosa from him and sit her in the highchair between them. The toddler wailed a protest until Bowie offered her a cracker.

Once Addison and Emilia were busy coloring, Alayna relaxed a little. Her gaze tracked the hostess's movements as she seated another family. "I'm sorry for dragging you into everything today."

"You didn't. Sometimes things happen for a reason. After the kids eat and you get them settled at home, we need to talk, Alayna."

An anxious knot settled in the pit of her stomach. Surely Bowie wasn't going to rehash past hurts. But if he was…she owed him that much and more after everything he'd done today. She opened the menu. "Okay, we'll talk later."

The mac and cheese went over well with the girls, as did the dinosaur-shaped chicken nuggets and steamed broccoli. While Emilia and Addie ate, Alayna tied a plastic bib around Rosa's neck and then cut up a nugget and some steamed broccoli for her. The two-year-old chased the small pieces and the mac and cheese around her plate with a spoon.

Alayna finally sat down to eat her meal and glanced up to see Bowie watching her.

"I can't remember my mom cutting up anyone's food. Not even Carmelita's or Ciro's."

"She didn't need to. You always took care of them. I have to watch Rosa. She chokes easily, so I have to cut things up pretty small."

Rosa chose that moment to thrust her spoon in Bowie's direction. "Bite?"

"Yum." He acted like he was eating from her spoon and earned a grin.

They all ate in silence for a moment. When she could no longer bear the quiet she asked, "How are Carmelita and Ciro?"

"Fine. They both finished college. Carmelita is a buyer for a retail store in Los Angeles, and Ciro works in an insurance office. Ciro comes to visit now and then and crashes on my sofa. Carmelita has a boyfriend and rarely comes to San Diego, but calls twice a month."

"It sounds like they're doing well." After everything they'd been through, the way they'd been brought up… "They wouldn't have done as well if you hadn't been around to show them the way."

"I wasn't around, Alayna. I got through college by working two jobs, even with the scholarship. I sent money home to Carmelita when I could after setting up a post office box she could use so Moira couldn't get her hands on it. But that was all I could do for them. Then I joined the Navy and shipped out as soon as I finished training."

"You set a good example by starting and finishing school, Bowie."

He shook his head. "I haven't been around to set an example in a long time. What they did, they did on their own."

She studied his expression. He was so different. Harder. Not a surprise considering everything he experienced in his job—in his life. Had what she'd done been a part of that too? It certainly changed her. The parts he didn't know about had changed her more.

"Ciro is truly okay?" she asked.

"Yeah. He surprised us all by bouncing back as quickly as he did."

Alayna swallowed against the painful knot in her throat. "I'm so very glad."

Addison slipped out of her seat and came around to her. "I have to go potty," she said in a loud whisper.

"All right, honey."

"Me too," Emilia said, and slid out of her chair.

Alayna looked at Bowie. He smoothed Rosa's hair, earning another smile from the toddler. "We got this. Don't we, Rosa?" He reached for the plastic cup of milk with a lid and straw and held it for her. She leaned forward and latched onto the straw.

When they returned, Bowie was wiping Rosa's sleepy face and gummy hands with a wet wipe he'd probably gotten from the waitress. He removed the bib from around Rosa's neck and lifted her out of the highchair. He sat back down, propped her on his thigh, and cuddled her in against his side. Alayna stood to go around and take her.

"She's fine. You and the girls finish your meal, Alayna."

He sipped iced tea while Rosa yawned and cuddled close against him.

"She doesn't normally take to strangers so easily. Especially men."

"She's taking her cue from you. She can tell by your body language and tone of voice that you don't perceive me as a threat. You aren't going all momma bear protective when I get near any of them."

His patience with them also went a long way to easing any distrust the girls might feel.

But there were tensions beneath the polite words she and Bowie exchanged. A distance she couldn't ignore. Old hurts and past regrets were certainly part of it, but he'd changed, too, and what had happened between her family and his had to have played into it. And it *had* been nearly a decade.

For her, the pain seemed fresh and sharp. It all came back in a rush as soon as she laid eyes on him. How could that be?

The girls fell asleep in the car on the way to the apartment complex. As they got closer to home, Alayna's nerves stretched taut. She wiped her damp hands on her slacks as he pulled into the parking lot.

He studied the older building with its tired exterior and sparse landscaping. It was all she could afford.

"What floor are you on?" he asked.

"Second floor. Apartment Two-oh-seven."

"Give me your keys and I'll go up and check it out." He held out his hand.

Did he really think it was necessary? His deadpan expression was answer enough. She handed him the keys. "The entrance code is five-four-seven-eight."

"Lock the doors, Alayna. If anyone approaches the car, push the alarm button on the key fob, and and I'll be right back."

ONCE INSIDE THE apartment complex and inside the elevator, Bowie found his thoughts fixed on Alayna. Seeing her again was harder than he ever thought it would be. She'd handled herself pretty well at the bank and at her ex's house. Though she'd been wild with worry for her girls, she held it together. She impressed him.

Her girls were well behaved and maybe a little too trusting. The older one, Emilia, was more wary than the little ones. Addison was a corker, miss personality. Rosa, the little one, seemed hungry for attention.

And Alayna... She was more beautiful now than she was in high school. He remembered digging his fingers into the heavy weight of her hair and covering her mouth with his own. They'd been so hungry for each other. He couldn't say he wouldn't want to do it again, feel that way again. But with those memories came others less pleasant.

But he couldn't delve into them and the emotions they triggered while he was checking out their apartment. He needed to stay focused.

The elevator doors opened, and he stepped out into a wide hallway. The floors looked like hardwood but were actually tile, and worn in spots. The walls could use a coat of paint, but things looked clean enough. As he walked down the hall he glanced at apartment numbers mounted above the doors.

He paused outside Alayna's door and tried the knob. The door was locked. He used the key. The door opened easily. A light in the kitchen shined into the living room.

The apartment looked like a bomb had gone off inside. *Shit!* What the hell were these people after? Bowie reached for his phone and dialed 911. Again. He asked the dispatcher to contact Detective Gray, then closed the door and walked back to the elevator, but decided to take the stairs to get back to Alayna and the girls more quickly.

Once outside he stood by the car and waited for her to unlock the door. "What is it?" she asked.

"Someone's broken into your apartment."

Alayna's eyes widened. "You're kidding."

"No. I've called Detective Gray. He'll be here any minute."

"My God, what's going on?"

"I don't know, but you and girls need to get out of town for a while, at least until the cops find your ex and figure it out."

"I can't, Bowie. I don't have the resources. The police have frozen my bank account. I have to go to work every day to support the girls."

"Call and tell them you've got a family emergency. Or at least send the children to visit your parents until this thing has blown over."

"I can't send them to visit my parents. I don't... We've been estranged for a long time."

A momentary rush of satisfaction hit first and as quickly subsided. As much as he hated Harold Wieland's guts, Alayna needed her parents. What had caused this? "I'm sorry, Alayna."

"I almost called them when Aaron left me just after I found out I was pregnant with Rosa."

The words hit him like a punch. "He left you while you were pregnant?"

"Walked away. I didn't blame him. Things hadn't worked for a long time."

The careful composure of her expression didn't hide a damn thing.

He glanced back behind him at the girls, sound asleep, and paused at Rosa. "It's his loss, Alayna. You're better off without him, and so are they."

"Yeah. We are. Otherwise, my girls and I might have been caught up in whatever it is he's involved in and be dead like Bliss." Her voice shook on the woman's name.

Bowie flipped open his phone and dialed Detective Gray again. "I'm taking Ms. Wieland and her girls to my apartment. Her children are exhausted and they've experienced enough trauma for one day. If you need to talk to us, we'll be there." He rattled off his address.

"Okay. Harper's still in the wind."

"I figured so. There was no sign of forced entry at her apartment. The lock had to be picked. I used the key to unlock the door but didn't go in. The place was…" Aware of Alayna listening to his conversation, he settled on, "…it was pretty messed up."

"You'll need to bring Ms. Wieland to the apartment in the morning, She'll need to do a walk through to see if she can tell if anything is missing."

"Call and I'll bring her over." He put his hand over the phone and looked at Alayna. "You don't work on Saturdays?"

"No."

"We'll be available whenever you want to see her."

"All right."

He started the car and pulled out of the parking lot.

"You can take us to a hotel."

"I have a king-size bed big enough for the four of you, plus a sofa I can crash on."

After a long silent pause, she asked, "Why are you doing this?"

He glanced in her direction. "Because you need a safe place to stay, and I have one."

She fell silent again. "Is that the only reason?"

Uncertain of what she was asking, he formulated a reply that said all and nothing. "There are three reasons in the back seat, and one sitting up front with me."

For a moment he thought she might break down, but she controlled it. "Thank you so much."

He heard a "but" in there somewhere.

After a long pause, she said, "I know what you do for a living… You protect people who can't protect themselves. You take out the bad guys."

"Sometimes. We do rescue and recovery too."

"I don't want to get you tangled up in anything that could affect your career."

He wondered how far to go with her. "You're partly responsible for me choosing this career."

She gasped. "How?"

"After you cut me loose, I followed the plan we decided on together, except I went to Austin. I worked my ass off and got my degree, and then I enlisted to serve my country. Back then, if we'd gotten married, it would never have occurred to me to go into the Navy and do what I do."

She looked away. "We were different people then."

"Yeah." They were both dancing around the elephant in the room. It had already been a day filled with trauma. Now wasn't a good time to deal with the past.

Luckily he pulled into the apartment building parking area just then, putting everything on hold while they unloaded the girls and took them up to his apartment.

While Alayna gave the girls a quick bath, Bowie put fresh sheets on the bed and tossed a blanket onto the couch to make a bed on the sofa. He laid out some of his T-shirts for them, including Alayna.

It wouldn't be the first time he'd shared his clothes with her. And the girls needed something clean to sleep in.

He had just taken a seat on the couch when the three girls ran out to tell him good night. His T-shirts were huge on all of them, but Alayna had tied a knot in the shirts to keep the bottoms from dragging the floor. The three smelled of soap and baby lotion. Emilia spoke for them all. "Mommy said to thank you for letting us sleep here and for giving us your shirts to wear."

She sounded so prim, Bowie had to smile. "You're welcome."

Addison and Rosa hugged his neck. Emilia did so hesitantly. He offered her an encouraging smile. All three ran back into the bedroom, holding the hem of the shirts up. Their dainty feet pattering against the hardwood floor had him smiling until a thought repeated itself in his head.

They could have been his daughters. He and Alayna had talked about the family they would build together after they finished college. The regret that they weren't his was more painful than he wanted to acknowledge.

CHAPTER 5

ALAYNA STOOD IN the bedroom doorway, taking in the living room. The whole apartment was a masculine living space, with no feminine touches anywhere.

The fawn-colored leather couch and love seat faced each other. The coffee table was a wooden footlocker stained and sealed with polyurethane and set on legs. The walnut end tables, one at each end of the couches, held square, box-shaped lamps. An entertainment center stretched across one wall with a flat screen television and a stereo system.

A desk sat opposite with a laptop and printer on it. A recliner angled in the corner, a stack of books on the floor beside it, and a floor lamp to one side. The artwork on the walls was of old patents filed for machines in walnut frames. The only things out of place were the tackle box and fishing rods propped in a corner next to the recliner and the large duffel packed for his trip.

Nerves made her palms sweat and her breathing shaky. She sauntered into the room and sat at the end of the couch, leaving two feet of space between them.

Bowie set aside the electronic tablet he was working on. "They're asleep?"

"Yes. They were out like a light as soon as I got them settled." She studied his face. "You really need to put some ice on your jaw. You have the start of a bad bruise."

"I've had worse in training. It'll be okay." He leaned forward to rest his elbows on his knees. "I think you need to get out of town with the kids, Alayna. I know you need to work, but your children's safety, and yours, are more important."

His chocolate brown eyes still had just a hint of gold around the iris. She had dreamed of his eyes, dreamed of *him,* for years.

Imagined him holding her when she was hurt, lonely, grieving.

"I was at the bank today cashing a check," he continued, "because I was going out of town. Some of my team members were going to go with me, but they all had to cancel. I have a cabin rented at Big Bear, and I was going to hit the grocery for supplies tomorrow morning. You and the girls can come with me. There are three bedrooms and a couch bed, so there's room. By the time we get back, the cops may have figured out what's going on."

"How long would you be staying?"

"Ten days."

She couldn't take off ten days. "That's almost half a month's pay, Bowie. My daycare still has to be paid, whether the girls go or not. I have to pay my rent. My utilities."

He started to lay a hand on her knee, but changed direction at the last moment and placed it on the cushion next to her. She wished he'd touched her. It might have broken through this invisible wall he'd erected between them. A wall her family had built by their actions. And had forced her to build, too.

"Look, we'll talk to Detective Gray tomorrow and work something out."

They'd be spitting into the wind. All the police cared about were Aaron and the money he'd taken. "What had you planned to do up there?"

"Fish, canoe, read, jog around the lake, take naps, and work a little. When I get back, I'll be walking into a new assignment, and I'll be working long hours getting my team organized and in sync."

She looked away. "You see what my life is like with three children. It's organized chaos most of the time. You wouldn't get many naps or get to read much."

"I think I can handle it. And I know you can. I watched you

handle a lot worse today."

Most of the time she was just putting one foot in front of the other and praying she didn't mess up.

"Why can't you contact your parents, Alayna?"

"I had a falling out with my father and brother. As soon as I graduated from high school I moved out of their house, and I haven't been back since." She couldn't tell him the biggest part of that without revealing the rest. She couldn't face it yet, because it would only make him angry. But would it cause him as much pain now as it still did her?

"They haven't seen the girls?"

"My mother and sister Joanna talked about coming out, and Joanna visited briefly one time, but Mom never did."

"What about your brother?"

She shook her head.

"What happened?"

If she told him now, just when he was inviting them to go with him, he'd either think she was angling for sympathy, or it would set him off, and he'd want to go after Harry and Matt. It wouldn't do anyone any good. "It's done, and I'm not interested in burying the hatchet, Bowie." Not unless it was in her father and brother's cold, merciless hearts. "I can't take the girls out of state. Aaron has a signed order from a judge barring me from doing so."

"His legal issues might have a bearing on that soon."

"But not right now. He's tried every way he can to take them away from me. He doesn't want them, and Bliss wasn't the mothering kind, but he wants to hurt me more than he wants to do what's right for them."

"Why?"

Wow. She didn't want to bare her soul for him about her marriage. "We've been making each other miserable for a long time. He blames me for everything. I blame me, too. I should never have said yes when he asked me to marry him. I could have saved us both a lot of heartache." She brushed her hand over her face. "We've got three beautiful, incredible, daughters, and I don't regret that part one bit. But I hoped once he married Bliss he'd move on and be happy. For some reason, though, he's still intent on punishing me."

Bowie grasped her wrist, his jaw working. "It isn't his place to punish you for the failure of your marriage. He had a part in it, too."

His touch both soothed and triggered the sharp pain of a loss that still seemed fresh, even after ten years. "I know he did. And he tried for the first three years. So did I." She'd clung to Aaron because she had no one else. But she hadn't loved him enough. It was hard to remember the feelings she had for him back then after the recent years of conflict between them.

"I'm tired, Bowie. I need to think things through. I'll let you know about the trip to Big Bear in the morning." Withdrawing from his touch, she stood. She hadn't had time to process what happened today. She'd tried to keep her mind on the girls instead. But now everything was catching up with her, and she needed five minutes alone. "Thank you for letting us stay."

He stood. "There was no way I would have dropped you at a hotel and driven away. There's someone out there searching either for your husband or for something he has. Or he's gone rogue and is on the run. He either tore the apartment up, or the guys after him were looking for something they think he may have passed on to you. Think about that while you make your decision."

She didn't need him to remind her of her responsibilities. Everything she did was for her children. They were all she had, all she cared about now.

She paused at the bedroom door. "I wasn't jealous of Bliss. And I never had anything against her. I wanted her and Aaron to be happy together." It would have gotten him off her back. "I just worried she wouldn't watch the children as closely as she needed to. But she did when it counted. She didn't deserve to die." Her composure started to crumble, but she breathed through it. "I don't know how I'm going to tell the girls she's gone."

"As long as they don't start asking questions, you don't have to tell them right away, Alayna. Give the police a few weeks to find out who killed her. Then you can tell them the bad person who did it was caught."

It made sense, and it gave her a good excuse to put it off. Rosa and Addison wouldn't comprehend what happened, but Emilia… She was old enough to understand. She'd taken care of her sisters in Bliss's place.

"Whatever Aaron is twisted up in—he's never seeing my children again. I'm taking him back to court, and I'm going to fight for that. They could have been killed." If only Aaron could stop hating her long enough to love his children. She understood why he felt shortchanged—why he felt she hadn't loved him like he wanted her to. She hadn't. But she'd tried. And their children never had a thing to do with the shortfalls in their relationship.

"Put some ice on that jaw," she said as she left the living room.

She closed the bedroom door behind her, tiptoed past the bed where the girls lay sleeping, and went into the bathroom. She sat on the toilet lid and rocked while she wept silently. Wept for Bliss. Wept for her girls. Wept from exhaustion and rage. After ten minutes, she called a halt to her meltdown, wet a washcloth, and pressed it to her eyes.

How many nights had she spent crying in the bathroom over the past six years? It had to end. If Aaron truly was guilty, he'd be going to prison. She wanted freedom from his vindictive anger, but she'd never wish prison on him, because of their daughters. She couldn't imagine taking the girls to visit him in jail.

If he wasn't convicted, she had to find a way to neutralize his ability to intimidate and manipulate her. She'd continue to tape him every time they spoke, and gather evidence against him so the police would finally believe her about his threats. She should have done it all along.

But none of this would be relevant if he was dead.

CHAPTER 6

A LAYNA CRACKED AN eye and counted heads. Both eyes flicked open, and she bit back a murmur of concern. If not confined to her room, her youngest child had a tendency to slip out of her bed and wander. Luckily Rosa hadn't figured out how to unlock the deadbolt at home. But there was no guarantee she wouldn't figure it out here at Bowie's apartment.

Alayna slipped out of bed as quietly as possible and went to the bedroom door. She peeked out. The blanket and sheets Bowie had laid out the night before were folded neatly at one end of the couch, and a soft murmur came from the direction of the kitchen. She followed the sound.

The kitchen, all stainless steel appliances and white cabinets, gleamed. Black quartz countertops contrasted nicely with the cabinets. An impressive collection of herbs and spices clung to one side of the refrigerator in round magnetic containers.

Rosa sat on one of the barstools in front of the island, and Alayna's heart skipped a beat until she realized a belt secured the toddler to the seat. Thank God it wasn't a backless barstool.

Rosa pretended to feed her monkey dry Cheerios out of a bowl while eating them herself. She carried on a jumbled conversation with the toy only the two of them understood. But she did hear the words good, baby, and eat.

Bowie was buttering bread and putting the slices on a baking sheet while bacon sizzled in a skillet. A carton of eggs sat on the counter.

He noticed Alayna as soon as she entered the room. "Coffee's ready if you'd like a cup," he said. His attention rested on her bare legs, and she felt that warm brown gaze on every inch of her skin before he swiveled back to the stove to turn the bacon.

"Bacon is the girls' favorite."

"I guessed that when Rosa woke me demanding, 'Bacon!'"

Alayna laughed at his imitation. "She's a little bossy."

She grinned at his raised brows and the quick, crooked smile he flashed her…and finally, there were his dimples. She poured a cup of coffee to hide the heat suffusing her face, adding some milk to the cup. "Can I help fix breakfast?"

"I've got it. But I'm guessing Little Bit needs a pull-up change."

Of course she did. But she was getting better about asking to go to the bathroom during the day, though it was still hit or miss if she made it. She still slept too soundly at night. "I'll take care of that right now."

She placed her coffee cup on the island next to a bank envelope. A phone number and a woman's name were written across the envelope in a feminine hand. Her stomach lurched, followed by a dropping sensation. Bowie was a single guy. Of course he'd have a little black book of numbers.

She tried to ignore the ache in her belly and unbuckled the belt around Rosa's waist, then hiked her up on her hip.

It took only a few minutes to undress Rosa, clean her up, and dress her in fresh shirt and pants from the diaper bag. She was setting out Addison's clothes when Emilia stirred. Rosa wandered back out, her monkey under her arm.

Alayna slipped into her clothes and helped Addison dress while Emilia pulled on her things. By the time they emerged from the bedroom, Bowie had Rosa strapped back into her seat and had served her two strips of bacon and a piece of oven toast. He helped the girls up on the stools and set similar plates in front of them.

He scooped eggs onto their plates and then filled one for Alayna as well. "The eggs are hot girls, let them cool," he warned.

"You're very efficient," Alayna commented as she warmed her coffee.

He flashed her a smile that gleamed white, and her stomach tumbled. "I'm a SEAL, darlin'. I'm trained to be efficient."

She shook her head at his cockiness, and he grinned.

He poured orange juice for the girls and for himself. "I seem to remember you don't like orange juice. Or has that changed?"

"No, it hasn't changed." She took a bite of egg and chewed.

"I'm out of apple juice. Sorry. I have milk and—"

"Coffee's fine, Bowie."

She waited for him to settle across from her with his food. "Do you have someone who'll be upset with you for acting as a babysitter for us?" She'd phrased the question so it wouldn't sound like she was pumping him for information about his private life.

"No. I'm in and out of the country a lot. It isn't fair to expect anyone to wait for me to wander through."

"Sometimes it isn't about quantity but quality, Bowie."

"Yeah. I remember we used to spend some quality time together."

Her heart leaped as images of some of those moments rushed through her thoughts like a slide show. Her mouth went so dry, she had to work to swallow her food. It took every ounce of courage she possessed to look at him.

His features were sharp with interest. "When are you going to tell me why you broke it off, Alayna?"

She reached for her coffee and took a drink.

"I know it had something to do with your father. It always did. He hated my guts. He had his cop buddies stop me every chance they got and search me for drugs and weapons."

She frowned. "You never told me that."

He shrugged. "What could you have done about it?"

She shook her head. Nothing. She couldn't do anything. It was horrible to be so powerless.

"I kept waiting for one of them to plant something in my car, or claim they'd found it on me, but they never did."

"They didn't have any reason to hate you. But my father hated that I loved you. He hated you more than he loved me. And Matt was already…you know how he was. I couldn't ask you or your family to forgive my family. I was so ashamed of him."

"Down, Mommy!"

Grateful for Rosa's interruption, Alayna went to the sink to moisten a dishcloth to wipe her hands and face, then untied her from the barstool and lifted her down.

Addison swung down off her stool like a monkey and took her baby sister's hand. "Let's go play match, Rosa."

Emilia climbed down as well. "I want to play too."

"I hope that means matching objects or pictures or something," Bowie said, brows raised.

She chuckled. "It does."

His phone rang as she sat back down. He spoke briefly, then hung up.

"That was Detective Gray. He wants to do a walk-through of the apartment in an hour."

"Okay."

THE DESTRUCTION AT the apartment was much worse than he'd imagined from his brief glimpse of the living room the night before. Drawers, cabinets, and closets hung open, and their contents dumped and systematically destroyed. Fingerprint powder stained door handles, knobs, and broken objects.

As soon as Detective Gray and his partner left, Alayna went into the kitchen and got a box of garbage bags from beneath the sink. Bowie followed her into the children's room, where clothes were tangled with the broken lamps and crushed toys. Alayna searched through the mess for clothing for the children and stuffed the useable ones into one garbage bag. He did the same with the broken toys and trashed belongings.

Stuffed animals and dolls had been ripped apart and their cotton strewn across the floor. Someone had systematically searched for something. But what?

They worked in silence for some time. "Has your ex-husband been here to visit the girls?"

"Just to pick them up."

"Could he have put something in one of their toys?"

"I don't know." Lines bracketed her mouth and her eyes looked tired. "But if he did, whoever ripped the girls' toys to pieces must have found it."

Why wasn't her ex's house trashed and shredded like this? Because whoever did this knew it wasn't at his house. And the only one who knew for certain was her ex. Unless he told someone he'd hidden something here. Why would he put the girls at risk? They were his children. It was his responsibility to protect them. Anger gripped him, and heat rushed into his face.

He looked up from tossing another Barbie doll onto one of the beds in a keeper pile while he scooped the broken things up with a dustpan and dumped them into a garbage bag. Why would the man destroy his own children's toys?

He couldn't say aloud what he was thinking. Alayna was already dealing with too much. But Aaron either lost his temper when he couldn't find what he was looking for, or he got pleasure from destroying her apartment.

When she reached for another small blouse, she nudged aside a broken piggybank with her toe and the few coins left inside it jangled. She studied it for a long moment before picking up the coins and putting them in her pocket.

"When did you tell the daycare center we'd be back to pick the girls up?" Bowie asked.

"A couple of hours. And I told them to call the police if Aaron shows up."

He tried to tell himself the satisfaction he felt was on the girls' behalf, but he lay awake a long time last night going over the things Alayna told him. The girls deserved better from a father than broken toys and ripped clothing. This Aaron guy was a fucking bully and an asshole, and deserved whatever he got from the police or anyone else hunting him.

The one room in the apartment remaining untouched was the kitchen. Maybe the asshole had been worried about getting cut if he broke glass, or maybe he'd still been inside the apartment when Bowie opened the door and figured the police wouldn't be far behind.

Damn. Now Bowie wished he'd gone inside and looked around before going back downstairs. But the girls and Alayna were in the car, and he'd been antsy about leaving them alone.

Damn it! This protection detail was turning into a two-man job. But he had no one for backup.

Alayna called the daycare to check on the girls and extend the time they needed to stay, and they worked steadily until they reached her room. Liquid makeup stained the bedspread and sheets. Lipstick smeared the dresser mirror. One tube, pale pink, lay crushed and ground into the carpet.

"I suppose it was lucky that I only owned two tubes of lipstick. Otherwise they could have painted the room," Alayna commented, her tone flat. She took pictures with her phone, just as she'd done all along, then tucked it into her back pocket. "I'll have to run by the police department to get a copy of the report so I can file a claim. How long do you think it'll take for them to have a report ready?"

"At least a few days."

"Detective Gray said they've unfrozen my account, so I can pay my rent and utilities. At least we'll still have a roof over our head."

"That's good."

Something crunched under his tennis shoe, and he bent to pick it up. It was a frame with the girls' picture in it. Though the glass was gone, it was still in good shape. He placed it back on the nightstand and picked up the empty drawers and put them back in place.

Alayna picked something up tangled in the bedspread at the foot of the bed and stood looking at it for a long time. "Emilia made this for me in kindergarten. Why would he want to destroy something like this?" The plaster piece had Emilia's handprint and her name written in uneven letters across the bottom. One side had been broken off, and with it two of the fingers.

"Because they're assholes."

Tears glistened. "Will you help me find the other piece? I can glue it back together."

She'd been so controlled until now. Too controlled. Too calm. Holding everything back.

Bowie tossed the things he'd picked up off the floor onto the bed and eased up to hold her. She buried her face against his chest, and a sob like a hiccup shook her. The plaster thing dug into him as she clasped it against her. He ignored his discomfort, rubbing her back and working his fingers beneath her hair to caress the back of her neck.

Had his mother ever loved him and his brother and sister the way Alayna loved her kids? Everything but the kitchen was destroyed, and she was crying over a gift from her child. No way would Moira have worried about something like that.

He rested his cheek against her hair and breathed in the scent of her shampoo, some kind of citrus fragrance. "We can fix it, Alayna. And the rest are just…things. The insurance company will make it possible to replace a lot of them, and you can start fresh. You and the kids are what's important."

"How many times can someone start over?"

"As many times as it takes, sweetheart."

She leaned back to look up at him, her lashes spiked with tears. "Why don't you hate me like he does?"

So she suspected it was her ex who did this. He'd hoped she wouldn't think about it. "I could never hate you, Alayna." *You were my first true love. The only one.* He'd never allowed another woman close enough since then. But she owed him an explanation for what she'd done. She loved him. He knew she did, but she'd broken it off, refused to see him. Though he supposed it should have been the other way around considering everything her father had done. He still deserved to know why.

She'd already taken too much of a beating today for him to add to it, but he'd bring it back up when she was stronger. "It was a long time ago. I'm still in one piece."

"I'm sorry."

"You already said that outside the bank." Her tear-washed eyes were killing him. Every instinct urged him to comfort her.

"You read my lips?"

"Yeah." He hugged her tight, then eased up the pressure. She fit so perfectly against him, her head just beneath his chin, her arms around his waist. Just as she had years ago. "I was on my way over to you when the van stopped behind your car."

"You saved me."

"I seem to remember you kicking one dude in the leg and the balls and elbowing him in the stomach. You just needed a little help with the other guy."

She gave a half-hearted bark of laughter. "If only I'd known martial arts or something." She pulled away to reach for a sleeve that had been torn off a blouse and used it to wipe her face and blow her nose. "We need to finish up here and get the girls. I have to call and talk to my boss." She paused at the bedroom door. "It isn't too long a drive to the lake, is it?"

Relieved she'd agreed to go, he said, "About three hours. We'll get the girls some coloring books, and I'll download a movie. They can watch it on our way up."

BOWIE WAS TOO good to be true. He had everything figured out, which made her feel both relieved and wary. She was more nervous about spending time with him than she was about calling her boss and telling him she needed to get out of town until the police found her husband and arrested him.

Spending time with Bowie meant answering questions. Something she didn't want to do. If she told him the whole sordid story, he might go off on a rampage of revenge against her father and brother. And he might think she was trying to avoid admitting her part in it.

Once she was in the kitchen, she keyed in Willard Kappes's number and pushed send.

She hesitantly told him everything that had happened.

"It's okay, Alayna. You're due two weeks paid vacation since you rarely take time off unless one of the kids is sick. I think it's wise for you to make yourself scarce until they find Aaron. He's unstable, and a danger to you and the girls. If he's desperate and on the run, he may think you will be his way out."

He wouldn't. He knew what she had on him. And she knew partly what he'd been looking for. Not information about money, but something more personal. She had the pictures and the doctor's notes.

Her boss, having dealt with Aaron in the past, understood what she was dealing with. But he also might be worried that Aaron would show up at his office looking for her. "Thank you for understanding, Mr. Kappes. I really appreciate it."

"If there's anything we can do for you, just give us a call."

"I will. I finished typing up the brief for the Richards' case before I left on Friday. And the letters and paperwork for all the other current cases are caught up."

"I've told you before how excellent you are at your job. But your grasp of the law goes beyond that. You could go back to school and get your degree."

"With three young children, sir, I don't think I'd be able to carry the load. Maybe when I get them all in school."

"When you're ready, let me know. I'll write letters of recommendation and help you find some grants to pay for it."

"Thanks so much, Mr. Kappes."

She hung up and leaned back against the counter. She'd been dreading the beans and meatless spaghetti she'd been expecting to eat in her near future. Now she didn't have to worry about stretching a two-week paycheck to cover a month.

But there were other problems. Her past attachment to Bowie made things worse than if they were total strangers. She was even more vulnerable because he seemed to be the same protective, caring man he was when they parted.

How could she stop loving a man because her family didn't want her to? How could they hate him because of his nationality and his skin color? How could her father and brother expect her to live with them after she learned what they were capable of?

And now the man her father and brother hated served their country in a way neither of them ever had or ever could. The rage and pain she felt toward them so many years ago reared its head. Bowie had been the better man back then, and he still was. They weren't fit for him to wipe his feet on.

But with everything going on right now, she needed to keep her distance.

She couldn't afford to get too close to him. She'd never survive when he walked away again. Her girls would be brokenhearted too. As he said himself, it wasn't fair to ask a woman to sit around waiting for him to wander through.

If she ever decided to marry again, it would have to be to someone who could provide stability, and who would be there for them all. Someone she hadn't wronged so completely.

She had nothing to worry about. Bowie'd keep his distance. He had enough on his plate being a SEAL. He wasn't interested in a ready-made family.

What would their relationship have been like if her brother and father had left them alone? Would they have toughed it out through college and followed their dreams? Would they have been able to handle the added stress of a family?

After ten years, she had no way of knowing. But she was plagued by what-ifs.

CHAPTER 7

BIG BEAR WAS one of the most beautiful areas in California. The lush greenery of the San Bernardino National Forest rolled across the distant hills and circled the lake. It had been a couple of years since Bowie and the team were here for a four-day weekend to fish, drink, and play poker.

Alayna spoke from beside him as she took in the panoramic view of the lake below while they approached the small community. "It's really beautiful. The girls have never seen mountains like this. I've never brought them up here."

"It's hard to drive and keep an eye on everyone at the same time."

"Yes. That, and they were all so little, there wasn't much they could do."

"Don't say that too loud," Bowie said in a whisper. "Addison thinks there's nothing she can't do, and Rosa is her sidekick."

"You've been with them twenty-four hours and just discovered that? I have to watch them both like a hawk."

"I used to know a girl who was just like them." He shot her a look. "I don't remember you ever backing down from anything."

She remained silent, her expression introspective. "I learned to be little more cautious. There are repercussions for everything you do in life."

Bowie shot a quick glance at Emilia via the rearview mirror.

Surely Alayna realized her caution had rubbed off on her eldest daughter. The six-year-old spent most of her time observing everyone around her and waiting for cues from her mother or the other girls before answering or acting.

Bowie asked, "Who's hungry?"

"Me!" For once Rosa beat Addison. Rosa and Addison had a competition going to see who got the most attention.

"What about you, Emilia? Are you hungry too?" He made a point of asking because she so rarely said anything or replied to questions.

She glanced up at the rearview mirror. "Yes."

"Have you ever had home-cooked tacos?"

"Mama fixed us some. Rosa and Addie made a mess."

"I bet they were younger. They're bigger now, and they won't make a mess. Will you, girls?"

"No." This time Addison won the race.

"And we'll have longhorn pancakes and sausage for breakfast in the morning. Have you ever had longhorn pancakes?"

Emilia smiled. "No."

"It's about time, then."

"What's a longhorn?"

Bowie shot Alayna a look. What the hell? You could take the girl out of Texas, but you couldn't take Texas out of the girl. Or so he'd always believed.

Alayna laughed. "It's a type of cow raised in Texas, honey. It has big horns. A long horn pancake is the shape of its head with big horns."

Addison mooed, making horns with her fingers. Rosa joined in, and together they created an ear-splitting racket of moos.

"I'll show you a picture when we get to the cabin." After a beat of silence, he said, "You really did put Texas behind you when you left."

"I had to. Things at home were…" She shook her head. "I finished my paralegal degree at college while I worked afternoons and weekends at a law firm, and I took some classes in California law when I moved here. Then I landed my job with Mr. Kappes.

He's been wonderful."

"What about your mom, Alayna?"

"We haven't spoken in ten years. Joanna called unexpectedly a couple of years ago. She told my Dad she was going to Galveston and came to visit. That was right after Rosa was born. She stayed three days, then went back. She's only called a couple of times since then."

"I'm sorry."

"I keep hoping they'll eventually realize what a lowlife piece of excrement Harry is and walk away."

Wow. Her father, who who insisted on being called Harold, would shit if he heard the way his daughter referred to him. Her bitter, unhappy expression told the rest of the story. Whatever had happened between them, it was something major. And based on her reaction, it wasn't over.

He couldn't think of a single comforting thing to say to her. He didn't have the happiest family life growing up. Just the opposite. But he and his siblings had covered each other's backs, knowing there was safety in numbers.

As though she read his thoughts, she said, "You mentioned Moira the other day. How is she doing?"

"She's living with a guy she met online. He's ten years older and needs someone to take care of him. I wish him luck with that."

"Have you talked to her?"

"Not in a couple of months. That's about how long it takes her to run short of money and call. Now there are three of us working, she spreads the mooching out among the three of us."

"I'm sorry. I hoped she'd changed." There was real regret in her tone.

"Not going to happen. We just leave her to it and hope she stays where she's at."

Five minutes later they pulled into the driveway of the cabin. Nestled back into a framework of trees, it looked like a regular bi-level house until they opened the front door. A large stone fireplace drew the eye the moment they walked into the living room. Too bad it was early summer and already too warm to build a fire. But maybe they'd have a chilly night or two.

Wide wooden beams crossed the ceiling. Beadboard wainscoting, painted white, covered the lower part of the walls, while the upper half was a warm gold to match the stone fireplace.

The chairs and couch were sprawling, overstuffed leather pieces guaranteed to be comfortable enough to sleep or sit on. The coffee tables and end tables, sturdy, wood-framed pieces perfect for the mountain atmosphere, looked heavy enough to withstand some wear and tear.

He'd learned from hanging with Langley and Trish Marks's three kids, the key to keeping children happy was keeping them busy until they crashed for a nap.

Unloading the car was the perfect time for that. They all had their own backpacks with toys, books, and little girl necessities. Bowie lined them up and slipped their packs on their shoulders and sent them scooting back into the house with Alayna to organize their play space on the round breakfast nook table, which had more than enough room. He followed them into the kitchen, wheeling two coolers of food to unpack later, while the girls got settled.

He rolled Alayna's bigger suitcase into the master suite, where she and the girls had access to a bathroom of their own, then hefted his duffel over his shoulder and climbed the stairs to the second floor. The bedroom under the eaves, where he'd slept before, had been updated a little, as had the bathroom across the hall with sandstone-colored tile and chrome fixtures. The warm desert colors went well with the deep green comforter and shams, and looked more masculine than the two bedrooms downstairs.

It would work well having the ladies' domain downstairs while he had the upper floor. Separate but handy. If he was downstairs in close proximity, he'd be too fixated on Alayna sleeping with only a wall between them.

At least the girls' presence kept his thoughts from wandering in that direction more than a couple of times an hour. But it didn't keep him from being aware of Alayna, wanting to touch her, wanting more. He was eaten up with the need to know if they could recapture the lightning in a bottle they'd known before. Memories clamored in his head, breeding curiosity. Could it really have been that perfect? And if it was, why the hell did she break it off? Before this was over, he was going to—by God—find out.

He tossed his clothes into drawers, stowed his duffel in the closet, and secured his Sig Sauer P226 on a high shelf beneath the extra pillow and blanket stored there, and went back downstairs to bring in the two last bags of staples they'd gotten at the store and check how the girls were doing.

Alayna was cooking hamburger, onions, and peppers in a skillet and had unpacked the coolers.

"Need some help?"

"I'm good, unless you want to cut up some tomatoes."

"Tacos!" Rosa yelled from her seat at the table.

"You said the magic word in the car, and nothing would do but that I get right on it."

Bowie laughed. "It sounds like Rosa likes tacos. Do you like tacos, Rosa?"

The master of one-word answers replied, "Yummmm," as she wiggled little people on her fingers.

Bowie chuckled. The kid was killing him. All of them were. He was already getting attached. "We can eat outside on the back patio, and I'll hose everybody down when they're done."

Alayna laughed. "Sounds like a plan."

A RAINBOW SHONE in the mist from the sprinkler Bowie had hooked up to the hose out back of the house. The girls were in their bathing suits taking turns leaping through the water. With their blond hair, dark with water and stuck to their heads and shoulders, they looked like water nymphs.

The girls' laughter eased the anxious knot that had taken up residence in the pit of Alayna's stomach since leaving her apartment earlier. No, it had been there since the attempted kidnapping at the bank, and had gotten worse with every additional catastrophe.

But they were out of reach and anonymous for at least a week. And no one but Detective Gray knew where they were. She could relax.

Or could she? Her attention strayed to Bowie, stretched out in the sun on the lounge, his gaze focused on the girls, his mouth crooked in a half smile.

Had she ever seen Aaron that besotted with his daughters? Perhaps Emilia when she was first born. He'd been so happy then. He had less time when Addison was born, since joining a new real estate firm and having more responsibility thrown at him. When he walked away while she was pregnant with Rosa, she'd been grateful, and glad he never even tried to bond with their youngest child.

She could have saved them all a mountain of heartache if she'd just filed for divorce before then. Her gaze rested on Rosa while she danced with excitement as she waited her turn to leap through the water. She wouldn't have had Rosa. That alone made the hurt worth bearing.

The sun dropped behind the distant hills, and a chill tinged the air almost immediately. Five more minutes and she'd call them in to dry off and get dressed. She'd feed them a light meal, get them interested in a game, and let them watch a few minutes television before bed. They'd sleep soundly tonight.

Bowie spoke close to her ear, "What are you thinking about?"

His warm breath fanned her cheek and sent chills through her. "How lucky I am to have them. No matter how bad things get, they're all that matters."

He shifted a chair closer to hers and sat down. "But you deserve something for yourself, too."

Her heart drummed hard. It took her several seconds to build up enough courage to look at him.

The careful control of his features made it impossible for her to read what he was thinking, but his eyes held something else altogether. Something that scared the hell out of her. She wouldn't survive getting involved with him, only to lose him a second time.

"I have too much baggage, Bowie." Baggage she couldn't hope to share with him. It would be too painful for them both when it didn't work out. Besides, he couldn't be interested in her in that way. He just had a thing about taking care of people.

"The shit that's going on right now will pass."

"But the kids won't."

"I don't view your girls as an obstacle. Why should anyone else? They're doing okay with me, aren't they?"

They were. His steady, calm nature gave them an opportunity to enjoy him. Even Emilia seemed to trust him a little.

"I've been alone for nearly three years, Bowie. Actually a lot longer. Aaron had already left our marriage by then. I haven't dated anyone since the divorce."

"Why not?"

"I didn't want to make any more mistakes that could affect my children. The upheaval they've been through has affected all of them, but Emilia more. She's anxious so much of the time. Addison was only two when he left, and Rosa hadn't been born yet. But Emilia was there for all the stuff that went on during the implosion of our marriage. I tried to protect her from it, but I couldn't. Aaron has a volatile temper, and he's loud. Sometimes words can seem worse than a blow when you're only four."

"Have you made Aaron aware of how things have affected Emilia?"

"I've told him. Luckily, he's rarely home during the time he and Bliss have the children. Bliss never raised her voice to the girls, and they seemed to like and accept her." Another wave of grief and regret hit her. She wished she'd taken the time to get to know the woman better.

"Mommy. Cold," Rosa pressed her little body against Alayna, soaking her clothes. She welcomed the distraction.

"Yes, you are." She'd meant to call them in ten minutes ago, but had gotten sidetracked by Bowie. Alayna reached for a towel from the table, dried Rosa's hair and rubbed her little body until she was warmed, then wrapped the damp towel around her.

Bowie turned off the water and herded Emilia and Addison toward her.

She dried Emilia and Addison while Bowie took Rosa in. He was standing in the living room cuddling her, keeping her warm when the three of them came in.

"Burgers or hotdogs?" he asked.

"Hotdogs," Addison yelled as she ran into the bedroom.

He set Rosa on her feet, and she ran into the bedroom, dragging the towel behind her, barking like a dog.

"What about you, Emilia?"

"Hotdog, please."

He grinned at her, and a small smile peeked out at him before she walked into the bedroom at a more sedate pace than her sisters.

"She's like a little copy of you," he commented, and went into the kitchen.

By the time Alayna had all three dressed for bed, Bowie was taking the burgers and hotdogs out to put on the grill.

The smooth efficiency with which he seemed to do everything took so much pressure off her. Was he always like this?

After their quick meal of hotdogs, store-bought potato salad, and steamed carrots, she settled the girls in front of the television for thirty minutes of cartoons while she cleaned up.

Bowie disappeared upstairs and returned wearing running shorts and a T-shirt. His legs looked long and muscular in tight shorts, his stomach taut in the tank-style T-shirt. "I'm going for a run. I'll be back in a little while."

"Okay."

He leaned down to whisper in her ear, setting every nerve alight in her body. "You still remember how to use a gun?" At her nod he continued. "There's a Sig upstairs in the closet on the shelf under the blankets. It's loaded and ready. Lock up behind me. I'll case the neighborhood and make sure everything looks okay."

A dropping sensation struck her stomach. "You don't think…"

"No. No one knows we're here but Gray and his partner. I'm

just being thorough and getting the lay of the land." He gave her arm a gentle, reassuring squeeze.

"Okay." She pressed a hand to her throat where her heart still pulsed, fast and hard.

Emilia looked up from her coloring project at the kitchen table, her expression anxious. "He'll come back, won't he, Momma?"

"Yes. He's just going for a run. He has to stay fit for his job."

CHAPTER 8

BOWIE STRETCHED TO loosen his muscles, then took off at an easy jog down the street to the east. Cars were parked sporadically along the road, others in slots in front of the houses.

As he jogged, Bowie scanned for any occupied vehicles and anything out of place. He'd studied several pictures of Aaron Harper. Mid-thirties, sandy hair, blue-gray eyes, even features. But he had a weak jaw, and he didn't exactly knock himself out staying in shape. What had Alayna seen in him?

The street stretched quiet before him. He raced through the darker pools of shadow cast by the tall, mature pines growing in nearly every yard, increasing his speed after he cut around the corner, finding his rhythm.

He ran around the block and passed the house again. Lights from the television flickered against the blinds, and he imagined the girls watching cartoons. Nothing moved around their rental house or any other. Everything was as it should be.

He extended his running path to include the next block ahead, then cut back again, his thoughts cycling toward Alayna again.

It was nearly four months since he'd been with a woman. Not that he hadn't had opportunities, but training BUD/S candidates took stamina, and by the end of the day he was tired. Partying no longer held the appeal it once did. In fact, in the past couple of years he'd partied less and less. He spent more time out on the ocean fishing with Doc than he did dating. His promotion had something to do with that...or had it just been a natural progression?

It was time to put aside that part of his life and get serious. He was more than ready for it.

It couldn't get any more serious than Alayna's situation. And her girls'. It wasn't just the two of them anymore. Whoever Alayna got involved with would have to take them into account. The four of them were a package deal.

The guy who wanted to build a life with Alanya would have to be patient with them all. Alayna because even after damn near three years, she was still raw from the divorce.

Her ex had done a number on her. On the one hand, when it came to survival mode for her and the girls, she was all in. In fact, her whole world revolved around them. But even he recognized that she needed a life outside her children. Or not exactly outside, but parallel to them. Other women seemed to find a way without damaging their kids. Alayna could do it, with the right guy.

The girls weren't an issue. They were sweethearts. Well-behaved. A little whiny at times, but hey, all kids were now and then.

Whiny kids drove guys crazy most of the time. It had triggered memories of his brother and sister for him, so he knew how to handle them and recognized why they were acting up.

But if she hooked up with some dude who didn't understand kids, or didn't have the patience to deal with them... Concern clouded his thoughts. He picked up the pace, his feet hitting the sidewalk with a distinctive tattoo.

His mother was never able to get it together. The guys she dragged home had always come before his or his brother and sister's welfare. But Alayna seemed to have the mother part figured out, but not the woman part.

What if she got snowed by some SOB a second time? Or worse, what if some asshole who liked little girls targeted her? Hell, it was known to happen. She was as vulnerable as Emilia. They were both marked with kind of inner bruise left behind by

Asshole Aaron.

It wasn't Bowie's business, though. She made it clear back in high school that she didn't want him. But it was perfect for a while. Until she stomped his heart to shit and left him wounded. Still, he saw the regret in her face as he walked off that day at the bank, saw her mouth the words, *I'm sorry.*

The scratching of tires on dry ground and gravel sent his thoughts into survival mode. He glanced behind him. Headlights threw his shadow before him as he darted between two cars and rushed up onto the sidewalk to make way for the car. The driver revved the engine as he passed him, his tires squealing as he turned the corner. The interior lights of the dash etched the driver's image in profile, but weren't bright enough for Bowie to see details.

A sense of urgency hit him, and he turned the corner in an all-out sprint, closing in on the house like it was the finish line at the end of a race. He tried the front door and found it still locked, then darted around to the back. Everything was secure.

He forced himself to walk up and down the sidewalk, cooling his body while his breathing slowed to a normal rate. It wouldn't do for him to burst into the house all worked up. He didn't want to alarm Alayna, but he couldn't shake the sudden rush of anxiety. Couldn't shake the need to see Alayna and check on her.

But he needed to keep his distance and simply protect her kids, protect her, until the cops gave the all clear, and then he'd go on with his life.

Once at the door he stopped. He would not give her another shot at breaking his heart.

He let himself into the house, then secured the door. He jingled the keys so he wouldn't startle her and entered the living room, eager to speak to her. The momentum of his emotions hit a wall of disappointment.

Alayna lay on the couch, fast asleep, her features relaxed for the first time all day. She'd been through a lot in the past few days. An unexpected tenderness rolled through him which he tried to ignore, but it didn't keep him from reaching for the throw on the back of the couch and draping it over her.

Movement at the bedroom door caught his attention, and he turned to see Emilia hovering there, every line of her small body projecting indecision.

"Can I get you something, Emilia? A drink of water?"

"No." Her large green eyes fastened on his face. "You came back."

Her words triggered thoughts of the moment they opened the laundry room door to find her standing guard over her sisters, her face beaded with sweat, her eyes teary with anxiety, while the other two clung to each other.

Bowie knelt to her level so he could look into her eyes. "I'm here to help you and your mom, and I'm not going to leave." The possibility of being called up flitted through his mind. If it happened, he'd deal with it. But right now Emilia needed to know she was safe.

Her measured gaze met his with a look older than her six years. "There was a big bang yesterday. It scared us, and Rosa cried, but I cuddled her and shushed her like momma does."

His mouth went dry. They could all three have been killed. His voice came out husky. "That was a smart idea."

"Bliss never came back."

The question in her eyes reached down into his gut and gave it a twist. "Bliss couldn't come back to get you, but I will, and so will your mother. There was an accident at the bank, and your mom couldn't drive her car, but all she talked about was coming to get you. And we did. She loves you so much, she'll never let anything happen to you or your sisters."

Emilia nodded. She placed a hand on his shoulder, then moved in tentatively to hug him.

Emotion gripped his throat. He held her and patted her back.

She released him and wandered back into the bedroom. He watched from the doorway as she climbed into bed and curled up against Rosa. He eased the door partially shut, leaving a crack so the living room light would act as a nightlight.

He glanced at Alayna on the couch. Her gaze was focused on

him, intent and thoughtful. She crooked a finger, and he tried not to read anything sexual into it as he strode over to her, but her drowsy eyes and flushed cheeks made it…and him…damn hard.

ALAYNA'S CHEST ACHED with emotion. Bowie sat on the edge of the couch and for several beats they stared at each other. She wanted to grab him and drag his mouth to hers and experience the heat she saw promised in his expression. He was too good to be true, and when something was too good, it always meant heart-ache.

"You're so good with her," she managed. She was using her children to keep him at bay, to keep her own emotions under control, when it was the very last thing she wanted to do. If she got involved with him, she'd have to tell him things she didn't want to admit.

His Adam's apple bobbed. "It doesn't take a psychologist to figure out what's going on. Her father left and didn't come back, Bliss locked her in a room and didn't come back. You're all she has, and she's scared."

And she'd brought another man into their lives who would eventually leave. Why hadn't she heeded her instincts, thanked him, and walked away? Because she felt like she owed him something for what happened after they broke up. She didn't want to acknowledge the rest.

She was afraid for her children's lives, for her own. She and Bowie were the only defense against the people who killed Bliss. Only Bowie and her.

Alayna shoved up and tucked a pillow behind her, then looped her arms around her knees. "All I can do is keep reassuring her, Bowie. I could tell her Bliss was hurt badly so she won't feel like she abandoned her and her sisters."

He lowered his voice to a rumble. "She already knows some-thing happened to Bliss. She heard the shot. They all did. Eventually you'll need to tell them the truth."

Alayna ran her fingers through her hair and pulled at it. They were so young. They cared for Bliss. She was part of their lives. She wished she'd given the woman more of a chance. "I'll tell them tomorrow."

"I know you want to protect them, Alayna. I do too. But they'll be okay. They're young."

She hoped so. "I know you practically raised your brother and sister."

"I fed Carmelita her bottles and changed her diapers when I was seven. She was four when Ciro was born. Two years later Mom sent us to stay with our father in Mexico, hoping he'd keep us, but he couldn't even afford to feed us, and there was no one to care for Carmelita and Ciro but me. Every summer she shipped us off, and every school year he brought us back."

Her heart ached for those children. "I'm sorry, Bowie. I don't remember you ever telling me about those visits."

His dark brows knotted in a frown. "I didn't want your pity, Alayna. Not then, and not now. We all three survived it, and we're all responsible adults. Like I said, kids are resilient."

"And you still insist you're not responsible for helping your brother and sister succeed?"

Bowie shrugged one wide shoulder. "They did the work. I just tried to help as much as I could. Then when I went into the teams, they realized I needed them more than they needed me."

"Your work...you said you'd be working long hours once these two weeks are over. And don't SEALs get deployed a lot?"

"Sometimes. Depending on the mission, my deployments can stretch anywhere from a few days to six months. Sometimes I have to leave at a call without explanation. And I know the life isn't for everyone." He leaned forward to brace his elbows on his knees.

"Is that why you're not married?"

He looked away. "Partly. I just haven't found the right woman. She'd have to be comfortable running the show while I was gone, and willing to welcome me back after my absences."

And the worry of the deployments would be torture. It would

take a very strong woman to face that alone. She knew what alone meant all too well. She fought to keep her thoughts from going to places too painful to think about.

"Are you going to stay in until you retire?"

"I don't know. I've got seven years in. Retirement is twenty. Thirteen more seems abstract right now. But I plan to re-up next year for four more."

And what if something happened to him during one of those deployments?

She'd known he was alive and living his life, had pictured him doing just that numerous times during the five years she struggled through college, though she hadn't known he was in the Navy. After marrying Aaron she'd refused to allow herself to think about him, because she was afraid to compare what she and Aaron had with what she'd been forced to throw away. She'd been desperate to be satisfied with her marriage.

But now, knowing Bowie put his life in danger so often…

"If you meet someone and have a family, will you continue with your team?"

"I'll have to make that decision if it happens."

She smoothed the blanket over her knees. "Does your family write to you, send you care packages, and things like that?"

"They rarely know where I am, Alayna. We're not allowed to say."

How could they bear it? And why would he choose to be isolated from his family? He had a good relationship with them.

She pressed her forehead against her updrawn knees for a moment, then forced herself to straighten. "You didn't choose this because of what happened between us?" *Please tell me you didn't.*

"Why would you think that?"

Because she made the choice to isolate herself from her family because of it.

She looked up to find him waiting for her response. "Because it's the only thing we didn't plan together."

CHAPTER 9

ROSA'S SMALL FINGERS clutched Bowie's hair. Her fragile legs hung over his shoulders, and he rested his hands on them to hold her secure. Her heels occasionally drummed against his pecs when she got excited, and every once in a while, she'd lean down and rest her cheek atop his head. It made him smile every time she did it.

She smelled like little girl and the sunblock Alayna slathered all over the girls' fair skin.

A breeze cooled the air and made the afternoon pleasant, though on occasion it brought with it the scent of wild animals and manure.

"What is that, Rosa?" Alayna asked in an attempt to get her to speak.

"Cat."

"What kind of Cat?"

"Big cat." Rosa threw her arms out and around.

Bowie couldn't help but smile, and knew she was gesturing even though he couldn't see her.

"It is a big cat. It's a mountain lion," Alayna said.

Rosa made a claw and growled.

Within the enclosure, the rocky terrain simulated the mountain lion's real habitat, all but the woven matt the cat lay on. He raised his head and blinked his golden eyes as though to say *don't interrupt my nap*, then lowered his head and went back to sleep.

A few minutes later, when they paused beside the snow leopard enclosure, Rosa wiggled atop his shoulders. "Down." One of the large cats lay in a hammock strung between two trees, while the other stretched out on the ground beneath, her large paws folded atop her chest like she was playing dead.

Bowie grabbed Rosa's hands and let her slide down his back while Alayna caught her and set her on her feet. She gripped a log safety railing taller than she was and called out, "Kitty-kitty-kitty." The two large white Snow leopards with their distinctive black spots ignored her.

"Sorry, baby, they don't understand 'kitty,'" Alayna said. Bowie grabbed Addison as she swung over the safety railing, saving her from a spill, and set her on her feet.

Alayna shot him a look of gratitude and bent to caution her. "Stay off the railings, Addison. They're there to keep you from getting too close to the animals." She spoke to all three children. "These aren't pets like our neighbor Mrs. Kutzera's cat, Freckles. These are wild animals. The only people they're used to being around are the people who feed them. They're here because they've been hurt and can't live in the wild anymore. But they aren't tame enough to pet."

"Bear," Rosa shouted pointing to the enclosure next door. She ran to the next fenced-in area and peeked from under the top rail to see the animals.

The word sounded more like bar than bear. "Sounds like a little Texas slipping into her accent," Bowie murmured as the rest of them followed her.

Emilia, acting like a little mother, bent to repeat the word more clearly. "Bear, Rosa."

"Big black bear."

Wow, a whole sentence. She was doing pretty good for being just a few months past her second birthday.

He placed a hand against the small of Alayna's back and felt the warmth of her through the lightweight cotton shirt. "I believe Rosa can say a lot more than she does, but chooses not to. With two older sisters to do all the talking for her, what's the point?"

"You're probably right, but she needs to communicate for herself, and be independent. I'm not really pushing her, I just want her to build her vocabulary."

"Once she learned to talk, Carmelita never shut up. She still hasn't. When Rosa's ready, she'll start chattering endlessly and you'll long for the quiet."

She smiled for the first time since they left the house. Understandably, she dreaded telling the girls about Bliss when they returned to the house. He'd hoped the trip to the zoo would get her mind off it for a while.

"Does Rosa like music?"

"Yes. All three girls do."

"I'll download some songs on my MP3, and we'll encourage her to sing. Music is the universal language."

Alayna gaze fastened on his, a half smile curving her lips. The warmth in her eyes, her expression, set off a chain reaction of longing and need inside him. Was it real, or was it just an echo of what he felt for her years ago?

Addison gripped Bowie's fingers and leaned against his leg. He looped the arm around her small shoulders and earned a smile. These girls were a source of entertainment, and a much-needed distraction when he got too caught up.

He scanned the people around them, looking for anyone showing interest in their small group. The three large guys he'd been tracking since they arrived stood forty feet behind them at one of the cages. All three were large, with dark hair, and wore sunglasses. Something about them set off his radar. They seemed out of place with the families and couples touring the facility.

"Mommy, can we have a ice cream cone?" Addison asked.

"When we get back to the cabin."

"But I want one now."

"We have ice cream at the house, Addison. There's no reason to spend money on it if you can have it when we get home."

Addison pouted.

Alayna gave her what Bowie had labeled as The Mommy

Look. Addison's head dropped, and she studied her feet.

Bowie's phone rang, and he tugged it free of his pocket. Recognizing Detective Gray's number, he activated the call.

"We're at the cabin," Gray said as soon as Bowie identified himself.

"What's up?"

"I need to see you and Ms. Wieland."

Bowie looked up and down the path they were walking. "We'll be there in about half an hour."

"We'll wait." It had to be something important, otherwise the two detectives wouldn't have driven three hours to have a face-to-face sit-down.

"Gray's at the house. He wants to see us." He swung Addison up on his hip. "We'll go get that ice cream you want, Addie."

"Good."

"Me some, too," Rosa said.

Alayna mouth parted in surprise, then she beamed. "Two sentences in a row!"

They made their way through the facility, and were halfway to the car when Rosa pointed toward the east end of the parking lot. "Daddy!"

They both whirled to look where she pointed, while Bowie scanned the parking lot for movement. All he saw was a row of vehicles.

"Is Daddy here, Mom?" Addie asked.

Her gaze met Bowie's "I don't see him. Rosa may have seen someone who looked like him, but he's gone now."

He hit the fob on his keys to unlock the SUV. He couldn't leave Alayna and the girls unprotected. "Let's get the kids to the car, and we'll drive around and look."

She waited until the girls were secure and the doors closed. "How would he know we're here?"

Bowie shook his head as he started the car and drove it around the parking lot in a slow search. "I don't know. The only people who know are my CO and the police. You didn't tell anyone else, did you?"

She shook her head.

"If it's him, he had to follow us here. If it's not…" He read the fear and worry in her expression. He scanned the parking lot again. "He's gone by now. There's no need for me to look around. And the police are waiting for us."

He thought about the guy in the car two nights before, peeling off and driving toward him fast enough that he'd felt compelled to dodge between two cars and run up on the sidewalk. Was it her ex? Or someone out to find him?

A GRAY, NONDESCRIPT, four-door sedan was parked on the street in front of the house. Detective Gray and his partner Detective Stansberry climbed out when Bowie pulled the car into the driveway. Alayna took the children in, settled them at the table on the back patio, and made each one of them an ice cream cone. By the time she finished, Bowie had brought the two detectives into the living room and offered them a seat.

Alayna sat on the couch where she could watch through the sliding glass door while the girls ate their ice cream.

"There's no easy way to say this, Ms. Wieland. We found your ex-husband's car. It was dumped in an area of the city where there were several abandoned warehouses. The car had been burned, and there was a body inside."

Aaron was dead. The father of her children, the man who had tormented and threatened her for the past three years, was gone.

Her ears filled with cotton, and Detective Gray's voice sounded muffled. Nausea rolled over her, along with relief.

Detective Stansberry laid a hand on her shoulder. "Are you okay, Ms. Wieland?"

She swallowed against the nausea. "I don't know. I can't believe this is happening."

Stansberry went into the kitchen.

Gray continued, "We won't know for certain if the person in the car is your ex-husband until we compare DNA to samples from his house or dental records."

"You—you don't need to take a sample from one of my children?"

"No."

She felt relieved they'd be spared that.

"The body was very badly burned. We're hoping they can use dental records, but if that doesn't work, they'll extract what they need and verify it was him in the lab."

Dear God. First Bliss and now Aaron. "If they can't, then what?"

"We keep investigating and try to identify him in other ways."

"Who could have done this?" She sipped water from the glass Detective Stansberry handed her.

"We're looking into it, Ms. Wieland. Your ex-husband embezzled a lot of money from a lot of people. Some of them are very angry. Dangerously so."

Her eyes strayed to the girls outside. Their father—might be dead. Probably was. Their stepmother had been murdered. They'd lost two people from their lives and didn't know it yet. Her heart pulsed at her temples and throat.

"I haven't told them about Bliss. I was going to tell them today, after the zoo." She struggled to regain her composure.

"I'd suggest you hold off telling them anything until we get further into our investigation."

Did it make her a coward to jump so quickly at his suggestion? She didn't care. She wanted to spare them... For all his faults, he was their father.

"Would there be any reason for your ex-husband's prints to be all over your apartment?"

"No. He comes to pick the girls up, but has never been past the living room."

"We found his prints in several areas. Including your bedroom and the girls'. Based on the evidence, he was the one who trashed the place. There were no other prints anywhere, other than yours and the girls."

She had suspected, but hadn't wanted it to be true.

"Do you have any idea why he would have done that or what he might have been looking for?"

"No. If I knew why he did this, other than to hurt me, I'd tell you. If he was looking for something…I don't have a clue what it could be. And if I did know, I'd hand it over to you. My girls mean everything to me, and I would never put them in this kind of jeopardy."

Detective Stansberry leaned forward in his chair. "We noticed you'd cleaned the place up when we went by."

How would they know that without someone letting them in?

"You didn't really expect me to leave it like it was until we got back, and let my girls walk in to see their room and the rest of their home destroyed, did you?"

His lips compressed. "No, of course not."

"Bowie and I went through everything, saved what we could, and threw out everything that was broken. He even cut up our clothing and destroyed the children's toys. Why would he do that?"

The two shook their heads. "Did you pack them a bag when they went to their father's? Do you still have them?"

"We left them at his house. I assumed since the house was a crime scene nothing could be removed, so I didn't ask about them."

"Would you mind if we went through the girls' things here? The toys you brought. Just in case?"

"No. You're welcome to look through everything, including what I brought with me. We're in the two bedrooms on this floor."

"Thanks, we appreciate it," Detective Gray said as he shot Detective Stansberry a look. The two went into the bedroom Emilia and Addison were sharing.

Bowie sat on the couch next to her. "I guess Rosa didn't see Aaron at the zoo."

"I can't believe he might be dead. But then I also can't believe anyone would kill Bliss. Why would someone want to hurt her? She was harmless. Kind of ditzy, but she tried to be good to the girls. We didn't have anything but Aaron in common. I didn't really give her as much of a chance as I should have."

"The killers might have wanted to know where Aaron was. Or the location of whatever he was searching for at your apartment."

"But what could it be? He only grudgingly gave me child support. There's no way he'd give me anything of value."

Bowie shook his head. "Did the kids have any electronics he allowed them to use at his house?"

"An iPad, but they weren't allowed to bring it to my house, it had to stay at theirs. The girls had toys and clothes he bought for them, and those had to stay there too."

Bowie raked his fingers through his hair, his expression harsh with control. "You don't have a computer at your house."

"My laptop is in the shop. I had to take it in last week." A dropping sensation hit her stomach, and she placed a hand over it.

Bowie's voice dropped to a whisper. "Are you sure he couldn't have put something on it?"

"It's my work computer. He wouldn't have access to it."

"Are you sure, Alayna? You're helping the kids get ready to leave and go to his house, and he's waiting in the living room alone. How long would it take for him to put something on it using a flash drive?"

She bit her lip, nerves dancing like an aerobics instructor in her stomach. "We'll pick it up when we get home and check it. But I don't see how or why he'd do that. Once he got it on there, when would he have access to it again to get it off?"

"When he broke into your house and trashed it."

He was right. And if they found it on her computer—whatever it was—they'd think she had something to do with Aaron's criminal activities.

Bowie's gaze met hers, conveying the same thoughts. "It's a long shot, but one we can check."

"Okay."

The children came in the same time the two police detectives finished their search of the second bedroom. Alayna put on a Sesame Street program for them, and the four adults went outside.

"How long will it take to get a DNA match?" Alayna asked.

"It will take several weeks, Ms. Wieland, but the dental identification may come in in a few days."

"The men who attacked me? Have you found them?"

"We have some leads we're following," Gray said, but for the first time he didn't meet her eyes.

"We can't stay here hiding out indefinitely. What would you suggest I do?"

"The only thing you can do. Go back to your life."

She clamped her lips together to keep them from trembling. "And hope they don't try again? Hope they don't take one of my children instead?"

Detective Stansberry attempted a soothing tone that didn't work. "If your ex-husband is dead, and he was the one who hired them, they won't have any reason to try again. And if it wasn't him, but someone meaning to use you for leverage, he's dead now, and it won't do them any good."

"Unless it wasn't him in the car. Or whoever was after him thinks I know something. Maybe I should take out a full-page ad in the paper. 'Alayna Wieland knows nothing about her ex-husband's misdeeds. Please leave her and her children alone.'"

"If it isn't him, we'll know in a few weeks at most, and he'll be wanted in connection to the death of whoever's in the car. We'll find him," Detective Stansberry said.

"I don't find much comfort in that, Detective. You can't even find the men who tried to take me."

Detective Gray answered for them both. "Our hands are tied, Ms. Wieland." His cell phone rang, and he stepped away from the group to take the call.

She focused on Stansberry. "You'll need Aaron's parents' contact information. It's in my address book in the bedside table. While you're searching my apartment again, you can get it."

"I'll need you to sign paperwork giving us permission to search your apartment again."

Gray rejoined them, his features harsh with tension. "We need to go."

"Let me get the paperwork." Stansberry strode off to the car.

Gray returned to the conversation they'd been having. "If it had been anyone but your ex-husband who trashed your apartment, we'd have some wiggle room, but with the fingerprint evidence, we don't."

A crash sounded from inside and a plaintive, "Mo-o-o-m-m-m," stretched out immediately afterwards. Alayna threw the screen door open and hurried inside.

FRUSTRATION AND RAGE burned through Bowie's patience. "You have an attempted kidnapping as wiggle room," Bowie said. "An attempted kidnapping you don't seem all that interested in investigating."

"You're wrong, Lieutenant. And what makes you think she's completely innocent in all this? Why else would her husband trash her apartment if she didn't have something hidden?"

"Alayna would never, *ever* put her children in danger. If you'd taken the threat to her more seriously when it happened, instead of devoting all your attention to Aaron Harper's crimes, you might have caught up with him before someone else did. Those men could have been your lead to Harper, or at least to one of the people after him."

Bowie loomed over the detective. "You've left Alayna and her kids vulnerable to attack because you were too busy following the money instead of the threat." Bowie took a step closer to Gray. "I go back to work in a little over a week and a half. She'll be alone with three children to protect. Totally alone. Think about that while you're driving back to San Diego." He ground his teeth in frustration. "If something happens to any of them, I have a few friends in very high places who are going to hear about it."

Bowie opened the screen door and stalked inside.

CHAPTER 10

THOUGH BOWIE ATTEMPTED to put his anger behind him, the girls seemed to sense his mood and were quieter than usual. He downloaded a movie for them on his computer and hooked it to the television while he and Alayna sat at the kitchen table and decompressed.

He poured her a glass of wine while he grabbed a bottle of beer from the fridge for himself.

"They think I'm involved, don't they?"

He couldn't see the point in holding back a warning. "Yeah, they do."

She shook her head. "I'm not. One minute they're saying Aaron might have hired those men to kill me for the insurance money, the next saying someone might be attempting to use me for leverage to get their money back and now they think I'm involved with whatever he's doing." She shook her head. Gripping the wine glass like it was an anchor, she said, "If I had access to all the money they keep talking about, I wouldn't be worried about making my rent."

Bowie spoke before she got worked up. "I don't believe he's dead."

Alayna's head snapped up.

"If it was me, and I was a ruthless son of a bitch with access to bundles of cash, I'd put someone in my place and give myself time to find whatever the hell it is I've lost. Do you think Aaron might be capable of killing?"

She fell silent for a moment. "When we first met, I would never have believed it. It wasn't until he started getting more and more clients, the pressure started building—"

"You have your doubts too?"

"Yeah. After everything that's happened in the past three years, it just seems too...easy." She raked her hair back from her face with one hand and propped her elbow on the table. "And even if it is him in the car, there are still the people looking for the money he stole. I'm the only one left they can blame." She sucked in a deep breath.

She hadn't shared nearly as much information with him as he wanted. "What about your ex's family?"

"They live in Pennsylvania, and I've only visited with them a few times. When we first got married, and after Emilia and Addison were born, they came out for a week each time. Warren is quiet, and Gloria is...a little uppity. But California is a long way to come for a visit, and Aaron wasn't interested in them coming out after the divorce. His mother calls now and then. And I've set up FaceTime for her and the girls several times. I've even invited them to come visit.

"Gloria wanted me to bring the girls out to see them. But the court order kept it from happening, even if I'd been so inclined. I always worried they'd be waiting on the other end of the trip with a signed custody order."

Living with the constant fear of having her children taken from her made her wary. He couldn't blame her. "They wouldn't have been able to get custody. You're a good mother, Alayna."

"I try to be." A weary frown crossed her features. "You know we're going to have to go back to San Diego. Aaron's parents will be flying in to represent their son. They're his next of kin. They'll want to see the kids."

"I know. I want the girls to at least get to swim in the lake."

"And you haven't been fishing yet."

"I fish all the time with Doc, one of my buddies. We were

coming down mostly to play poker and drink beer. A lot of the guys have kids now, and our beer-drinking days are numbered."

She smiled and shook her head. "All the money you've spent on this place will go to waste. You could stay and enjoy it. I can rent a car and drive back alone with the girls."

He shook his head before she even finished speaking. "Not happening, Alayna. Besides, being here alone wouldn't be nearly as entertaining." He pointed toward the girls in front of the television. "Look at Little Bit, she's singing along with the others and dancing." He laughed at Addison's butt-twitching antics and Rosa's attempts to emulate her older sister. Even Emilia was getting in on the action, a little more gracefully than the other two.

"They're great kids, Alayna. They wouldn't be as great without you. If Aaron's family doesn't see that, it's on them. Their son is the one who's under investigation for embezzlement."

"Unless they find something hidden in the apartment. Do you think he may have trashed the place to draw everyone's attention away from something he left there?"

Bowie couldn't deny the thought had occurred to him. "This is the second time they'll have had access to the place. If they do find something, your lawyer will counter that the person who broke in had time to conceal it under cover of damage. They have Aaron's fingerprints to prove it was him."

ROSA'S SOFT BREATHING, like the distant sigh of a wave, might have soothed her to sleep, but Alayna's thoughts dwelled on Bowie, lying upstairs in bed. Every time he touched her, whether it was just a brief, light pressure of his hand against the small of her back, or leaning down to whisper something in her ear, she ached with need.

She couldn't block out her still-vivid, visceral memories of what they had in the past. In an attempt to turn off the feelings triggered by thinking of him, she forced herself to look at her current situation.

Was Aaron alive, or wasn't he? Was it safe to take the girls home when the police were more interested in looking at her as a criminal than they were in looking for the men who tried to kidnap her? Why couldn't she shake free of the stranglehold Aaron had over her life? She never had anything to do with his business. Had struggled for so long to break free of the iron hold he had on her.

He kept dragging her and the girls back. He could do whatever he wanted by using them as leverage. But now she had a chance at a life. If he was arrested…or… she couldn't think about his death. She wouldn't sink to Aaron's level by thinking it was okay to move on without regret if he was dead.

But it would be a relief not to have to constantly keep her guard up every time he showed his face at her house or called her on the phone. She was so tired of him, of his anger, and his need to lash out at her. His need to manipulate and maneuver her as though they were still married.

If he was still alive, where would he hide? Who would he turn to for help? She needed to think it through, so she'd have a direction to move in. She wasn't going to hide out and wait for something else to happen to her children or her.

Unable to lie there and stew any longer, she slipped free of the bed and padded softly to the living room, where a lamp still burned. She made certain it stayed lit every night, so if one of the girls woke in the middle of the night they'd be able to find their way to her room.

She went into the kitchen and turned the light on. Once she put the teakettle on to heat, she found a cup and a tea bag. She sat down at the kitchen table and pushed aside the collection of puzzles, coloring books, crayons, and colored pencils. Drawing a writing pad toward her, she fished through the flotsam until she found a pencil.

It had been some time since she moved in Aaron's circle, but she knew some of his closest friends, plus his partners. She wrote down four or five names as she remembered them. She'd known some of the wives, and she thought they might be more apt to talk to her. She wrote them down too.

She remembered the teakettle just in time to keep it from screaming and poured the hot water in her cup. As she turned to take it back to the table, a large, male form appeared at the bottom of the stairs, and she nearly dropped the cup. "Jesus, Bowie. Make a little noise. You scared me."

"Sorry. You couldn't sleep?"

She shook her head.

He moved past her to the refrigerator and got a bottle of water. His sleep pants, tied loosely, hung low on his hips, and his tank-style T-shirt hugged his torso like a layer of skin. His shoulders looked a yard wide, the muscles in his arms bulging as he sat down across from her and cupped his water bottle in front of him.

Try as she might, she couldn't drag her eyes away from him. He was beautiful. His body perfect. She knew from memory that his hair was thick and little coarse to the touch. His skin smooth and warm. His lips and tongue as talented as his hands. She lifted her tea and took a cautious sip to moisten a mouth so dry with desire she couldn't have swallowed without it.

Bowie waited for her to put the cup down, then laid a hand over hers, his brown eyes focused on her intently. "What have you been working on?"

"A list of Aaron's friends and business associates who might offer him help."

"Put it away for a while, Alayna." He ran his thumb over the back of her hand.

That small caress drained the strength from her limbs and had her heart leaping.

He raked his fingers through his hair from front to crown, thick, straight layers falling back into place like a sable's pelt. "I've been thinking too much to sleep too."

She glanced up. His nose was thin, the nostrils flared, his forehead broad, and his jaw strong. His mouth was a thing of beauty. She could see the imprint of his Spanish heritage on his features, but his Caucasian DNA marked them as well. She never tired of looking at him.

"I've never forgotten what we had before. Have you?"

"No. I haven't forgotten." Dear God, how could she forget?

"Do you ever think about what it could have been like for us?"

All the time. "Yes."

Her stomach tumbled with nerves. And was that hope?

"After all this stuff is over, I'd like for us to date again. If you're up for it."

Could she date Bowie? She wanted him with a hunger she hadn't felt since...since they were together in high school. Dating seemed a tame pursuit in light of the emotions roiling inside her.

The girls wouldn't have to come into it. Would they? She was rationalizing to keep from thinking about how much the girls would be hurt if something happened to him. If he deployed, and he left them. She wanted to say yes but... "How can you forgive me so easily after what I did?"

"We were young, high school. It was a big commitment for us both. Your family has nothing to do with us now."

They'd been in love. So in love. She'd never stopped loving the boy. But he was a man now. A man committed to the Navy and serving his country. He was different. Could she feel as deeply for him now as she had before?

And what about his family? After what Matt did to Ciro... She'd have to tell him eventually. And afterward? There was no way they'd accept her. How could he accept her?

"I haven't had a date in three years, Bowie."

"I'd say you're due one, then." His half smile flashed his dimples and punched her just beneath her heart, stealing her breath.

"I don't suppose all the things we've been doing together with the girls could be called a date?"

"No. A real date would be just you and me doing something we both enjoy, together."

She could think of one or two things right at this moment she'd like to do with him. She told herself for years that those feelings had been forever deadened by everything that happened in her marriage. But Bowie jumpstarted them again with a vengeance. It was both a blessing and a curse.

She focused on their hands, because he'd somehow captured both of hers. She loved the darker tone of his skin, so warm against her pale hands. "What if we've built up all those memories to something they're not? We may not be the same with each other."

When she met his eyes, he leaned forward, inviting her to meet him halfway. His gaze held hers, challenging, compelling. It seemed to take her forever to stand and lean across the table. His lips, warm and light, brushed hers, then separated, then came back for more.

She raised a hand to his jaw, his stubble prickling her fingertips, and she slid her hand behind his neck, drawing his mouth harder against hers. Their tongues tangled, and desire swept through her like a brushfire. With quick, darting movements, he drew her tongue into his mouth. When she thrust her tongue forward, he sucked on it.

Rivulets of sensation worked their way downward, and she hummed beneath the pressure. An ache of need built in intimate places that had been a stranger to arousal for a long time.

He broke the kiss, his lips warm against her cheek, her throat. "If you were on this side of the table with me, I'd already be inside you, Alayna."

She couldn't deny that. The fire of need he triggered inside her was still there. But they were adults now. Both of them had responsibilities. He to his country, his calling. Her to her children.

And then there was a past he knew nothing about. A past that might change everything between them.

She eased back down in her seat and took a sip of her cold tea. Inside, the need and frustration hammered away at her self-control and made her hand tremble. "I'd have to be in a coma not to want you."

His quick smile flashed strong, white teeth and showed off his dimples. She wanted to grab him and drag him in for a longer duel of lips and tongues.

"But—?" He frowned, his features serious.

She wanted to tell him then, but if she did, it might destroy everything building between them. "We need to move slowly, Bowie. Make sure there's more between us than the attraction."

"Agreed. I don't know why you ended it…"

She owed him at least a partial explanation. "Because Harry Wieland is the most bigoted, hard-core son of a bitch on the planet. You should know that yourself. He's a card-carrying white supremacist, and he's raised Matt to be the same. He'd have found a way to either put you in the ground or have you spend the rest of your adult life in jail."

DAMN. HER BITTER tone said more in a few words than a long conversation could hope to.

So her father had used something against her to make her break things off. Whatever it was, she'd truly believed Harold Wieland would kill him or worse.

She continued, her hands moving nervously over the edge of the pad she'd been writing on. "In college, he kept tabs on me. He hired people to keep tabs on me. After that first semester, I went up to UT to search for you, but you'd gone to a different school. I tried to find you. Your mother wouldn't give me your number or tell me where you were. Your sister wouldn't either. I searched for you online. Called friends. No one could tell me how to find you."

"I didn't really have any friends I stayed in touch with. And you'd cut me loose." They'd all known how torn up he was over her.

"They would never have told me where you were."

"No, they wouldn't have. They didn't tell me you'd come around, either."

Her eyes looked liquid with regret. "Why didn't you ever try to call me?"

"I believed you were finished with me. So I moved on." Or had he? Dating one woman after another. Sleeping with—he wasn't sure how many women. Empty sex and a life filled with training, work, and deployments.

He ran his fingers through his hair. "It wasn't easy. It took a while." The admission came hard. Just because he'd forgiven her didn't mean he wasn't wary of leaving himself wide open to being hurt again.

"I'm so sorry, Bowie."

"You've already said that." But he was damn curious what the hell her father had done to force her to break it off. Threatened to kill him, possibly. But that wouldn't have been anything new. He'd threatened him to his face a number of times. But for Alayna to turn her back on her whole family, it had to be something major. She'd have to tell him when she was ready. But damn, it was hard not to push.

"I have a day on the water planned for tomorrow, if you're up for it. I thought I'd take you and the girls out in the canoe. I have life jackets for the kids and us, and small fishing rods we'll be using off the neighbor's dock for just a little while. Are they squeamish about worms?"

"Emilia probably, but I don't know about the other two."

"If we were staying longer, they could go to the water park and swim."

"I know what a sacrifice it is for you to give up the house to return to San Diego."

"I've contacted a friend, and he and his family are going to come down and take it over from us. So I won't be out as much. They'll be here before we leave on Wednesday. They have a son and two girls."

"Good. I'll strip the beds and remake them. That way they'll be good to go."

"I'd appreciate it. Langley and Trish are the best. You'll like them."

Alayna went to the sink to empty her teacup. Unable to let her go quite yet, Bowie followed her. He eased in behind her and encircled her waist with his arms. Alayna leaned back into him, and he rested his chin against her hair.

"Langley and Trish, they're close friends?" she asked.

"Yeah, they are. They're as much family as Carmelita and Ciro. I've been introduced to your world through the girls. Wednesday will be your first introduction to mine."

"What are you going to tell them about us?" She placed her hands on his forearms and rested her head back against his shoulder. His body stirred at her nearness, the scent of her shampoo, the fragrance of the lotion she used after her shower. Because he couldn't fight the urge to taste her, he bent his head to nip her earlobe and felt her answering shiver.

Would Langley remember him talking into his beer a time or two back in the day as he'd become maudlin over the memory of their breakup. "I'll tell them we were involved years ago and just recently found each other again." Then he'd catch some shit from Langley when he put two and two together and figured it out.

"Trish, his wife, was a social worker for several years, and now she's doing something similar for the SEALs, making sure they're getting the services they need if they're injured, that kind of thing."

"I'll look forward to meeting them."

She turned in his arms and aligned her body to his. He'd been semi-hard before, but came to full attention in a heartbeat, and there wasn't a damn thing he could do about it.

Her voice took on a husky tone he knew for the past. "I suppose we need to go to bed. It sounds like an active day tomorrow."

Bowie didn't attempt to hide his smile.

A blush stained her cheeks. "Separately. Trust me, you'll want to take things slowly. And I haven't been on birth control in a long time. I haven't needed to be."

If he'd gotten her pregnant before college, her father really would have killed him. With three children already, she wouldn't be in any hurry to have another. And he wasn't ready for that responsibility either. He didn't want his child to experience the same feelings of abandonment he had. He didn't want to dish that out to Alayna's girls, either. But he couldn't walk away without knowing what they could have.

"I promise to spend as much time preparing for our dates as I do my missions, so there won't be any reason to worry." He focused single-mindedly on the bottom curve of her lip, and bent his head to catch it between his lips and nip it just a tiny bit before running his tongue over the spot. "I've wanted to know if we could have the same fire between us. It's been driving me crazy."

She caught her breath. When he took her mouth full on, she hesitated, then slowly rose on tiptoe to plaster her body to his.

He cupped her ass and held her against him, the hard heat of his erection, covered only by the thin cotton sleep pants, nestled between her thighs. Heat rose in his cheeks, and his breathing grew ragged as she pressed her hips forward to rock against him. She was so close, the sleep shirt she wore a flimsy barrier. The thin ridge of elastic at the top of her panties would only take a moment to snap. He could imagine her raising her leg over his hip and he'd be inside her in a second.

It was she who pulled back, her cheeks flushed and her mouth berry red from the pressure of his. "We're flirting with danger here." She hid her face against his shoulder. "And as much as I'm enjoying it, it wouldn't do for either of us to wake up in the morning with regrets."

She pulled away from him, but there was reluctance in the way she moved, and her color rose as she glimpsed his obvious condition. "I'm going to say good night right now, so things don't get out of hand."

"Sleep well, Alayna." But he wasn't going to sleep. She'd relit the fire in his blood, and it was going to take more than a few kisses to quench it.

CHAPTER 11

AS BOWIE DIPPED the oar in the water on one side of the canoe, Alayna did the same on the other from the front of the canoe. They had a rhythm going that sent the vessel forward. With the girls sitting in the center of the craft between them, where he could keep a close eye on them, he was able to enjoy the activity of rowing and the scenery. They followed the verdant shoreline dotted with clustered rocks, the water calm and glassy smooth.

The novelty of being in a boat had worn off pretty quickly for Addison and Rosa, who were playing Barbie in the bottom of the canoe. But Emilia was transfixed as she studied the water. One the edge of the lake, a small deer suddenly eased out of the under-brush and bent its head to drink. Emilia caught her breath and turned to look over her shoulder at Bowie. He put his fingers over his lips. "Don't scare her."

"Momma, look!"

Hearing Rosa's high-pitched voice, the deer startled and looked around.

Emilia shushed Rosa, "Be real quiet, or she'll run back into the woods." The deer's large ears twitched, and she continued to watch the drifting canoe for a moment.

Her mouth moved like she was chewing something.

"She's chewing gum," Addison said, with such conviction Bowie leaned forward, head down, hiding his expression with the narrow brim of his boonie hat. His shoulders shook as he tried to stifle his laughter. He glanced up to meet Alayna's eyes and saw her wrestling with the same urge as she covered her mouth.

"She's eating something," Emilia said in a stage whisper.

The doe turned away and disappeared into the brush.

Emilia's smile was bright with excitement. "She was beautiful, wasn't she, Momma?"

"Yes, she was. They don't come out during the day very often. We were very fortunate to see her."

"If deer chewed gum, what kind of gum would they chew, Addison?" Bowie asked as they started paddling again.

"Bubble gum," she answered.

"What flavor?"

"Cherry."

"Deer like cherries, strawberries and blackberries, and all the edible berries that grow wild. They also like tender shoots off trees and bushes, and nuts, acorns, and mushrooms, too."

"We ate mushrooms on pizza," Emilia said. "It was good."

"Maybe we'll have pizza tonight for supper. Unless we catch enough fish to fix."

"Yumm," Rosa contributed her favorite expression. Bowie laughed.

Half an hour later, Bowie baited hooks and got the girls settled on the dock, fishing poles in hand. He sat with Rosa and helped her hold the pole.

"Tell me about your friends who'll be coming tomorrow."

"Langley is a Master Chief, and Trish used to be a social worker. As I told you, she's recently switched jobs. They've been married fifteen, maybe sixteen years. Tad, their son, was only a little older than Emilia when I was transferred into Langley's unit. And the girls were tiny. Tad's thirteen now, and the girls, Jessica and Anna, are eleven and nine, I think."

"Wonder what their secret is for being married so long?"

"She and Lang give each other space when it comes to their work, but they're a unit when shit hits the fan or something's going on with the kids. They talk to each other, *really* talk to each other, when they're together. We can't really say anything about the missions we go on, but it's still like they're in tune with each other."

"That's a blessing."

Bowie hesitated for a moment. "We used to be like that."

They had, but… "We were young and uninhibited and talked about a lot of things we shouldn't have, and didn't talk about the things we should."

"Like?"

They fell silent for a moment their attention on Addison's line as the float bobbed.

"I didn't want you to know how horrible Harry and Matt were. I was ashamed."

"I was ashamed of my mother, too. But I still told you about her. Warned you about her."

"What was I…?" She grabbed Addison's arm as she started to pitch off the end of the dock.

"Mom!" Addison leaned back, the line on her pole taut and she gripped it with both hands.

Bowie leapt to his feet, set Rosa down beside Alayna, dropped her pole onto the dock, and rushed to help.

Instead of taking the pole from her, he sat down beside her and helped her hold on. With his help, she reeled in the line. The tip of the little pole bent, and Bowie half expected it to break, but it didn't. Two minutes later a crappie about eight inches long surfaced.

"Wow, Addison. It's big enough for us to have for supper tonight."

Addison's mouth parted in shock. "We can't eat him!"

"Why not?"

Addison scrambled to her feet. "His mom and dad will miss him."

Taken back by her comment, Bowie couldn't formulate an answer.

Alayna laughed out loud. "Your expression is priceless."

He studied Addison's face. "If you don't want to eat him,

we'll turn him loose."

Her relief was obvious "Okay."

He raised the fish out of the water and waited for it to swing toward him, then took the fish off the hook. "Do you want to drop him back in the water?"

Addison cupped her hands and accepted the fish. She pitched it underhanded off the dock into the water and smiled as he swam away. When she turned to Bowie, wrapped her arms around his neck, and hugged him, he knew he'd handled things well.

ALAYNA'S NERVES STRETCHED taut as she checked on the girls behind her. Fastened in her car seat, Rosa whined crankily and fought against the restraints that held her in place. After being out in the sun and on the water for three hours, all three girls were tired and hungry. Her two-year-old just expressed it more vocally than the others. She caught herself continuously checking Bowie's expression.

Bowie soothed her by saying, "We're almost to the house, Rosa. What do you want to eat once we get there?"

"Taco," she said, distracted for a moment.

"I'll fix you a turkey taco when we get to the house, baby."

Five minutes later, when they pulled into the driveway, Rosa was in a full-on meltdown and screaming. Emilia had her hands over her ears and looked close to tears herself, while Addison shouted, "Make her be quiet, mommy."

Bowie bailed out of the car and unhooked Addison's seat re-straints and helped her out of the car while Alayna helped Emilia. Bowie released Rosa's, and she reached for him. He scooped her up and lifted her free of the seat, cradling her against him. He handed Alayna the key to unlock the door.

While he fixed sandwiches and a tortilla wrap for Rosa, she dealt with the cranky two-year-old by bathing her face with a washcloth and talking to her in a calm, soothing voice.

Twenty-five minutes later the girls had finished their sandwiches and Rosa was slumping in her lap, half asleep and fading fast.

Bowie said, "I don't know how you do this alone."

"It isn't a question of how. When you're alone and you're all they have, you just do it. Just like you did with Carmelita and Ciro."

"I remember being trapped in the house with them for days at a time while Papa worked. Maybe that made the logistics easier, but being isolated made me crazy. I dreaded going to Mexico every summer. I took off one time and stayed gone for three days to keep from going."

"What happened?"

"When Moira finally found me, she beat the shit out of me and dumped me at the border. I had to call my father to come pick me up. I was twelve."

Alayna couldn't imagine dropping her child off alone in a strange place and leaving him. What if he'd been kidnapped or killed? "I'm sorry, Bowie."

"It's part of the past. And since my father died I haven't been back. I haven't seen Moira in three years, either. I send her money every couple of months to be sure that continues. Besides, the money's really the only thing she cares about."

She understood what it was like for family to be a burden. She'd chosen to dump her own because of it. "It's easy to block out what they've done as long as they're out of sight, or you don't have to communicate with them. But it doesn't make the hurt go away."

His silence spoke louder than words.

"I'm determined to be as good a mother as I can be. But after everything you went through, having to care for your brother and sister, I can't imagine why you'd give dating me even a thought."

"I never blamed Carmelita or Ciro, Alayna. They had even less control over our lives than I did. Your kids aren't an issue."

"They're a lot of work. If we got truly involved, it would be a lot to take on—on top of what you already have going on in your life. Not to mention all this with Aaron. You need to give it some thought." She nodded toward Rosa, now limp in her lap. "I'll be right back." She laid the toddler in the middle of the bed and pulled a lightweight blanket over her.

Emilia and Addison played a board game at the coffee table, but she suspected they'd be nodding off in minutes.

By the time she had everyone occupied, Bowie had cleaned up and was loading the dishwasher. It seemed all they did together was care for the girls or occupy them. Maybe that was why she hadn't had a life outside of the children. It was so hard to find time for someone else when you already had three people demanding every part of you.

But she wanted time with Bowie.

She checked that the front door was locked, then went to the refrigerator to get a bottle of water.

Bowie grasped her hand and tugged her toward the back door.

"Is something wrong?" she asked as soon as he pulled the sliding glass door shut behind them.

"No." He took the bottle of water from her and set it on the table. "I just wanted…five seconds alone with you without kids." He looped an arm around her waist to bring her in close against him. "Just five seconds to show you we're already involved."

He cupped her chin to raise her face to him. The heat she read in his gaze set her heart to pounding. His lips covered hers in a soft kiss that drained the tension from her limbs and had her melting against him. He leaned back against the house and parted his legs to draw her in closer as the kiss deepened, heating up as their tongues touched and tangled.

It had been so long since she'd been kissed with such passion. A responsing heat flushed her skin and triggered a tempting tingle in intimate places long untouched and unfilled.

When thoughts of the past started to creep in, she quashed them by running a hand under Bowie's shirt and caressing the smooth skin and taut muscles of his abdomen and chest. He felt so powerful, so male. The wiry teenager with an abundance of sex appeal had matured into a handsome hunk who practically radiated sex, but it wasn't just the exterior that drew her. His patience and strength were what sucked her right in.

When his warm palm caressed her waist, her ribs, and cupped her breast, a sensual thrill raced through her, and her nipples beaded, hypersensitive and eager to be touched. He plucked at one with just the right amount of pressure, and rivulets of sensation trailed downward, building her need to an empty ache.

His lips left hers to find the sensitive hollow between her shoulder and neck. His warm breath feathered her skin, and she shivered. She raked her fingers through his hair, recognized the coarse thickness of it, and turned her mouth to his.

A slap on the glass door beside them caused her to jump. "Mommy?" Emilia's voice traveled through the glass, though muffled.

Bowie raised his head. She bit back a protest. His passion-sharpened features and the unfulfilled ache inside her gave her a jolt of regret.

"I'm sorry," she murmured as she pulled away and went to the door.

"Mimi is on the phone, Mommy."

Alayna's sensual high dropped so quickly her stomach tumbled, and she placed a hand against it. She pulled open the door and took the cell phone Emilia handed her. "Hello, Gloria."

"We'll be arriving in San Diego a little later than expected. Probably five o'clock on Wednesday."

"Do you need me to pick you up at the airport?"

"No. We'll be getting a rental car. But we'd like you and the girls to join us for dinner after we get settled at the hotel, probably around seven."

She'd have to feed the girls a light snack beforehand. Alayna's stomach started to cramp with nerves. "Okay. Where will you be staying?"

"The Courtyard Downtown on Broadway. Aaron's house is still a crime scene, and the police won't be releasing it for a few more days. Once that's done, we'll have it cleaned and move in there until something is resolved."

Though her tone was level, Alayna sensed the stress behind it.

"I wish we had room for you to stay with us, but I only have two bedrooms. One for the girls and one for me. And most of the time one of them ends up in there with me."

"We understand."

She moved further into the kitchen to see where Addison and Emilia were, then backed toward the sliding glass door again. "I haven't told the girls about Aaron and Bliss yet. The police came here yesterday, and they won't be sure for a few more days."

"I just can't believe any of this."

"I don't know what to believe either, Gloria. Aaron had the girls on the weekends twice a month. He and I didn't really have any other contact about anything but them."

"Who is Bowie?" she asked. "Emilia said you were there with him."

"He's a friend from high school. We recently reconnected."

"I don't really approve of you carrying on a relationship with a man in front of the girls."

Heat hit Alayna's face, and she caught her breath. "Not that it's any of your business, Gloria, but Bowie's on the second floor, and I'm sharing a room with Rosa. Our relationship hasn't really progressed to that point…yet. But I wonder if you expressed your objections to Aaron when he moved Bliss into the house six months before they were married and had the children over on the weekends."

Silence stretched between them. Alayna was tempted to shut the phone, but held on, though she was trembling with a combination of hurt and anger.

"Will we see you on Wednesday?"

"Yes. And I'll be bringing Bowie with me so you can meet him."

"This isn't really a good time for us to meet your boyfriend, Alayna."

She didn't really care if it was a good time or not. "I've been alone for three years, Gloria. I gave birth to your youngest grandchild alone. How long do I have to be alone before it's okay for me to move on?"

"Very well. We'll see you at seven on Wednesday."

Alayna hung up without saying goodbye.

DAMN, IT WAS hard enough to romance Alayna when the kids were continuously interrupting, but the telephone call had set her off. She was angry, but hurt with it. Clearly her ex-mother-in-law said something to upset her. If he could get her to share it with him, she might get past it.

It would be nice if, when they got back to San Diego, they could go out on a date, just the two of them, so they could have a conversation that didn't center around someone else's needs or wants and could concentrate on their own.

But now he understood Alayna's wariness about dating. Most guys wouldn't give her or the kids a chance, and those who did might be out for what they could get rather than what they could give. It was a two-way street most men would be wary of walking. There were some serious implications here for them all.

And the dynamics introduced when you added in-laws and an ex-husband to the mix, when she was used to going solo and couldn't even depend on her own family. Jesus!

He sauntered through the kitchen into the living room. Finding the room empty, he sat down on the couch and changed the channel to a movie. Alayna appeared from the bedroom.

"They've crashed for a little while. It could be an hour, or it could be ten minutes."

"Sit with me and relax for an hour or ten minutes…whatever time we have."

She sat, but she ran her fingers through her hair and held her head in her hands. "I told Gloria, my ex-mother-in-law, I'd be bringing you to dinner tomorrow night. Will you mind coming with us?"

"Of course I'll come."

"I think Aaron may have implied to his parents that I was un-faithful during our marriage."

"Why would you think that?"

"Gloria said she didn't like the idea of me carrying on a relationship with a man in front of the girls, like we were stripping off naked and having sex in front of my kids."

"Jesus!"

"They're going to make trouble, Bowie. I can tell. Aaron's filled their heads full of lies, and they're going to go after the girls. I can feel it."

He looped an arm around her, drawing her in against his side. She nestled in and clung in a way that spoke of fear. "They can't get custody. You're a good mother, Alayna."

"They can if they can prove living with me is a danger to them."

"Your ex-husband is responsible for all this. They can't take your children simply because you're caught in the crosshairs of a situation he created."

"They can try."

"Look, Trish worked in social services for years. When she comes down tomorrow, ask her about all this. See how much of a leg they have to stand on. Then call your boss and talk to him. You have resources they don't have, Alayna. Use them."

"I will."

He needed to ask Trish some questions as well. Would his relationship with Alayna prove a help or a hindrance? There was nothing in his background that would prove problematic. He'd had a background check for the military. If there'd been anything there, he'd have never gotten into the SEALs. And his military record was clean.

In the meantime, all he could do was offer her reassurance. He held her close and gave her what comfort he could.

CHAPTER 12

ALAYNA NARROWED HER eyes against the glare that danced across the lake. The aroma of grilling burgers and the lighter scent of fish done to a turn filled the air.

The Markses' girls, Anna and Jessica, were playing on the swing set with her three girls. Tad, their thirteen-year-old brother, was stretched out in one of the lawn chairs they brought, playing an electronic game.

Trish Marks's strawberry blond hair cupped her chin as she sat across from Alayna on the bench seat of the picnic table. She had a country girl prettiness, the sprinkling of freckles dusting the bridge of her nose making her look younger than mid-thirties. She certainly didn't look old enough to have a thirteen-year-old son.

They'd talked about their children and jobs while the men finished grilling the meat. The park was well-maintained, and the children were having a good time.

"So how did you and Bowie meet?" Trish asked.

Alayna hesitated for a moment. How was she supposed to explain that one? Somehow she thought Bowie would want her to keep it simple. "We've known each other since middle school, but we hadn't seen each other since graduation. We ran into each other at the bank."

Trish's blue eyes widened. "Wow. What are the odds?"

"Yeah. It was really a bolt out of the blue. He's doing me an incredible favor by allowing the girls and me to spend time here at Big Bear with him. I needed to get away for a few days, and his friends had to cancel their plans to join him here, so he brought us instead."

"And he took the girls fishing instead," Trish said.

Alayna couldn't help but smile. "Yeah. I wish you could have seen Addison's expression when she caught that huge crappie, but it wasn't nearly as entertaining as Bowie's when she said she couldn't keep it to eat because his mom and dad would miss him."

Trish laughed. "Kids are so entertaining when they're that age."

"Yeah, they are. Bowie's been really wonderful with the girls."

Trish looked up from folding and unfolding her napkin. "He's never dated anyone with kids before."

They hadn't really been out on a real date yet. How much could she share with this woman? They'd only just met. "He said it wasn't really fair to get serious and then expect the woman to adjust to his wandering through between deployments. Or something like that."

"But he's made an exception with you."

Had he? With his overdeveloped sense of responsibility, he really wouldn't think he had a choice about bringing them here. She bit her lip. "We haven't really been out on a date yet."

"It'll happen. He keeps looking over here with that eagle eye of interest, even when he's talking to Langley."

"Maybe he's worried I might tell you some his deep, dark teenage secrets," Alayna teased.

Trish grinned. "Gossip, yum. Spill it. These guys are like vaults. The only people they talk to are each other. Most of the time."

"I imagine you get your husband to talk, and you seem to have done okay with me so far." Trish was very easy to talk to. "I know I'm not like the other women Bowie usually dates, am I?"

Trish studied her for a moment. "I know the others were out more for a good time than a relationship. When you have children, it changes everything."

"Yes, it does. I haven't dated anyone since the divorce three years ago because of that. Officially, Bowie and I are just thinking about dating." She could tell herself that, but what about the hot and heavy petting session they had in the kitchen, and the other out back of the rental house?

Trish looked away, but not before Alayna caught a slight shift in her expression. "You said your youngest daughter is two."

"She'll be two and a half in another month. Aaron divorced me while I was pregnant." Her gaze shifted to Rosa, watching as Jessica pushed her gently on the swing. It had been a rejection of her and of their child. It hurt her more for Rosa than it ever had for herself.

"I'm sorry." Trish laid a hand on her arm, drawing her gaze back to her face.

She hated feeling the need to defend herself because of Aaron's action. "He was already involved with someone else when he left."

Trish folded her arms along the top of the table. "Bowie told us about your ex-husband."

Alayna bit her lip again. "I know how close you and your husband are to him. He thinks of you as family. I don't intend to cause Bowie any trouble. I know his commitment to the SEALs comes first."

"That isn't exactly the way it works, Alayna. When you're married to or involved with one of these guys, it's a conscious choice to either accept what they do and support them or walk away."

Well, that left her a little breathless. If she were alone, without children to worry about, she'd already be invested in a relationship with Bowie, but because of the girls, she had to think with her head, and not with her heart—or any other part of her anatomy.

"Though they didn't really have a choice, my children accept what Langley does and everything else that goes along with it. But to Langley's credit, he's made a conscious effort to do the best he can when he's home to stay bonded to the kids, and to me, too."

Trish looked down at her linked hands folded on the table.

"In the six years I've known him, Bowie hasn't bonded to any woman for more than a few weeks. He's a serial dater. But he certainly seems to be at home with your girls." Trish tipped her head in the direction of the grill.

When had Rosa decided to go to him instead of swing or come to her? Watching Bowie hold Rosa, his arm securely under her bottom and her head on his shoulder gave her stomach a tumble. He rubbed Rosa's back while Langley flipped the burgers.

She hadn't realized until now how hungry her youngest child was for male attention. Aaron ignored her much of the time. His reasons were clear to her, but he was damaging their child because of his guilt.

She spoke around the knot in her throat. "I haven't gotten involved with anyone because I didn't want it to affect the girls if things didn't work out. Bowie's made a point of showering all three of them with attention. Emilia is very quiet, and he's even drawn her out. Addison is a little more precocious, and makes it impossible to ignore her."

Trish took a sip of her iced tea. "It looks like the girls might have made up their own minds about him."

It was. "He's just so damned irresistible. He always was."

Trish laughed. "They all are. Just wait until you meet the rest of the original team members. Even though they've moved on to teams of their own, they still stay in touch. They've gone into battle together, covered each other's backs. They'll be friends for life."

"Does your husband lead a team too?"

"No. He's the Lieutenant Commander's executive officer."

"That's a big deal, isn't it?"

"Yeah. He's worked hard for it, but it was his work on this particular team that led him to it. They were an exceptional bunch except for one."

Alayna couldn't help but ask. "What happened to him?"

"He was arrested for assault and a host of other things, and is doing six years in a military prison. When he's released, he'll receive a dishonorable discharge."

The betrayal of what he'd done would have been hard for the rest of the guys on the team. She understood how it felt to be sold out by someone you trusted. "That couldn't have been easy for any of the men."

"You're right. It hasn't been. They were the ones who took him down and turned him in."

Something doubly hard. "Have any of them seen him since then?"

"I don't think so."

How hard would that be for him to be cut off from the men he'd served with, the men he had called friends? "How much longer does he have?"

"Less than a year, I think."

"Do you think he'll want to see the rest of his team once his time is up?"

Trish shook her head. "I don't know. I'm not sure that would be physically safe for him, or the other guys. But emotionally, and mentally it might be cathartic for them all. Including Derrick."

She understood that. "Why did you tell me all this?"

"I know who you are." Trish leaned forward and rested her elbows on the table. "When the guys first get through BUD/S, they celebrate...a lot. Bowie hung out at our house quite a bit. One night he had too much to drink and told me all about you."

That was almost worse than having Trish know her ex-husband might or might not have been killed, and his body and car burned.

Trish rolled the napkin into a tube. "You're the only woman I've heard him wax poetic about...ever. That was six years ago."

Her throat was too blocked by emotion to speak. "I never wanted to break it off with him. I did it to protect him." She was tempted to tell Trish about her father and brother, but decided against it.

"Eventually things will get back to normal, and the two of you will have time to make up your minds about whether you want to pursue a relationship." Trish rose and stepped out of the picnic table bench seat. "I think the guys are done with the grill. I'll call the kids over to eat."

Alayna moved to set the table and offered to take Rosa from Bowie.

"She's fine with me." He said as he sat her down on the bench and pulled a plate in front of her. "Hamburger or fish, Rosa?"

"Fishhh."

Bowie looked up. "Think she'll eat it?"

"I haven't seen her turn her nose up at anything so far. And if she doesn't eat it, I'll eat hers and she can have a burger and some mac and cheese."

Tad reached the table and pumped his clenched fist into the air, "Mac and cheese! Score!"

She and Bowie looked at each other and laughed.

Bowie shook his head. "I think it's universal. If they'd played their cards right, the Romans could have continued to rule the world just through the supply and demand of mac and cheese."

Langley laughed as he put a plate down with fish on it, then another with hamburgers. "You could say the same for Mexico and the taco. I think my children would gladly subsist on pizza, tacos, and mac and cheese.

"Tacos!" Rosa announced, in a dictatorial tone.

Bowie groaned, "You've done it now, Lang. You said the word. We'll never hear the end of it."

"What?"

"T-A-C-O-S." Bowie spelled the word, "are currently Rosa's favorite food. And once she gets them on her mind…"

"Rosa, look what I have," Alayna said quickly to distract her. She put a spoonful of macaroni on her plate, a piece of fish, and some grilled asparagus.

"Taco!" Her bottom lip popped out.

Bowie rose from his seat. "How about a fish taco? I think we packed the tortillas before we left the house. I'll be right back." He jogged to the car and returned with a plastic-wrapped package of flour tortillas.

"Anyone else want a fish taco?" he asked.

"I do," Emilia said.

Bowie was back with the tortillas and sauce, quickly cut up two pieces of fish on two tortillas, put a slice of cheese on each, and put them on the grill for a minute. He scooped them off, sprinkled lettuce and tomato over the melted cheese, squirted a little of his sauce on them, rolled them up like a wrap, cut them in half and put one in front of Rosa and one in front of Emilia.

Emilia thanked him. Rosa took a big bite, chewed and grinned. "Yummm—Good taco."

Jessica, Anna, and Tad laughed and earned a fishy grin in their direction.

When he sat down beside her, Alayna put a plate covered with a helping of everything on the table in front of Bowie. He always went the extra mile for her and the girls. "Thank you for heading off a tantrum."

"No problem." He smiled. "I may start carrying tortillas in my pocket everywhere we go."

Alayna laughed and gave his arm a squeeze.

Conversation flowed freely around the table as they talked about everything there was to do here in Big Bear, and some of the local restaurants they'd talked about trying. While she and Trish were cleaning up, the men took a walk with the kids.

Alayna approached Trish about the children and her in-laws. She told her everything that had happened thus far. And the possibility that Aaron might still be alive.

"When will you know?"

"They said in a week or so." She took a deep breath. "My ex's parents are flying in today. We're supposed to meet them at seven for dinner with the girls. I think if he is dead, they'll file for custody of the girls."

Trish's mouth sagged in shock.

"I think Aaron has told them lies about me. My boss had to file a restraining order to keep him from coming to the office and harassing me. Since he couldn't catch me going out on him, because I wasn't, he wanted to imply I was having an affair with my boss, since he was the only man I saw every day.

"It wasn't true. And he couldn't make it so. I think he harassed Mr. Kappes, hoping he'd fire me, and if I didn't have a job and a stable home, he could gain custody. When that didn't pan out and Mr. Kappes filed the restraining order, he finally quit coming to the office.

"When he got married again, I was relieved. I thought he would concentrate on his marriage and his wife and leave me alone. But he hasn't.

"I know you don't know me, but I swear to you, I was always faithful to him. Since the divorce, all I've had time for is my job and my children. My daughters mean everything to me. I think of them first, always.

"After what happened at the bank and the break-in at the apartment, if Gloria and Warren go before a judge, they could say I can't provide a safe environment for the girls, they could take them away from me."

"The danger would have to be clear, present, and ongoing before a judge would give them permanent custody, Alayna. As long as you're able to show you're taking precautions and putting their welfare ahead of everything else, they won't take your children."

Those few words helped to ease the panic burning in her chest.

"Aaron tried several times to take them. So I've had meetings with DCS before. It's terrifying every time. Even when you haven't done anything wrong, and you're doing the best you can, you're always thinking in the back of your mind, you'll say the wrong thing, or because you're struggling to make ends meet, they'll decide the parent with more money can do more for them. Now Aaron has destroyed things throughout the apartment, it looks barren. The children are going to be so upset when we go back."

"He broke in and destroyed their things?"

"Yes. The police found his fingerprints throughout the apartment. They believe he was looking for something. But I don't have a clue what it could be. The police came and asked permission to search the apartment while the children and I are here, and

I gave them permission. There's nothing there. Bowie and I cleaned the place up, and if there'd been anything, we'd have found it."

"Change your door locks, get a dead bolt, and demand a copy of the police report from the break-in, with the information that your ex is suspected of being the one who broke in and destroyed your property. It's proof that he's aggressive toward you and the children."

"I will. I've also been to the daycare center. And the preschool and elementary school where Addison and Emilia go, and discussed the situation at length with the principal, secretaries, and teachers. If Aaron shows up there to try and take the children, they'll call the police. And his parents aren't on the list of people who can pick them up. The only people who're on the list are the daycare owner who runs the bus, and me."

"It sounds like you're doing everything you can, Alayna."

"I'm nervous about going back. Even when you haven't done anything wrong, the police have a way of making you feel like you have. If they only knew how little we had to say to each other when he or Bliss came to get the girls. Aaron would never have voluntarily given me anything. He refused to pay his child support on time, even when he was threatened with jail time, and called to harass me on a regular basis."

"Do you have that documented?"

"Yes, the court documents about the child support are public record, but he was careful about the harassment, and without a witness besides the girls, the police wouldn't do anything. I did finally record a conversation we had a couple of weeks ago." She heard the weariness in her own voice, and raked her fingers through her hair. Just talking about it wore her down.

"Did he ever get physical with you or the children?"

Alayna looked away. "Not the children. Only once with me." Once was enough. She glanced up. "Don't tell Bowie any of this. He's always had a thing about protecting women. I don't want him worked up over something that happened three years ago. And I don't want him always seeing me as someone he has to protect.

I've been working hard to put a lot of things behind me, and I now I think I finally have…I don't want it raked back up."

Trish remained silent for a long moment. "Things you bury have a way of raising their nasty heads when you're least prepared for it."

She knew all about that. "The men bury their battle wounds, too, don't they?"

"But that doesn't mean it's good for them. Have you ever thought about seeing a therapist?"

"I don't have time. I have the girls and caring for them, and I have a full-time job. I don't want them in daycare any longer than they have to be."

"No friends you can switch out with for a play date?"

"If I had just one child, but asking someone to take three is a bit much."

Trish nodded. "I understand. I can still give you the name and number of a couple of therapists, just in case you find the time."

When the men returned to the picnic area, it was time to take their leave. Bowie and Langley did a handshake and shoulder bump. He looped an arm around Trish's shoulder and guided her a few feet away to have a private conversation.

While Jessica and Anna took the kids up to the car and strapped them in, she turned to Langley. "I'm so glad I got to meet you both, and your children." She offered her hand.

Langley shook it. "Good to meet you too," he said with a smile.

"The beds have been changed and the bathrooms and kitchen cleaned. We left some bread and milk, condiments, and lunch meat in the refrigerator."

"But took the tortillas."

Alayna laughed. "It used to be waffles. You haven't lived until you have to make waffles with peanut butter and raisins for lunch every day for a month."

Bowie rested an arm around her shoulder. "I'm ready if you are."

"Yes, I'm ready."

"So did the great and powerful Trish give you some sage advice?" Bowie asked.

"Yes, to keep doing what I'm doing and things should be okay." *And that you waxed poetic about me when you were drunk.* She should have told Bowie about the pictures and run away with him right after high school. But the pictures had been damning. He'd have gone to jail. She made the only decision she could have made at the time.

But that was the past, and they could have another chance. She had to believe that.

CHAPTER 13

BOWIE BUTTONED HIS shirt and finger-combed his hair one last time. The black slacks and button-up, long-sleeve white dress shirt seemed the best way to go. The black tie with tiny silver-gray diamonds woven into the fabric was conservative but dressy. A gray blazer made it a classic look. He threw his jacket over his arm and checked that he had his wallet and keys.

Wary of dropping the girls off at the apartment and leaving them, he'd swung by the super's apartment, talked to him about a new door lock and dead bolt, and got him on board. The super promised to install it tomorrow morning.

Alayna opened the door, and he was struck her flawless skin and flushed cheeks. In that pale green dress and off-white heels, she looked cool and classy. She'd braided her hair into a rope and looped it into a figure eight at the nape of her neck.

"You look beautiful," Bowie murmured as he leaned forward to brush her cheek with his lips.

"So do you," she whispered.

He flashed her a smile. "That's handsome, sweetheart."

"I have to get Rosa's shoes on and I'll be done. Have a seat."

Emilia sat on the couch crumpling her dress at the sides over and over.

Bowie sat down next to her. "What is it, Em?"

"Someone broke in and broke my toys and my piggy bank and

stole my money. All mom found was a little change."

"How much do you think you had in the bank?"

"Over twenty dollars. I helped Rosa and Addie clean up their toys, and sometimes brushed their hair and put on their shoes. Mom paid me a quarter every time. Then she took me to the bank, and we changed the coins to five-dollar bills. She said all she found was thirty cents."

He'd been with Alayna when she picked the coins up off the floor. If Aaron Harper had really broken in and trashed the apartment like the police thought he had, he was a fucking asshole. If he stole his child's money, that made him a fucking slimy bastard on top of it.

"If I had the twenty dollars, I'd give it to momma to buy Rosa and Addie's toys back."

She sounded so grown-up, and so sad. If Aaron Harper had been in the room, Bowie would have punched his face in. "What about your toys?"

"I like to watch movies and read books. They didn't tear up many of my movies, and I go to the library at school to get books."

"You're a good sister for looking after them, Em." He tucked a blond strand of hair fine as corn silk behind her ear. "Do you know what insurance is?"

She shook her head.

"Insurance is something you pay for every month, to fix your car if you have an accident, or replace the contents of your house or apartment if you have a fire or break-in. Your mom will fill out a paper explaining to the insurance company what happened, and they'll give her some money to buy some of the things back."

"Do you think mom could get me a *Beauty and the Beast* movie?"

"I bet she will if you ask her." If he didn't get it before then.

"They tore up my clothes. They must not have a little girl like me."

It was hard for Bowie to swallow past the lump in his throat. "Someone who rips apart your clothes and steals your money doesn't deserve a little girl like you."

Alayna ushered Addison and Rosa out of the bedroom as he spoke. Alayna's eyes met his, then dropped away.

Bowie rose to help Alayna herd the children down the hall and into the elevator. On the way to the hotel the silence stretched between them. Even the children were quiet. Rosa, sitting directly behind him clung to her monkey and sucked her thumb.

Where the girls sensing their mother's tension and his? Seeing their room empty of most of their clothes and toys had been traumatic, too. Alayna had obviously done a lot of explaining to try and make the experience less upsetting for them.

He broke the silence with, "I spoke to the super of your building. He's going to get right on the new lock and deadbolt tomorrow morning."

"Thank you for thinking of it."

"You were busy with the kids and other things." He reached for her hand and gave it a squeeze.

She caught and held it. "My ex in-laws may be a little difficult."

He glanced her way. "It isn't your responsibility to apologize for anyone else's behavior. You don't have any control over them."

"Well, just in case."

"I promise not to hold it against you."

She smiled slightly. "I appreciate it." She paused. "Warren is okay, but...."

Jesus, Gloria Harper must be hell on wheels if she cowed the kids and Alayna before they'd even seen her. Luckily they were going to a family pizza place. The kids would be busy eating, and he'd stuck a coloring book and crayons in Alayna's ever-present backpack.

"It's going to be okay." He wasn't going to sit by while they ganged up on her.

A faint smile tipped up the corners of her mouth, then disappeared.

The restaurant was in full swing when they arrived. The waitress led them to a large table in a back room. In the corner sat a couple. The man was thin, his blond hair liberally sprinkled with gray, his dark slacks, white shirt, and gray blazer very similar to Bowie's. His wife sat straight-backed and tense beside him, her silver hair lighter than her husband's. Her purple dress contrasted becomingly with her hair and skin.

The couple rose as Alayna and the children reached them. Their body language remained stiff as they hugged Alayna, but warmed as they greeted and hugged each one of the children. At Alayna's introduction, Warren Harper shook Bowie's hand, and Gloria Harper gave him a cool nod.

A waiter brought a booster seat for Rosa, and they all settled in at the table. The first few minutes were taken up with ordering food. The waitress had barely left when Gloria started grilling Alayna about the Emilia and Addie's school progress and Rosa's daycare situation.

Was she asking because she was interested, or was she fishing for information and a reason to contest custody? The muscles of his neck and shoulders knotted with the need to step in and set her straight.

"I wish you could have brought them out east to visit us," Gloria said.

"Aaron had it set up with the court that I couldn't take the girls out of state, Gloria."

"Why did he do that?"

"I wish he was here so you could ask him. I never tried to gain sole custody, and never threatened to leave the area."

Gloria looked down her thin blade of a nose. "You really shouldn't talk about this in front of the girls."

Color stained Alayna's cheeks. "I was just answering your question."

Warren cleared his throat. "How is your job going, Alayna?"

"It's fine."

"Are you still working for that Kappes fellow?"

The fact that he knew her boss's name was very telling. Bowie reached for the hand clenched in her lap and gave it a squeeze.

"Actually, I work for three different lawyers in the firm, Warren. Mr. Kappes, Mr. North, and Mr. Sullivan. I've researched and written briefs for all of them."

"I didn't realize it was a partnership."

"They've been practicing together for twenty years."

"How old are these fellows?"

"Mid-fifties."

Warren frowned, then his gaze shifted to Bowie. "How did you and Alayna meet?"

"We ran into each other at the bank. But we've known each other since junior high."

"You're from Texas, too."

"Yes."

"What do you do for a living?"

"I'm in the Navy."

"I was too, many years ago. I only stuck it out for four years, but it taught me some discipline and focus."

"It has me too."

The food came, and for a short time they ate in peace. In the middle of the meal, Alayna rose to take the girls to the restroom.

"You said you ran into Alayna at the bank," Gloria said.

"Yes."

"That must have been a surprise."

"Yes, it was. We hadn't seen each other in ten years."

"And she just decided to go off with you with the children over the weekend?"

"No, Mrs. Harper, she didn't. I know you haven't spoken to the police about the circumstances surrounding your son's— disappearance. And Alayna can't tell you things in front of the children, but I can tell you now so you'll have a clearer picture of what's going on.

"Your son embezzled funds from the estates of some very powerful people. While we were at the bank, two men attempted to kidnap Alayna by forcing her into a van. Luckily I was still in the parking lot, and we were able to fight them off. It was suggested at that time they may have been hired to hold Alayna hostage to put pressure on your son to return the money he's stolen.

"After the kidnapping attempt, Alayna asked me to accompany her to your son's house to get the children. We found Bliss dead—murdered—and the girls locked in the laundry room. Bliss was killed protecting the children. That should tell you the kind of people Aaron's angered."

Bowie thought it best not to mention the break-in and her son's part in that. The woman looked shell-shocked.

"The police will tell you all this tomorrow when you see them. Or they may try to be a little more sensitive than I have. But the truth is, your son is an embezzler and may have gotten his wife killed and put his ex and their children in deadly danger. In light of that, I would think you'd cut your ex-daughter-in-law some slack, since all I've seen her do since all this came down is the best she can to keep her children safe and care for them.

"She went to Big Bear with me to get out of town with the children in the hopes the police would find your son and the men who tried to abduct her before she came back. The children had been through a trauma and needed a distraction.

"When the police came down to notify her they'd found Aaron's car and he might be deceased, she knew you'd be flying in, and thought you'd want to see the girls. She hasn't told the girls about Bliss's death, or that their father might be gone because there's a possibility it wasn't him they found in the car. And she didn't want to upset them if they discover it isn't.

"I don't know your son. I've never met him. But in light of everything that's happened, in your shoes, I'd start questioning what else he may have been…less than truthful about, at least for your grandchildren's sake."

To her credit, Gloria Harper's hand shook only a little as she reached for her wine and took a sip. "We'll be discussing everything you've said with the police tomorrow."

"I'm sure you will."

Alayna came back to the table, and Warren and Bowie rose to help her get everyone settled once again.

The meal passed in a less confrontational manner. And when

they rose to leave, Bowie offered to pay the check.

Warren shook his head. "Thank you but I've got it. You were our guests." He placed cash in the folder holding the bill.

Rosa reached for Bowie, and he lifted her in his arms.

"The girls seem very comfortable with you, Mr. Ramirez," Gloria said.

"I like children, and they seem to like me."

"I like you, Bowie," Addison said.

Bowie chuckled. "Thanks Addie. It's always good to be liked."

Emilia slipped her hand in his in a silent show of agreement, and he gave it a gentle squeeze.

Gloria Harper hadn't completely been cowed by everything he'd told them, he surmised from her imperious tone as she said, "If you wouldn't mind taking the children to the car, I'd like a word with Alayna alone."

Great. "Sure, Mrs. Harper. Addison, hold Emilia's hand, and what?"

"Don't let go."

"You got it."

ALAYNA'S STOMACH CHURNED, and the one slice of pizza she'd eaten seemed to be stuck at the base of her throat.

Gloria surprised her by saying, "The children were very well-behaved tonight."

"Thank you. They're good girls."

"After we've met with the police tomorrow, we'd like to come over to your apartment to visit with them. They'll be more comfortable at home than in a strange hotel room."

What would they think of her barren apartment? The detectives were certain to tell them about the break-in. "Certainly. I can text you the address so you can find us." She pulled her phone out, typed in the address, and heard the chime from Warren's cell phone. "What time should we expect you?"

"Our appointment is at ten in the morning."

"We'll look for you at noon or a little before then. After your visit, there's a park a few blocks from the building. We can drive the girls there to play and take a picnic lunch. The girls and I do that most weekends."

"That sounds nice. Thank you."

Gloria was being so polite it made her nervous.

"We'll walk you to the car," Warren said, and took her arm.

Gloria continued to talk. "The police said that once they had released the house, we could stay there. Do you think it will disturb the girls to go there?"

"I don't know. We'll have to play it by ear and see." She drew in a deep breath. "Bowie told you what happened, didn't he?"

"Yes, he did," Warren said.

Now she understood why Gloria was being nice to her. It didn't matter. She still didn't trust her. Aaron had learned his vindictive hatefulness from his mother. She'd seen too much of it firsthand. And Warren would never stand up to his wife. He was too weak.

They exited the restaurant. The air, cool and crisp, cut through her dress, and she shivered.

"Bowie and the girls are waiting. We'll see you tomorrow. Good night." She barely waited for their reply before rushing to the car.

CHAPTER 14

ONCE THEY WERE home, Alayna left Bowie in the living room while she got the girls ready for bed. Rosa and Addison raced back out to the living room to say good night, but from the laughter coming from the outside the door she suspected Bowie was playing with them.

It was as she was tugging Emilia's pajama shirt over her head the six-year-old asked, "Why doesn't Nana like you, mama?"

She tried to answer her children's questions with at least a grain of truth. "Nana is just upset because mama and the three of you don't live with daddy anymore."

"I don't like Nana."

"Why not, Emilia?"

"Because she talks mean to everyone."

"Sometimes when people are upset about other things, they take it out on everyone around them."

"Like Brandon at school. He picks on the girls because we won't play with him."

"Why won't you play with him?"

"Because he picks on us."

Alayna bit her lip to keep from laughing. Brandon needed to change his strategy to get the girls to like him.

"Do I need to talk to your teacher about Brandon?"

"No. She puts him in time out. You said Nana and Grandpa

are coming tomorrow. I won't let Nana be mean to Addison and Rosa."

"Nana isn't going to be mean to you. She loves you."

"She's mean to Grandpa. Doesn't she love him?"

"I'm sure she does." God help him.

"Daddy was mean to Bliss and made her cry."

Her heart skipped a beat. "When was Daddy mean to Bliss?"

"The day you came to get us out of the laundry room."

Alayna's heart fell. She'd complained so much about Aaron's treatment, but had never dreamed he'd be the same with Bliss.

"I'm sorry he was mean to Bliss. He wa—isn't ever mean to you or your sisters, is he?"

"He yells at us to be quiet, but he doesn't spank us."

"Good."

"Can I say night-night to Bowie?"

"Sure."

As she suspected, Bowie was playing a game with the girls. Something about hunting a bear.

"Sack time!" he announced as she came into the room. He knelt so Emilia could hug him good night, and she herded them all back into the bedroom. She turned on the night light while they all three climbed into bed. She made sure everyone was settled with the cuddle toys Bowie bought for them in Big Bear, then turned off the overhead light.

Bowie had unbuttoned the top button of his shirt and rolled back the sleeves. His forearms looked muscular and tanned. She wanted to curl up in his arms and be held for a moment. Instead she sat down beside him. "Thank you for telling Gloria and Warren. If it had come from me, they'd have resented me all the more for it."

"I get that. Has she always ridden your ass that way?"

"Pretty much. I married her precious boy, and she thought I wasn't good enough. Then, after the divorce, I wasn't good enough to be the girls' mother."

"Bet she's feeling the sting now she knows what he's done."

"She probably is. I can't believe it myself. Why would he do this? And how on earth did he think he could get away with it?"

"I guess when you're caught up in something that promises you everything you ever dreamed of, it's hard to imagine getting caught."

"Emilia said he was mean to Bliss on the day she died. It pisses me off knowing, that he treated her badly, and got her killed, too."

"A tiger can't change its stripes, Alayna."

"People aren't tigers. We have the intelligence and opportunity to change if we really want to. When we were first married, I just went along with everything Aaron wanted." She'd been thrilled not to be alone anymore. "Then, when I decided to go back to work, he started to change. He'd bitch about dinner being late, or that the baby was fussy, or anything he could think of to make me feel less than what I was. At the time I didn't realize it as a form of abuse until I was around his mother more and she did the same to everyone. He learned it from her. That's why I don't stand for it, and it always keeps us in a confrontation mode."

"I hope you didn't accept it from him, either."

"I didn't. But then he started having affairs. And I started pulling away from him further and further."

"What else did he expect?"

"That I'd take whatever he dished out. Because that's the way he saw me. And I suppose when we were first married I sold him that bill of goods. I'd lost my mojo, and it took me a while to get it back." Like five years.

"You changed, and he didn't."

"I couldn't let my girls see me as weak and willing to put up with crap. I don't want them to ever put up with being treated badly, either."

Bowie rested a hand on her back and ran it up and down her spine. "I find it very hot that you won't put up with any crap from me or any other guy."

She smiled. "Or their mother."

He laughed. "Or their mother." He drew her in close against him and lowered his mouth to hers. He tasted of the sweet tea he'd been drinking and him. Her heart raced, and an empty ache settled inside her, an ache she wanted him to fill. The kiss turned torrid, and she hummed beneath the sensual pressure.

When Bowie broke the kiss, they were both breathing hard. He rested his forehead against hers. "I feel like a teenager sneaking around to make out with my girl."

"I understand. Finding time alone with three children is a challenge."

"Unless you learn to be very quiet and buy a lock for your bedroom door."

Alayna chuckled. "Or they're all in school or daycare."

"Can we take time for just the two of us on Monday?" His lips found a sensitive spot just beneath her ear. "The kids will be in school, and you'll still be off work, won't you? We can go out for breakfast, go grocery shopping, make love in the afternoon."

Oh, God, he was such a temptation to her. "Bowie—I'm not sure either of us is ready for... *more.* It's been less than a week."

"How will we know unless we try?"

Now he had fallen back into her life, she was afraid to reach for what she wanted. What if this was all a pipe dream, and it just went up in smoke? After dreaming of being with him for the past ten years... After being eaten up with regret, and imagining all the what-ifs during that time...

She had to take the chance, even if she never loved another man again in her life. "All right, Monday. Unless the police come up with any breaking news."

"Agreed." He kissed her again. This time slowly, softly, and so thoroughly every muscle in her body went weak. She wanted to bring him in and feel his body cover hers, run her hands up his back and hold him close as he moved inside her.

Bowie caressed her knee and his fingers curled hot along the inside of her thigh. "I remember how as teenagers we couldn't get enough of each other. Couldn't stop touching each other. How 'bout I do that now?"

A hot, melting ache built between her thighs. "Bowie—" She couldn't seem to catch her breath. Rivulets of sensation rushed toward the intimate heart of her in anticipation of his touch while nerves dried her throat.

She trembled as she placed her hand on his thigh, mirroring the position of his. Touching him would be an unbearable pleasure. She'd probably go off just doing that and nothing else.

Bowie's pupils expanded, eclipsing the gold, and his eyes looked dark with passion. His chest expanded as he dragged in a deep breath and spread his legs in invitation. His thigh muscles tightened beneath her touch as she ran her hand inward and up.

When his fingers reached the apex of her thigh and brushed the crotch of her panties, she caught her breath, and her mind went blank to everything but the roiling need tormenting her.

Bowie leaned forward to nuzzle her cheek, then latched onto her earlobe and nibbled it. "Let me take care of you, Alayna." His breath caressed her ear, and she shivered. She spread her legs as he had done, and he brushed his fingertips against the thin, silky fabric covering her.

"You're so wet for me."

His words fed her hungry need to be touched, held, kissed. "Oh, God."

"Keep calling me that while I touch you."

He smothered her laughter with his lips and eased her down to the couch, her legs draped across his. He pulled her sandals free and let them slip to the floor. When she curled into him, he caressed her bare calves, knees, and thighs.

Her legs trembled as his hand slipped beneath her dress and spanned the width between her pelvic bones. It rested there, driving her crazy, while his mouth explored hers in deep, thorough, drugging kisses.

She threaded her fingers through his hair, and her hands trembled as she unbuttoned his shirt and explored the width of his muscular chest and shoulders.

When he finally slipped his hand beneath the fabric of her panties, she moaned her relief. He cupped her and rested his fingers against her until she moved beneath the pressure to guide his touch where she needed it.

He eased two fingers inside her, and the sensation of being penetrated nearly threw her over the edge. She rolled her hips against the gliding movement of his fingers, simulating what his erect penis would do better.

Her movements feverish, she spread his shirt so she could touch him, urging him closer as the sweet, sweeping pleasure built higher and higher. She hovered on the peak until release rolled over her, and drifted down off the high of sensual pleasure like a leaf caught and carried upon the wind until it tumbled and dipped steadily to earth.

Every muscle in her body felt warm, loose, and spent.

Bowie lifted his head to look down at her and smiled. He slowly withdrew his fingers and rested his hand on her hip. "They're gone."

Curious asked, "What?"

"The lines of stress between your brows and around your mouth. Now we've discovered the cure, we'll have to do this every time they come back."

She smiled and raised a hand to smooth the hair she had mussed while they made love. "You always have had magic hands."

He grinned. "Is that all?"

"No. I think it was all that salsa dancing we did together. We had just the right moves on and off the dance floor."

"When the time is right, we can get back in step with each other."

Throughout everything they'd been through in the last few days, he had a positive attitude. A never-give-up attitude. She needed to adopt it as well, and start embracing things.

She needed to embrace Bowie for as long as he was here. For as long as they could be together. This might be the only chance she had with him, and she was wasting it.

"Do you have a condom, Bowie?"

CHAPTER 15

BOWIE STUDIED ALAYNA'S features. His hard-as-stone erection had throbbed with glee at the question. She looked drowsy with sexual release, and so fucking desirable his entire body remained on DEFCON 1 alert.

He reached behind him to remove his wallet from a back pocket and flipped it open. It had been forever since he'd dated a woman who wasn't prepared for safe sex, and he hadn't needed to carry protection. When he pulled out the lone condom in his wallet, she smiled, rolled easily to her feet and offered him a hand.

His pants felt like a vise against his erection, and he got to his feet with a little less grace than she. "Are you sure, Alayna?"

He'd never known her to do anything without a great deal of thought. They dated two years in high school before they had sex—though they had done a lot of heavy petting. By the time they made love, they pretty much groped each other every day, and knew every inch of each other's bodies. But that was ten years ago. He smiled in anticipation just thinking about it.

She drew him down the hall past the girls' room to her own. She reached for a lamp just inside the door and turned it on, then shut the door. She was trembling visibly as she turned to face him.

He ran soothing hands down the back of her arms and drew her close. "What is it?"

"I know it's crazy after what we just did, but I'm a little nervous."

"We don't have to do anything at all but hold each other, if that's what you want."

"That isn't all I want." She nestled close for a moment, then turned to offer him the zipper of her dress and was surprised when his finger went to her hair first. He unpinned it, unfastened the braid, and spread it out over her shoulders.

Bowie found his hands trembling as he ran the zipper down. He bent his head to kiss the bend where her neck and shoulder met. She shivered in response. She tugged the dress down and let it slide off her arms to land at her feet. The dainty lace panties and bra were as light a green as her dress, and the rest of her was all delicious, pale, bare skin.

Bowie ran his hands over her shoulders and arms to her elbows and bent to rest his cheek against hers. She turned to find his mouth with hers, and he cupped her face as his mouth fed from the passion of the kiss. Their hands collided as they both reached for the last few buttons of his shirt and rushed to peel it off. He unhooked her bra with a quick, practiced move, and she shook free of it. When her lips touched the spot just over his heart, he thought it might beat out of his chest. She reached for his belt, and just the idea of having her touch him forced him to count to ten to keep from losing control.

She pulled his belt free, and he bailed out of the rest of his clothes as if they'd caught fire.

Alayna laughed and wiggled back on the bed in just the scrap of lace underwear he found sexy as hell. When he tossed the condom onto the nightstand and slid onto the bed beside her, the smile still lingered as she ran her fingers through his hair and looked into his face with an expression of tender amusement that grabbed him first by the heart, then lower. "No need to rush. I'm not going anywhere."

In an attempt to ignore the rampant emotions her expression had triggered, he took the closest beaded, rose-colored peak in his mouth and sucked. Alayna's indrawn breath spurred him on to the other. Her breasts were full, her waist slender, and her skin pale in comparison to his.

Responsive to his every touch, she caressed his shoulders and back with a restless touch and tangled her fingers in his hair while he worked his way down her body. He slipped her panties down her legs and off. As he licked, nibbled, and kissed, she made a sound somewhere between a purr and a groan.

When he pushed back up, she grabbed him and kissed him like he was the last cookie on the plate and she hadn't eaten one in a decade. He reached for the condom on the nightstand and ripped the package open with his teeth.

Alayna plucked the condom out of the package and rolled it over his erection. Bowie gritted his teeth and mentally broke down his Mk11 sniper rifle to filter out some of the pleasure from her touch before it threw him over the edge. He eased inside her, nestling in as deep as he could get, and the glove-tight fit of her gripped him.

As he began to move, she countered his thrusts with an eagerness that ripped away his control. They strained together in a quest for completion that drove everything else from his mind. With her breath ragged in his ear and the soft sounds she made as she built toward orgasm spurring him on, his own release rolled over him like a tsunami, and he came for what seemed like minutes.

He collapsed beside her, and she turned onto her side, facing him. He looked into her eyes, just as he had so many other women, but there was a difference.

How many moments of repletion had he experienced with other women? Zero. As soon as he'd gotten off, he was ready to hit the door, or move on to the next one.

He gazed into her pale green eyes and knew he'd never feel for another woman what he felt for this one. It was as though he'd come full circle and landed back where he started. When she leaned forward and kissed him softly, he knew he was sunk. He wanted to spend the next week in her bed.

He wanted to find out if they could reignite the passion they'd shared. But he hadn't thought what it would be like to be all in again. His heart began to pound and his throat went bone dry. God, he was such a pussy. It was just sex.

"I never thought I'd feel this way again." Her voice came out just above a whisper.

"It was good sex."

AFTER THE HEAT and passion in his touch, his kisses, those few words felt...devastatingly wrong.

She turned onto her back and studied the ceiling to keep from looking at him, though she ached for him to reach for her and hold her. Her heart began to beat in her throat and wrists. This sudden disconnect after their shared intimacy was like having a strip of her skin ripped off. "Are you going to spend the night?"

"It might not be a good idea for the girls to see me asleep in your bed since your in-laws are coming tomorrow."

Though his reasoning was sound, it still hurt. "You're probably right." She brushed her hair away from her face. What went wrong? Was he always like this after sex? She remembered shared moments of humor, and the high of being together, not this...distance.

"I'll be right back." He rose and went into her bathroom. The toilet flushed, and water ran.

As she lay there, the fleeting thought that this might be some kind of payback for her breaking things off years before flitted through her mind.

Bowie had never been divisive or underhanded. Never cruel.

Then what happened just now?

When he came to the door, she waited for him to come back to the bed, but he continued to stand in the doorway, his gaze focused on her, his expression shuttered. She hadn't felt naked until that moment. Turning her back to him, she rose and reached for the robe hung on her closet door, quickly slipped it on, and cinched the belt.

"You need to tell me why you broke it off. What your father

used against you to make you do it."

Silence stretched while she attempted to shift gears to the last thing she wanted to talk about after making love with him. And how was she supposed to tell him the worst of it? It had been her fault his brother was beaten nearly to death. It was a miracle he'd lived.

Bowie's mother had screamed at her and blamed her before she hit her father up for a fat paycheck to keep from turning Matt into the police.

She told him what she could. "Harry had Matt video us having sex, then threatened to have you arrested for statutory rape."

His lips parted in surprise. "You'd reached the age of consent, Alayna. That's why we waited so long, so the charges would never have stuck."

"Matt changed the date on the video. You were nineteen, I was seventeen, but the new date made it look like I was sixteen at the time. That difference in your age and mine for those few months meant the difference between consent and statutory rape. You'd have gone to jail and come out either in a body bag or as a registered sex offender. Harry would have found a way to make it happen. Your life would have been over."

She shifted, glanced away, then back at him. "Even if the charges didn't stick... You worked so hard to get your GPA up to qualify for a scholarship and financial aid. All the cops had to do was keep you in jail long enough for you to miss the registration date, and you'd have lost the money. And they would have done it. Without that money, you never would have been able to go. I wasn't going to allow Harry and Matt to destroy you, destroy your dreams. Your future.

"So I thought I'd go along with Harry until you were safely out of reach. I stayed away, went to a different school. And as soon as that first semester was over, I slipped away to UT, but they said you weren't registered. So I went to see your brother and sister and begged them to tell me where you were." She shook her head and sank down on the bed.

She wouldn't tell him about the "welcome" she received when

she returned from the trip. Or the semester she missed because of it. She never went back home again, just finished her education and walked away without a word to any of them. Then she moved to California because it was as far away from them as she could get. She sank down on the bed.

"You should have told me, Alayna."

"You'd have wanted to confront them, fight them, and you'd have ended up in jail. It would have ended the same way, Bowie." Ciro had only been the beginning.

Completely at ease with his nudity, he moved from the bathroom door to sit beside her. "You sacrificed your dreams to cover for me with Harry."

"I eventually made it through."

"You wanted to go to law school."

After that first semester of college, she hadn't been in any condition to cope with the pressure of law school. "When the girls are older, I may. Until then, every time I research a case for my boss, I'm learning the law. By the time I go, I'll know enough to get through my classes more easily."

He slipped an arm around her and drew her closer. "All that school I missed, moving from one school to another, staying at home to cover for Moira when she didn't come home, being dumped in Mexico when she wanted to shack up with first one guy then another, cost me those two extra years in second and fifth grade. They'd never have been able to fuck things up for us if we'd been the same age."

"If you hadn't missed all that time, we wouldn't have graduated together. We might never have dated." She eased in closer and rested her cheek against his shoulder.

"It wasn't just good sex, Alayna."

Relief flowed through her. "I know." She looked up at him with a hint of a smile. "It was fucking fantastic sex."

He grinned. "Come back to bed so I can make it up to you for being an asshole."

"We're out of condoms."

"We'll think of something." He kissed her and guided her back down on the bed.

CHAPTER 16

A LAYNA PRAYED FOR the hours she spent with Gloria and Warren to pass quickly. She had hoped they would play with the girls, but they seemed content to sit on a bench while she pushed Rosa on the swing. When Emilia and Addison decided they wanted to ride on the roundabout, she sat Rosa between her older sisters' legs and pushed the disk while she ran alongside them.

"Why don't I take over for you for a few minutes?" Warren yelled as she trotted by.

She wanted very much to say no thanks and keep going rather than sit with Gloria, but she really had no choice. "Sure."

"Do you do this every weekend?" Gloria asked.

"Not every weekend, but most Saturday mornings."

"It's no wonder you stay so slender."

Was that a compliment? Her very first from Gloria.

They fell silent, watching Warren propel the roundabout by grasping the metal bars and pushing it along.

"Why are you living in this neighborhood, Alayna?" Gloria asked.

She scanned the park. A black mother pushed her baby in one of the hard plastic seats on the swing. A Latina mother stood protectively at the bottom of the slide ladder while her son climbed it, then rushed around to the bottom as the boy sat down and prepared to slide down.

"It's not affluent, but I've never heard of any drive-bys or assaults, and truthfully, it's the only neighborhood I can afford."

"But surely Aaron gave you money for the girls."

"Five hundred a month, which was what the court mandated. I usually save it for emergencies. The police froze the account and confiscated what was in it a few days ago. They said they were investigating where the money came from."

The woman's searching look had her counting to ten. "I'll show you the paperwork of the custody and support agreement, but it's a matter of public record."

"I would have thought a judge would have placed the amount of support high enough that you could at least live in a better apartment."

"Aaron's lawyer saw to it he didn't."

"You asked for spousal support, didn't you?"

"No. I didn't want his money, Gloria." She'd just wanted him to move on with his life and leave her alone. She'd taken the child support for the girls in case they needed medical or dental care, but she wouldn't be beholden to someone who hated her for anything.

When Gloria continued to eye her, she drew a deep breath. "I'll gladly show you the paperwork so you'll know I'm not lying."

"That won't be necessary. It's just ..."

"Aaron told you I was taking him to the cleaners and led you to believe I'm an unfit mother who didn't deserve to give birth to the children, let alone have custody."

"He did say your demands were making it difficult for him."

"Only because he refused to pay the children's support on time. When he was three months behind, I took him to court to get it. That's a matter of public record too." She rubbed her hands over her face. "He resented having to give the money to me."

Gloria fell silent. "Why would he lie about something like that?"

"He's upset because our marriage didn't work out, and he wants to cut me out of his life, but as long as I have the children he can't do it. He thought if he made enough noise in court, the judge would see things his way. But the thing is…I always put the children first. Ahead of myself. Ahead of everything."

It had been her experience that men rarely put anyone ahead of themselves. They believed they were more important than anyone else.

The way Bowie acted the night before, after such wonderful lovemaking, gave her heart a twist. His need to know what had caused her to leave before was understandable. But she read more into it. He wasn't certain of her. And she'd earned that after what she did to him in the past. But how and when could she tell him what destroyed her relationship with her family?

"The police think you and the children may be in danger."

"Is that what Detective Gray said?"

"Yes."

If she was going to use what her son had done in an attempt to wrestle her children from her, she had another think coming.

"If he thinks I'm in immediate danger, that my children are in danger, why isn't he here doing something about it?"

The children ran from the roundabout to the teeter-totter. Warren put Emilia on one end and put Rosa and Addie on the other. Since the weight was out of balance, he pulled Emilia's end down.

"You could come to Pennsylvania with us."

"Aaron has a court order that makes it illegal for me from leaving the state with the children."

"When did he do that?"

"Right after the divorce." He'd said, *you're not taking my kids anywhere, bitch.* But she'd spare Gloria that.

"If Aaron's—gone, you can petition the court, Alayna."

She remained silent for a moment. "We have to wait until he's identified as the man in the car. Until we know for certain, the court won't allow me to do anything." She paused. "I'd be glad to bring them out for a visit, but I'm not relocating. I had a hard time starting over, Gloria. I had to study California law, and take college classes to be certified here. I don't have the money to do it again and work. Emilia is happy in her current school, and Addison in the preschool. The daycare they go to runs a preschool starting at age three for Rosa. I don't want to uproot them when they're doing so well."

"And I don't suppose you want to leave your boyfriend."

Gloria's snide tone triggered a flash of resentment, and Alayna strode to the teeter-totter. "It's time to eat, girls. You don't want to wear Grandpa out."

"Taco?" Rosa said.

"I'm sorry, baby, Mama didn't bring any tacos, only home-made nuggets, grapes, and potato salad. But we can have tacos tonight for supper. And I have a special desert fixed."

She half wished Rosa would throw a tantrum and give Gloria and Warren a good taste of what raising a strong-willed two-year-old was all about. Instead Rosa stuck out her bottom lip but remained silent.

They retrieved the cooler from the car, spread a plastic table-cloth over the well-used picnic table, and set out the food.

"Where's Bowie today?" Warren asked.

She mentally braced herself for another attack. "I think he's working from home today. He's preparing for a new assignment. I'm supposed to call him when we leave the park."

He glanced over to where Gloria and the girls were engaged in a game. "You never had an affair with your boss, did you?"

"No." She met her ex-father-in-law's gaze. "All I do for Mr. Kappes is research the law for his cases, write briefs and letters, and make sure everything is delivered or filed on time."

Warren nodded, his face crumpling with what looked like sor-row. He seemed to have aged years overnight. "My boy went off the rails, didn't he?"

She patted his arm. "I'm sorry, Warren."

"No, I am. The things he did can't be excused."

She'd dealt with Aaron's machinations, his threats, his relent-less quest to hurt her too long to believe he wouldn't rise from the rubble like a cockroach to continue doing it. "I don't know what drove him to embezzle funds. He drank a little socially, played golf mostly with clients, and played poker one night a week. Unless things changed drastically after the divorce…"

"He's been gambling, Alayna. Thousands of dollars' worth. He's been taking trips to Vegas with Bliss and losing big."

Shocked, she remained silent. They'd been homebodies with two little ones when they were married, except when he was making her life hell.

"I'm sorry. The last year of our marriage, he was gone most of the time. Working and seeing other women, including Bliss."

"You couldn't have stopped him. Gambling is an addiction, just like alcohol."

His gaze trailed to Gloria. "She doesn't want to believe it, even after Detective Gray told her about it. He told us about your apartment being broken into, too. She wants to believe it was someone else. She doesn't want Aaron to be responsible for destroying their things and putting the children in danger."

"The police will sort it out, Warren. Try not to worry too much. The super's going to put a new deadbolt on my door today or tomorrow. We're being careful."

"Good. Your boyfriend, Bowie… He seems like a good man to have around."

"Yes, he is."

"I'm glad you and the children have someone."

She stared at him in surprise. "Thank you." Although once Bowie went back to his full-time duty, she didn't know if they'd continue to see each other. He was already getting cold feet.

BOWIE LOUNGED IN the chair across the desk from Detective Gray. The open floor plan of the room didn't allow for much privacy. He wondered how they heard their suspects and witnesses above the ringing of phones and the rumble of other voices.

"Has she said anything about her husband?" Stansberry asked.

"She said her ex tried every way he could to punish her for their marriage not working. And he tried to take the girls from her."

"Anything else?"

"She made a list of people he might go to if he was in trouble."

Gray cocked his head. "Why would she do that?"

"She doesn't believe he's dead."

"Why not?"

Bowie remained silent for a moment. "I think it's because he hounded and tormented her so much, it's hard for her to accept that it might be over. But I agree with her. He isn't dead. Whoever's in the car, it isn't him."

"Why do you think that?"

"If I had a million dollars hidden somewhere, but I was having difficulty accessing it, and I had the cops and other assorted pissed-off guys on my ass, I'd kill someone, put them in my car, and burn everything in the hottest flames possible to obscure my identity. Then I'd do whatever was necessary to find the key to getting my hands on the money so I could get the hell out of dodge before the results of the identification come through."

Gray leaned forward and rested his elbows on his desk. "I just met with Harper's parents, and they're in complete denial that their son would be capable of embezzling money from his clients."

"You mean Mrs. Harper is adamant that he would never do such a thing. Her husband is probably just staying mum to keep the peace. I think he probably has a better grasp of what his son is like, since his wife is the same way."

Detective Stansberry leaned forward in his seat. "You met them?"

"Last night at dinner."

"You're getting rather cozy with the ex-Mrs. Harper," Gray said.

He'd managed to keep his cool when Gray called him out of the blue and asked him to come in. He'd known it would be to pump him for info, but the man could take a flying fuck through a rolling doughnut if the detective thought he'd betray Alayna in any way. "Which is your business because?"

"It isn't my business, but she's still a person of interest."

"In what way?"

"We're not at liberty to say."

Bowie studied the man, his mind racing. Alayna and the children were the only connections he had to Harper. And Gray knew he was alive.

Bowie reached for his phone and unlocked it with a thumb brush.

"What are you doing?" Stansberry asked.

"I'm warning Alayna that her ex-husband is still alive."

"We'd rather you didn't do that."

"I'm sure you would. You don't really give a damn what happens to her, but I do." His thumbs worked the keyboard on the screen, quickly typing out *He's alive.*

"We have people at the apartment building and people following her." Stansberry reached for the phone.

Bowie hit send and bounced to his feet so Stansberry couldn't grab it from him. "If this ambush you've arranged goes south, and she or the girls are hurt, you'll pay with your jobs."

He was on his way out of the door before they could stop him.

CHAPTER 17

EMOTIONAL EXHAUSTION DRAGGED at Alayna by the time they returned to the apartment. Gloria had stretched her patience to the last thread with her snide remarks and snippy comments. She was relieved to close the door between her family and her in-laws and lock it.

Emilia and Addison went into their bedroom to look through the toys they had left. Rosa climbed onto the couch, popped her thumb in her mouth, and, clutching her monkey, lay down. Alayna wandered over and touched the back of her hand to Rosa's cheek and forehead. She wasn't running a fever, but looked tired. "You okay, Sugar Pop?"

Rosa nodded, and when Alayna sat down, she crawled into her lap, straddled her hips and rested her head against her breasts. "Me want Boy." The way she said Bowie sounded more like Boy.

"He's coming over in a little while. He had to go somewhere first." But what if he suddenly just disappeared from their lives, as she had her family's? With his job, there was no guarantee it wouldn't happen.

Rosa was out like a light in less than ten minutes.

Alayna wiggled to the front of the couch cushion, got to her feet, and carried Rosa into her bedroom. Her baby girl's limbs were boneless in sleep as she lowered her to the center of her bed and pulled the soft throw she kept at the foot of her bed over her.

Alayna tucked her monkey beside her and stood for a minute, watching the steady rise and fall of the child's chest.

She closed the bedroom door and eased down the narrow hall. Addison and Emilia were sitting on the carpet putting a puzzle together. She moved onto the living room and froze. A man in a dark jacket and pants stood in the living room, his head covered by a baseball cap.

When he turned to face her, she gasped. Aaron's face was haggard, his jaw unshaven, and dark rings shadowed his eyes. His blond hair, now dyed a dark brown, was unwashed and clung to his head. His brows, so much lighter, looked strange.

"How did you get in?" she demanded.

"I've learned how to do a lot of things lately I never thought I would."

That vision of a cockroach rose up to taunt her. "I knew the body in the car wasn't you."

"Where is it, Alayna?"

"Where is what, Aaron? What the hell are you looking for?"

"A flash drive. Bliss hid it in one of the kids' dolls, but when I looked for it, it wasn't there."

"So you destroyed everything they had?" Contempt shot heat into her face and her anger exploded.

He took two big strides toward her. Fear launched her heart into her throat. This wasn't the man she'd married, not even the man who walked away from their marriage. There was too much desperation in his eyes, his movements. She backed toward the hallway to block his access to the girls.

"Just give me the damn thing and I'm out of here."

"I don't have it, Aaron. I haven't seen a flash drive in any of their things. You went through everything they own. It isn't here."

"You're lying."

"I don't have it. And the police have been through everything here twice more. If it ever was here, it's gone now."

His eyes narrowed, and he started toward her again. She grabbed the backpack she carried and held it in front of her for what little protection it offered. He lunged toward her and ripped it out of her hands, tossing it aside and gripping her arms so hard she had to grit her teeth. His breath smelled of whisky and the rage it seemed to trigger in him. "You have to find it. I need that information or I'm a dead man."

She twisted "I don't know where to look. You destroyed the whole place. It was probably thrown out with the trash you left behind. Why did you do that?"

He gripped her throat and shoved her back against the wall. She caught back a cry of pain as the back of her head connected with the wall. She couldn't breathe. Her heart rate soared, and she clawed at his hand as the pressure increased and dark spots floated in front of her eyes.

No!!! She grabbed both his ears and yanked his head forward. His nose hit her forehead, and he yelped and released her.

Aaron bent at the waist and held his face. He looked up and bared his teeth in rage. "Where is it?"

Coughing, struggling for breath, Alayna was unable to speak.

Aaron raised a fist.

"Daddy?" Emilia said from the bedroom doorway. He froze, but his bloodshot eyes continued to glare into hers. Like a switch had been flipped, he released Alayna and took a step back. "Em. How you doin', baby?"

Emilia didn't answer. Addison peeked out from behind the edge of the door. Both girls watched their father with fear and uncertainty.

"You've done a good job turning them against me," he complained.

"You did that all by yourself. I've never said a single word against you to them. They aren't blind, Aaron."

He swung away. "Find it or you'll regret it." His gaze settled on Emilia and Addison for a moment. "You can lose everything, like I have, if you don't."

Rage boiled up like bottled steam inside her. "Don't you threaten my girls! You didn't lose anything, Aaron. You threw it away. And now you've thrown them away, too."

He cut her off. "The people after me will do more than

threaten, Alayna."

He turned, and she searched for a weapon, for anything she could use to take him down. But there was nothing. She watched impotently as he strode out the door.

She ran after him. "Don't you ever come back here again. Don't ever come near any of us, ever again."

She stood trembling in the middle of the hallway until Mr. Gaines, her across-the-hall neighbor, popped his head out. "Are you okay?"

"Yes."

"You have finger marks on your throat. You need to call the police and report him."

"I will, Mr. Gaines."

She rushed back into the apartment to check on the girls. They clung together at their bedroom doorway, still traumatized by their father's appearance and behavior. She hurried to them, knelt, and gathered them close. "Everything is going to be okay. I promise."

"Your throat is all red, Mommy," Emilia whispered.

"You're talking funny," Addison added.

"It's okay." Even though she was trembling, and her breathing came in short, choppy gasps, the girls were scared but okay, so she was okay.

Her phone dinged, signaling a text. She ignored it and drew back to smooth Addison's hair off her forehead.

BOWIE KEYED IN the security code to enter the apartment building and pushed through the main entrance. He clenched his hand and wished for his Sig. He had to leave it secured in the car since the place was crawling with cops. Instead of waiting for the elevator, he rushed to the stairwell and took the stairs two at a time. He shoved the second-floor door open and stepped out into the hall. A woman and two men stood outside their doors, looking down the hall.

Bowie broke into a run to Alayna's apartment, and found the door open and a policeman stationed outside. EMTs were packing up their gear and leaving. Relief raced through him when he saw Alayna was in one piece, though she looked a little banged up.

The cop stopped him when he would have gone inside until Alayna beckoned to him and said, "It's okay." Her voice sounded hoarse, and it looked like it hurt for her to swallow.

He drew her close and held her for a long moment. "What happened?"

"Aaron showed up."

She turned her face up to him and the reddish-purple finger marks on the pale skin of her throat stood out in stark relief.

Jesus! "Are you okay?"

"I am now. The police are searching the building, but he's gone."

Bowie followed her to the girls' bedroom. "Bowie!" Addison and Emilia chorused together and rushed to him. He knelt to gather them close.

"It's okay, munchkins. Everything's okay."

"Is Daddy going to come back and hurt us?" Addison asked. "He hurt Mommy." A sob broke from her, and she clung closer.

His rage soared, and it was a struggle to keep his voice even. "No. He's not." *Damn* it. "I'm here now, and I'm not leaving."

When Addison had finally quieted, he glanced up at Alayna. "Where's Rosa?"

"She slept through the whole thing." The relief in her expression mirrored his own feelings. "Addison, why don't you and Em sit on the couch and rest, and I'll put your new movie in? Mommy needs to talk to Bowie and make some telephone calls. We'll be right there." She pointed at the small kitchen table the girls could easily see from the couch.

"Okay."

Luckily the television and DVD player hadn't been destroyed in the break-in. She put in *Beauty and the Beast*, their current favorite, and got them settled.

Leaving the two intent on the screen, she and Bowie went

into the kitchen.

"I locked the door, so he had to have picked the lock. He said he'd learned to do things he never dreamed he would. He was wearing dark pants and a dark jacket, a baseball hat, and running shoes. I walked in on him in the living room. He grabbed me by the throat and slammed me into the wall."

"Jesus, Alayna."

She looked at Bowie, her expression a blend of frustration and anger. "I'm tired of this. He as much as said that the people after him will come after us if I don't find what he's looking for."

"What's he looking for?"

"A flash drive full of information."

"You have your computer back."

"I've already checked it, and there's nothing suspicious on it. He wasn't interested in the laptop at all, so I'm sure there's nothing on it."

"I'll look again just to be sure."

"Fine."

He could tell by her tone it was anything but, so decided to take a figurative step back. "Come sit down and just relax for a minute." He drew her to the small table and pulled out a chair for her to sit.

She rested her head in her hands for a minute. "I got your text after he was gone and I'd called the police."

"Gray called me into his office around two. He was trying to be cagy, but I figured it out. He used you for bait to draw Aaron out. He was supposed to have men on-site to catch him."

"Well, Aaron waltzed in here without any issues and then obviously waltzed right back out. He's dyed his hair brown and let his beard grow out to darken the lower half of his face." She drew in a breath and raised a hand to her throat, her hoarse voice shaking. "I'm afraid for my girls, Bowie."

"They're going to be fine. I'm staying with you until they catch the son of a bitch."

A knock on the door interrupted them. Bowie rose to answer it. He glanced through the keyhole then back at her and the girls before opening the door.

Detectives Gray and Stansberry filed in.

Stansberry spoke, "We need to speak to you, Ms. Wieland."

Bowie saw the shift in Alayna's expression. Her eyes lit with rage. He was already in motion before Detective Gray could get close. He caught her around the waist, and every inch of her body went rigid. He felt like he had grabbed a live grenade and it was about to blow up in his face.

"Let me go, Bowie."

He lowered his voice to a rumble. "If you hit him, they'll arrest you, and you'll be playing right into Warren and Gloria's hands—and theirs."

She rested her forehead against his chest, hiding her expression from him, but her entire body shook with the effort to control her emotions. When she raised her head, her eyes were glassy with tears, but her features were taut with control. He stepped back to allow her to speak to the two men.

She sounded deceptively calm when she asked, "Did you catch him?"

"No."

"I'm calling my lawyer as soon as you leave, and I'll be filing a formal complaint against you and your partner, Detective Gray. And while I'm filing an assault report with your department, and a next-to-*useless* restraining order against Aaron Harper, I'll be filing one against you. You threw me—and, far worse, my children—under the bus, and deliberately cleared the way for him to assault me and threaten my children." She trembled visibly as she struggled to maintain her composure.

Bowie fought the need to comfort her. If he touched her, she'd lose it.

"For the last time, I don't have what you're looking for, and I don't have what *he's* looking for. It must have been destroyed when he went through the apartment, or was thrown out, or lost. I will not meet with you again without my lawyer present. Now leave."

Neither detective said a word as they turned and left the

apartment. Bowie closed the door behind them.

Alayna went into her bedroom and closed the door softly behind her.

It would have been better if she'd slammed it. The need to go into the bedroom and hold her rose in him, compulsive and tormenting.

He fought it down. He couldn't leave the children alone. He had to keep an eye on them. That's what she needed while she got her emotions under control. He kept telling himself that as he sat in one of the living room chairs and waited for her to come back out.

CHAPTER 18

ALAYNA'S RAGE HAD dissipated by the time she was dressed. She resented having to call Gloria and Warren and ask them to come over to the apartment to keep the girls while she went to the police station to file an assault report. She was still so afraid they might take the girls while she was gone and catch the first plane out.

It gave her no satisfaction to see the conflict of relief and pain in their expressions when she told them their son was alive, then that he had assaulted her. The horror in Warren's expression when he saw the bruises on her throat and arms made it difficult for her to maintain her composure.

How much worse could it have been if Emilia hadn't spoken his name and drawn him back from the brink? At least he still cared enough about the girls to try to control himself in front of them.

"I don't know how long it will take me. There's spaghetti sauce in the refrigerator, and the pasta is in the cabinet. Emilia can show you were it is. There's also French bread to slice for garlic bread, and a salad that just needs dressing."

"We'll take care of all that, Alayna. We'll keep them safe while you're gone," Warren assured her while he tentatively rested a hand on her shoulder.

When Rosa cried and clung to her, she almost wept herself.

"Mommy will be back soon. Em and Addie will be right here with you."

Addison and Emilia came to her to kiss her 'bye. "Come on, Rosa. Sissy and I want to play cars with you," Emilia tugged at Rosa's hand. Emilia, her little mother's helper. She'd probably saved her life by speaking to Aaron. How had she known what to do?

She gave a shaky sigh when Rosa slipped off her lap to follow her sisters into the bedroom.

Bowie hovered close as she got to her feet.

"Aaron's changed his appearance. He's dyed his hair brown and has allowed his beard to grow, so he looks scruffy. He's afraid and desperate and…not himself." Which was the truth. He had raised his voice, but never his hand, when they were married. All but their last night together as a married couple. She shuddered and ignored the pain of remembering.

Gloria spoke for the first time since entering the apartment. "We'll call the police if he shows up, Alayna." Her gaze rested on Alayna's throat for a moment, then shifted away. "He'll probably be safer in custody than being hunted by the people he's stolen from."

Bowie rested a hand against the small of her back. She gathered her purse and he held the lightweight sweater she'd laid out so she could slide into it. She murmured her thanks and touched his hand.

She paused outside the apartment, surprised to find a police officer stationed outside the door. "What are you here for?"

"Protection detail for you and your children, Ms. Wieland."

Aaron was unlikely to return now. But someone else might. It did relieve a little of the tight feeling of fear that had taken hold of her. She thanked him, and she and Bowie walked away.

Alone in the elevator Bowie ran a hand down her back. "I'm sorry I wasn't here, Alayna."

"You can't be with us twenty-four seven, Bowie. I don't expect you to be. We're not your responsibility."

His features blanked for a moment. "I care about you and the girls."

"I know you do." They were already falling in love with him. The way Rosa had asked for him this morning when they got back from the park was proof enough. But loving him could break their hearts. He put himself in danger for a living. It would be an instinct for him to put himself between them and any threat. Loving them could get him killed. She had to take steps to protect them herself.

Once they were in the car, she broached the first step. "I need to stop at the bank after we go to the police station. The main branch downtown."

"Okay."

When he didn't ask why, she was relieved.

She had been to the police station a number of times for her boss, collecting paperwork for various cases, and to file restraining orders against Aaron. Will Kappes sat near the entrance of the station, talking on his phone, and she gripped Bowie's hand as she approached him.

He ended his call and unfolded his tall, lean frame from the chair. He often reminded her of Jimmy Stewart, with his long arms and legs, big feet and big hands. His closely-cropped hair was sprinkled with gray at the temples.

"I'm sorry to interrupt your day, Mr. Kappes."

"It isn't a problem, Alayna."

She turned to introduce Bowie and the two men shook hands.

Kappes got right to the point. "Have you thought of anything we didn't cover in our conversation earlier?"

She shook her head.

"Have you been to the emergency room to have your injuries documented?"

"No, but the EMTs documented them and will file a report. I thought the police would probably document them as well, since I'm pressing charges and filing a restraining order."

"Yes, they will, but it never hurts to have medical documentation."

They spent a few more minutes going over the situation that

had unfolded inside the apartment, and all the other information the police had shared before and since.

Kappes turned his attention on Bowie. "You texted Alayna while you were in the presence of Detectives Gray and Stansberry?"

"Yes, to warn her to be on the lookout for her ex, but it was too late."

"Why had Gray and Stansberry called you into the office?"

"They called me in to pump me for information. They didn't tell me why, but after a few minutes of them beating around the bush, I had a hunch and texted her."

Kappes shifted his attention back to Alayna. "And they didn't inform you when they learned the body in the car wasn't Aarons?"

"I hadn't heard anything from them since we met at Big Bear and they notified me they'd recovered Aaron's car. Not one word…until they waltzed in demanding to talk to me *after* Aaron had come and gone, Bowie arrived, and the other cops were finished with us."

"So, they purposely gave you no warning."

"I'd say so."

Kappes' expression turned stony, and he led the way into the police station.

A few minutes later an officer came down the hall and asked them to come with him. When they reached the area where Gray and Stansberry usually worked, they were nowhere in sight.

The officer stopped at a corner office set apart by glass and metal supports, opened the door, and stood back for them to enter.

An African-American man rose from the desk in the center of the room. His hair was almost buzz cut, his shirt and tie a little wrinkled from sitting in the chair, but his dark brown gaze was direct. "Ms. Wieland, thank you for coming in." He extended a hand, and she automatically moved to shake it. "I'm Captain Brian Sherwood. My detectives reported what happened."

Yeah, sure they did. She introduced Kappes and Bowie, and he moved to shake their hands as well.

"Please have a seat."

They sat in straight-backed chairs designed to be as uncomfortable as possible.

Kappes spoke, "Ms. Wieland is here to file a grievance against detectives Gray and Stansberry. They had a duty to notify her of her ex-husband's current status. She had already described to them his abusive behavior toward her. By delaying that notification, they gave her ex-husband the opportunity to initiate a blitz attack where he assaulted her and threatened her children, terrorizing them all.

"By not speaking to her, they missed an opportunity to place an officer inside her home, where they could have captured Aaron Harper and ended this whole thing."

Captain Sherwood leaned forward to rest his arms on the desk. "A plan to set up surveillance had already been initiated. Some, but not all, of our officers were in place. Harper slipped out undetected with a group leaving the building."

"Your officers had time to call Lieutenant Rivera and ask him to come in for an interview, but no time to call Ms. Wieland and forewarn her?"

Captain Sherwood's features tightened. "Detective Gray was being cautious. He thought perhaps you'd call your ex and warn him if you knew about the surveillance."

God, she was so tired of Gray's shit. She reached into her purse and removed her phone. She turned to Bowie. "I need you to step outside with me for a minute."

He nodded and rose.

"We'll just be a minute," she murmured.

Once outside the office, his golden-brown gaze fastened on her face.

"I'm not asking for you to do this because I don't trust you, Bowie. It's just that—" Her breath hitched. "I love that you're protective of the girls and me. To hear this recording will upset you…"

"It's okay." He studied her face for a long moment. "I know what you're saying. You don't want me to break the guy's neck if we're ever face-to-face."

"You're right, I don't." Her anger at Aaron knew no bounds, but she was not going to allow him to take one more thing from her. "I want him to spend as many years as possible in prison so he can't get to me and the girls. You stopped me from doing something that could have gotten me arrested, and I don't want to have to do the same for you."

"I'll be here waiting when you're through."

She rose up on tiptoe and pressed a kiss to his cheek. "Thank you."

She returned to the office and closed the door, unlocked her phone, started the recording she made of Aaron, and turned it on speakerphone. His voice came over the speaker with as much venom as he usually spoke to her.

"Sooner or later you'll slip up and I'll get custody of the girls."

"What do you mean slip up? I don't drink, smoke, do drugs, or sleep around. In other words, I don't do any of the things you do on a regular basis. You may have more money than I do, but you don't love them the way I do. I'd give my life for them. The only person you're interested in is yourself. And the only reason you want them is because you want to hurt me."

"I haven't even started dishing it out, Alayna. I'll keep going until I get everything from you. You'll be begging me to stop."

"Like I did that last night."

"Shut up, bitch. You were asking for it."

"I left you with everything but them, Aaron. I just want to raise my girls and move on with my life. Leave us alone, or I'll go to the police."

"Go on. I have any number of guys who owe me. I can set it up so the judge and everyone else in the state of California will believe you're a lying whore because you are one. You lied to me our whole marriage. You promised to love me, only me."

"I was never unfaithful to you, Aaron."

"You don't have to fuck someone to be unfaithful. Every time we made love you were thinking of him. Do you think I didn't know that?"

"I wasn't. I tried to be a good wife. But I'm not your wife any longer. And I have undisputable proof of what you did that night. Leave me alone."

"You'll never have a life as long as I'm alive. I'll make certain of it."

She'd cut the phone off at that point unable to bear anymore of his threats. Silence stretched for a beat then two.

Mr. Kappes placed a comforting hand over the fists she'd clenched in her lap.

"I'm assuming he—assaulted you before you separated."

She nodded.

"Why didn't you file a complaint against him then?"

"He walked out that night and never came back. I found an apartment and moved out of the house the next week. He filed for divorce five weeks later, and I thought that would be the end of it."

"But it wasn't," the captain said, his tone flat.

"No." She stared at the industrial tile floor and fought to maintain her composure. "He wanted me to have an abortion, but I wouldn't." The raw emotion worsened the ache in her throat.

Kappes' grip on her hand tightened.

Shame and embarrassment roiled through her. Her boss was listening to every detail of what she had endured. What would he think of her from now on? "When he broke into the apartment last night, he was looking for a flash drive with information on it about how to access the funds he's stolen, but he also was looking for the pictures I took of my injuries and my doctor's notes from a few days later, too."

She finally raised her gaze to Captain Sherwood's face. "I would never help Aaron in any way. I hope you find him and put him in prison for the rest of his life. I don't want him near me, or my daughters, ever again. Every time Detective Gray interviews me, all he asks me about is the money. Maybe he needs to concentrate on finding Aaron and dealing with the people he's stolen from. But it was his responsibility to protect me and my girls from harm, too."

Sherwood messaged his forehead. "You didn't tell him about the earlier assault, did you?"

"No. But I did tell him about the threats to firebomb my car and to kill me. I offered to play the recording for him, right after the men tried to abduct me from the bank parking lot, but he wasn't interested. He wasn't even interested in the attempted kidnapping. All he wanted to talk about was Aaron and any money he might have given me."

"We've had to take Harper to court on three different occasions just to get him to pay the court-ordered child support of a paltry five hundred dollars a month," Kappes said. "That alone should have alerted him to the type of relationship Ms. Wieland has with Mr. Harper."

Sherwood didn't respond to that. "Have you had any contact with anyone your husband may depend on for help?"

Alayna hesitated. "My husband's parents. They're staying with the children so we could come here today."

"Are they aware their son is alive?"

"Yes. I told them."

"How did they respond when you told them what had happened?"

"His father seemed relieved. I couldn't read his mother's reaction. Aaron's father was apologetic about what he's done. I think he's genuinely upset and devastated by what's happened. He said yesterday at the park, 'My boy went off the rails, didn't he?' There were tears in his eyes."

"And his mother?"

"Gloria wouldn't meet my eyes or look at me this morning. She promised they'd call the police if Aaron came to the apartment. Her words were, 'I'd rather he be arrested than caught by the people after him.'" Not a word about the bruises he'd put on his ex-wife.

"Do you think she's talked to him?"

"I don't know, but they're very close. Judging from their attitudes, Gloria would be more inclined to protect him than his father."

Captain Sherwood rose to his feet. "I appreciate your being so candid about everything. I'll be supervising the filing of your assault report myself, Ms. Wieland. Your lawyer can file your complaint against my two officers."

"Thank you." The spring of tension released in the pit of her stomach.

BOWIE TILTED HIS head back against the metal edging framing one of the large office windows. What was so bad about the conversation between her and her husband that she didn't want him to hear it? Not knowing was driving him crazy. Crazier than knowing would have. Or would it?

She did have a point. He was protective of her and the girls. He felt guilty as hell for not being there when her ex made his surprise appearance. He was reasonably sure at this point that Gray and Stansberry had wanted him out of the way because they suspected Aaron Harper was going to make a visit to the apartment. But how would they have known?

When Alayna came out, he straightened in his seat.

"I have to go down the hall to be photographed," she explained.

She looked tired but not upset. He shot her a thumbs-up. A woman in the San Diego PD uniform carrying a camera approached her. She flashed Bowie an appreciative smile, then turned her attention to Alayna. "Come this way, please."

Willard Kappes exited the office and turned to shake Captain Sherwood's hand. Bowie rose as Kappes reached him. "I'm glad Alayna has you, Bowie. Keep your eyes peeled for Harper. I mean that." His gaze sharpened with a message he couldn't share vocally. "Alayna will need to go before the judge tomorrow at ten to get the restraining order signed."

"I'll see she gets there safely, sir." He and Kappes shook hands.

"Lieutenant, can I speak to you?" Captain Sherwood said.

Bowie sauntered into the office and Sherwood closed the door. "I've read your interview following Ms. Wieland's attempted abduction at the bank and the discovery of Bliss Harper's body at the residence. I'd like for you to go back over both with me."

For the next twenty minutes Bowie went back through everything that had happened at the bank and the house.

"You and Ms. Wieland have a personal relationship."

"We're getting reacquainted since we haven't seen each other in ten years." An idea struck him.

"Gray said the SDPD budget didn't stretch to a protection detail. So I stepped in."

He'd been on his way to Alayna's apartment when Gray called him in for a bullshit interview just when Gray was attempting to take Harper down.

Surely Gray wasn't as big a fuckup as he seemed. There were a lot of very rich people looking to get their money back, and extra cash would be a temptation. And how had he known Harper would be there? And had he actually allowed the man to abuse Alayna because he hoped Harper would recover the flash drive?

And how could Bowie suggest all that to Sherwood without pissing him off and making the situation worse for Alayna? But what if the Captain was just as culpable as Gray?

"I was called here for an interview when Harper showed up at Alayna's apartment today. Gray called me in. That was pretty poor timing."

"Off-post you're just a regular American citizen, Lieutenant."

Sherwood would have to do a lot better than that if he was trying to piss Bowie off. He kept his tone flat and even, "I'll be sure to remind the next terrorist I take down of that."

Sherwood's features tightened.

Fuck it. "Alayna was hurt, and the girls were terrified and crying when I got there. I could have had Harper tied up with a bow for you. Instead he's still out there, an active threat to them." He didn't have to say *your guys fucked up*. He stood. "Interesting that Gray knew Harper would be there today. He must be the only psychic detective in San Diego."

Sherwood continued to eye him without emotion.

"Are we finished here, sir?"

Sherwood gave him a curt nod. "Yeah, I think we are."

Bowie sauntered to the door.

"Lieutenant?"

Bowie stopped at the door and turned to face Sherwood again. "I hope you have a concealed carry permit for that weapon." Sherwood nodded toward the weapon holstered on his right hip.

Bowie reached into his back pocket for his wallet and withdrew the paper. Sherwood raised a hand. "Never mind."

Bowie slipped the paper back in place and his wallet in his back pocket.

Sitting outside the office, Bowie took some moments to shake off his anger.

As soon as Alayna appeared, he left his seat to meet her. "You okay?"

"Yes." Her hand moved restlessly along the strap of her shoulder bag.

Once they were in the car, he locked the doors before securing his seatbelt.

Alayna's pale green gaze searched his face. "Something happened while I was gone?"

"Yeah. Just a back and forth with Sherwood." He hesitated, trying to decide how much to share with her. "It could be just an overactive sense of distrust on my part, Alayna. Maybe I'm reading more into the mistakes Gray has made trying to pursue your ex."

"Since I don't trust Detective Gray any farther than I can throw him, why don't you tell me what you think?"

Bowie ran a hand over his hair, roughing it up and smoothing it back down. He ran through his conversation with Captain Sherwood, and his conclusions about Gray.

Alayna remained silent for a long moment. "You're a wise-ass."

"Well...yeah."

"I really like that about you."

He chuckled.

"Gray searched your apartment twice and came to Big Bear to search your things there. But to be objective, all of that could be construed as an attempt to be thorough."

She closed her eyes for a moment. "But the surveillance thing today was suspicious."

"Captain Sherwood insinuated that they wanted me out of the way since I'm just a regular citizen while on American soil."

Her cheeks flushed. "Those fuckers put me and my children in danger on purpose."

He had rarely heard her swear, even in high school. Yeah, she was very, very upset.

"Do you think the detectives' incomes might be being subsidized by one of the people Aaron stole from?"

"That could be a possibility." That she was following the same lines of thought as he was without any encouragement... They were either paranoid or on to something.

"There's no way we could prove any of this since we don't have access to the list of people Aaron's embezzled from. We won't have access to that information until they've brought an indictment against Aaron and named the injured parties."

"I might know someone who can find out." Would Tess want to investigate this mess? It wouldn't hurt to ask. "I'll give her a call later and ask if she's interested."

Alayna's silence invited more information, so he continued.

"Her name is Tess Kelly, and she's a buddy's wife. You might have read some of her articles. She's a reporter on the San Diego paper, and specializes in the crime beat."

"Yes, I have. Her husband is deployed?"

"Yeah. But he'll be home soon. We'll get together with them. You'll like them both." He started the car and pulled out of the parking lot, heading into town.

Bowie waited in the lobby while Alayna disappeared toward the back of the bank with one of the employees. He took a moment to call Tess Kelly Weaver and fill her in on Alayna's situation.

Regret came across in her tone. "Another reporter here is covering the story. I'll ask him if he has inside info about the clients involved. I do know that Masters, Chumley, and Evans is freaking out about this. Some of their clients are a little cutthroat, and that a junior partner was granted enough access to do this... None of them are happy." She paused. "How did you get involved?"

"I hate to say this to you, Tess, but this has to stay off the record unless Alayna says otherwise."

"Understood."

"Alayna, Harper's ex-wife, and I knew each other in high school. I'm helping her and her kids out. There was a kidnap attempt on Alayna in the parking lot at the bank." He mentioned the bank location.

"That was her? The police withheld the victim's name."

"I happened to be there when it went down. There was speculation that it might have been an attempt to pressure Harper into giving up the money."

"If you're protecting her and her children, you need to be careful, Bowie. I did hear Grady say some of these guys aren't your average businessmen. I'll pump Grady for a client list for you."

"Thanks, Tess. It will stay between me and Alayna, no one else."

"I can't promise it will be for free. He may want a tradeoff for more information."

"That will be up to Alayna."

"Fair enough. I'll tell him that."

He switched gears. "When Brett gets home, I'd like us to get together. I think you'd like Alayna."

Silence hung between them for a beat. "She must be special if you want Brett to meet her."

"Yeah, she is."

"I'll mention it to Brett, and if you're available, we'll do it."

"Thanks, Tess. You know how to reach me."

Alayna appeared carrying a heavy plastic gun case. His brows rose. When she reached him, he gripped her elbow. "Are you sure you want that in the apartment?" He'd been careful every time he was there to secure his weapon where the kids couldn't get to it.

"Yes, I am."

"How long has it been since you shot it?"

"Last year, when I got my concealed carry license. I brought the pistol from Texas when I moved here. It's been locked away in the bank ever since."

"The Harpers are going to voice some objections if you bring it in while they're there."

"Then I'll wait until they leave, but I'm not going to be defenseless again if their son, or anyone else, comes into my home and threatens me. You can't be with us twenty-four seven." The resolve in her expression knotted his stomach.

There would always be times when he wasn't around to protect her or the girls. Today was proof. It would only be worse when he returned to base to work with his new team and they deployed. Frustration ate at him. He didn't want this for her. But at least he could make certain she was prepared.

"We'll go to a shooting range tomorrow so you can practice."

"Okay."

CHAPTER 19

WHEN BOWIE PULLED into the parking lot they both seemed to take a deep breath.

Alayna took stock of everything that had transpired in the course of the day. As hard as she'd worked to whip her life into order, it seemed it would never be anything but chaos.

Why couldn't people be open and honest? Why did everyone have a hidden motive? It didn't seem like capturing Aaron or the people who tried to kidnap her were on Detective Gray and his partner's agenda at all.

Their captain probably had a hidden motive as well. To cover his men's asses, and his own.

And Aaron certainly had motives that didn't include the well-being of his children. Then there were his parents.

And Bowie was caught in the middle along with her. She was putting him in danger. If he was caught up in the maelstrom of her life, it might damage his career.

Bowie exited the car, searching the parking lot before he walked around to open her door. They walked toward the apartment building with his hand against the small of her back. She could feel the pressure of each finger, and felt it through every inch of her body.

She dreaded seeing Warren and Gloria.

Alayna's phone rang, and she tugged it free of her pocket as they crossed the parking lot to the entrance. It was Mr. Kappes.

"I've been contacted by one of the people Aaron embezzled money from, Karrick Gilman. He'd like a sit-down meeting with you tomorrow afternoon after you've gone before the judge for the restraining order."

"Did he say what he wanted?"

"He hinted he's going to offer you a monetary incentive to try and find the money Aaron has stolen."

They stepped into the lobby and she paused to speak to Kappes. "You know this man's reputation?"

"Yeah. He's dangerous."

Gilman wouldn't have to pay her for the info. She'd gladly give it to him if she had it. "But I don't know where it is."

"I know that. But I can say that to him from my office, and he'll think I'm putting up a wall between you and him and maneuvering to negotiate for more money. He needs to hear it directly from you. And once you convince him you don't have any connection with your husband's dealings, word will spread, and maybe the rest of the pack will direct their attention toward the man responsible for all this."

"From what I've gathered from the detectives, these are all very rich businesspeople. None of them are going to want it to be common knowledge they were taken in by a crooked real estate agent. And if they're crooked themselves, like he is, they'll be doubly pissed and want revenge. And the way the detectives have been tiptoeing around things, I think some of the people may be as dangerous as Gillman, or more dangerous."

"Well, Gilman is a at least approaching you in good faith, and you may end up with one less person breathing down your neck. And I'll be there as a witness."

"All right. What time do I need to be in your office?"

"Noon tomorrow."

"Okay." She looked up after shutting off the call.

"Bowie…" This just kept getting more and more complicated. Eventually he was going to hit his limit with issues and he'd walk away.

The elevator door opened and they stepped inside.

Bowie hit the button to close the door. As soon as it was shut, he hit another button and the elevator jolted to a stop. "Whatever you're thinking about, let it go, Alayna." He backed her against the elevator wall and pinned her there with his body. Her heart raced, and her legs went wobbly.

His gaze delved into hers, hot and steady with need. His lips found hers with heated determination. After a second of surprise, her resistance crumbled. They clung together, their lips and tongues sparring with reckless abandon. His erection pressed into her stomach, and she wanted to lock her leg around his hips and hook him in.

The kiss went on and on, vaporizing every thought about anything but him, and leaving an aching need to have him fill the emptiness in its place.

Breathing hard, he broke the kiss and cupped her face. "Feeling better?"

"Yeah." She laughed.

"I told you that every time you get that stressed look, I was going to do something to remove it."

Physically he was as closely in tune with her now as they'd been in the past. She rose on tiptoe to press her lips to his again, with tenderness and caring. She'd missed him every day for ten years.

"If there weren't cameras in here…" He pressed warm lips to her forehead, then released her to start the elevator again.

CHAPTER 20

ALAYNA RAN WATER in the teakettle and set it on the stove, but didn't turn the burner on.

Bowie eyed her as she sat across from him at the kitchen table. She'd been quiet throughout dinner. They'd stopped to buy a new board game for the girls, and he played it with them after they ate while she cleaned up. Then came bath time and bedtime.

And now, with the elephant in the room, the Glock pistol in the hard case sitting before him, she seemed to have withdrawn.

"Would you like something to drink?" she asked.

"No. I'm okay." He touched the top of the box. "Are you sure you want to do this?"

"Yes." She left the room and returned with an old towel. She retrieved a box from under the sink and a microfiber cloth from one of the kitchen drawers, and after smoothing the towel out, she reached for the gun box and placed it before her. Next she withdrew a key from around her neck, unlocked it, and flipped it open.

Her expression was somewhere between sad and determined. "I'd hoped not to have to have a gun in the house ever again, but right now I feel safer having it here."

She withdrew the Glock 19 and the magazine, leaving the box of bullets where it was. Pulling back the slide, she checked the chamber, then dismantled the weapon.

She handled the weapon and the tools to clean it with a proficiency he hadn't expected. She screwed a bore brush onto a cleaning tool, then picked up the barrel of the pistol.

She glanced up to study his face. "I carried a concealed weapon my last three years of school in Texas." She dropped her attention back to the weapon that looked so foreign in her hands and ran the brush through the barrel several times.

Bowie's heart hammered hard. "Why?"

"I brought charges against my brother for aggravated assault. He went to prison for eight years."

"Jesus!" He couldn't hold back the exclamation. "Jesus! Why the hell haven't you told me about this before?"

"My family is so screwed up. More screwed up than yours ever was." She reached for the toothbrush in the kit to clean the slide of the pistol. "It was Christmas break after the first semester of college. I was staying at an apartment with some other girls until classes started back and my room at the dorm became available again. When I walked into the apartment two days before Christmas, my roommates were out and my family was waiting for me." Mindful of the solvent on her hands, she hooked a lock of hair with her pinky and guided it behind her ear. "We got into a heated argument because I refused to go home. It was then that I laid out everything that Harry and Matt had done and warned my sisters to watch their backs. Harry slapped me so hard he knocked me off my feet. Not one of them tried to defend me, not even my mother."

There was a slight tremor in her hands as she traded the brush for a cleaning rod and soft patches of cloth. Using a tiny bit of solvent, she cleaned the parts of the pistol. "I was on my way to work after they left. Outside the apartment complex, Matt stepped out of the shadows. I told him we didn't have anything else to say to each other. He said he was going to solve my issue once and for all. If I put the love of a…Latino…ahead of my own family, I didn't deserve to be a member of our family. I told him judging anyone because of his nationality was stupid since we weren't pure white bread ourselves. I said I didn't want to be associated with the family any longer.

"He accused me of seeing you again and brought up the pictures again as a threat. I told him you were worth ten of him because you didn't resort to lying, cheating, or blackmail to get what you wanted, you worked for it. I told him I was ashamed of him and my father."

She put the body of the pistol down and folded her hands on the table. "He punched me in the face. I wasn't expecting it. He'd never hit any of us before. Everything went black for a moment. Then he was standing over me, punching and kicking me. I tried to crawl away, but he just kept on and on. Some of the neighbors ran out, but he didn't even seem to notice. Some of the guys grabbed him and dragged him away, but he was able to stomp on my arm, and it just snapped." She touched a faint scar on her forearm. "I passed out. Someone called the cops and he was arrested."

Bowie's throat felt thick and his face stiff with the effort to contain his emotions. "I'm sorry, Alayna." He struggled to take a deep breath.

"I'm not. There are a lot of things I wish I'd done differently back then, but standing against Harry and Matt isn't one of them. I did, however, learn that standing by your principles when it's convenient is a whole lot easier than when it's not."

She went back to cleaning the gun, slowly pushing the solvent cloth through each working mechanism, then drying it thoroughly with clean patches and the rag. He remained silent, waiting for her to finish.

"Because he'd been convicted of assault for a bar fight, and because of my injuries and the descriptions of the attack from witnesses, the prosecutor wanted to charge him with attempted murder, which would have carried a sentence of ten to fifteen, but they came to a plea deal of eight years for aggravated assault.

"He was paroled for good behavior after seven. He'd already spent a year under house arrest before the trial, and they counted that as his eighth year.

Bowie couldn't seem to get enough air in his lungs.

"My sister, Joanna, called to warn me that he was out, and I got my license to carry here. She calls me any time he goes out of town so I can be prepared."

Bowie gripped his hair with both hands. "Ciro and Carmelita have never said a word to me about any of this. They had to know."

"I don't blame them. They were protecting you against a family of bigoted assholes. They heard the rumors Harry and Matt where spreading about our relationship, attempting to stir up trouble. Without your and my presence in the community to fuel things, and with Matt's conviction, everything died down, because by beating me, he unmasked everything he and Harry were about.

"People started distancing themselves from Harry, and his building supply business had started to tank before I moved out here, so there is some justice."

God, her father deserved to lose everything for what he'd done to her, and for every moment of pain and loneliness they'd both endured. "He beat you because you loved a Latino." There was no way he could filter the bitterness out of his tone.

"No. He beat me because I refused to ignore that he and my father are ignorant, bigoted white supremacists, and I threatened to tell *everyone*."

Bowie leaned forward and gripped her hands. The smell of the solvent lingered between them. "I've done some hard things, dangerous things. I've had some close calls. And I've always been prepared to do whatever it takes to get the mission accomplished. But I can't imagine you having to do the same thing, alone, here."

"You were just the catalyst, Bowie. It was bound to happen sooner or later. I wasn't blind to what they are, I just tried to ignore it. Once I accepted that I couldn't live with them any longer, I had to leave. And my father couldn't stand the fact that I wasn't under his thumb any longer."

Because he needed something to focus on, he reached for the pieces of the Glock. He applied gun oil where it was need, wiped away the excess, inspected the mechanisms, and then reassembled them, placing the pistol back in the case.

"We were so good at sneaking around to see each other back in the day. I knew he hated my guts and that he meant to keep me away from you no matter what it took."

She nodded. "Well, he succeeded." She stood, cleared away the debris, locked the gun case, and replaced the cleaning supplies under the sink.

While she was washing her hands, he slipped his arms around her waist, rested his chin on her shoulder, and then turned his head to find the sensitive spot just behind her ear with his lips. She dried her hands and relaxed back against him.

He breathed in the vanilla scent of her shampoo. "Running into you in front of the bank was the luckiest thing that's ever happened to me." They'd lost ten years, but they could try and make up for some of it.

She turned against him. "I'm still the daughter of a man who believes the white race is better than all the others. That it's okay to threaten, bully, and attack different nationalities. Your family will never accept me because of that, Bowie."

She hadn't had any contact with her family for ten years, surely that was enough. "You had no ties to the white supremacist group, and you've cut ties with your family because they still do. You've done everything you can to live outside that belief system. It'll be okay."

"You know it isn't that simple."

She was right, but Ciro was the one who would have to decide whether Alayna was the one who needed to be forgiven. When his brother was attacked so many years ago, Bowie hadn't blamed Alayna. He'd known who the responsible party was, even though they couldn't prove it.

Her stressed expression had returned, her movements slow and careful.

"How's the neck?"

"I think I need to take some Ibuprofen."

"And a hot bath might help. I'll keep watch while you take it."

While she settled into the warm water, he stowed the gun case in the top shelf of her closet, then made her a cup of hot tea, since she couldn't have any wine with the medication. He wandered into the bathroom and placed the cup and saucer on the edge of the tub.

Alayna's skin shone creamy and smooth, and her nipples beaded like cherries, but the bruising around her throat was darkening. And now she'd told him about her brother's assault, he noticed a scar on her upper arm, and his eyes wanted to linger on the longer one on her forearm. It was driving him crazy, knowing she'd tried to crawl away while Matt continued to punch, kick, and stomp her. He leaned down to kiss her.

"Just relax and let the meds take effect. I'll be in the living room watching a ball game and keeping an ear open for the girls." And any possible intruders. His Sig rested within easy reach on his hip, but he'd relish the opportunity to pound on someone right now. *Bring it on, fuckers.*

He muted the ballgame. And though he tried to relax, the muscles in his shoulders and neck tightened into rocks. He rolled his head to loosen them. Her suggestion that SEAL brass would take a negative view of his being involved with her had drilled its way into his brain and was rattling around in there like a song he couldn't shake. But it didn't hold water.

He knew Team members who were married to immigrants from tough places. Guys who'd had numerous marriages. Guys who slept around like they were trying for a Guinness world record. He tried for that for a couple of years himself. The brass didn't really care about your personal life, because it came second to the job. It would be okay. They'd see how she took her own family on and came out the other side.

By the time Alayna emerged from the bedroom, he'd gotten his head back on straight. Or at least he thought he had until she said, "I think you must be an expert on women. You seem to know what I need before I do." The light robe she tied at her waist did nothing to hide the soft shape of her breasts. She bent to pick up one of the children's toys and place it on the table and flashed pale skin cupped in something red and lacy.

He grew hard instantly. "I'm not sure any man can be an expert on women."

Her green eyes settled on him. "You seem to be more in tune than most."

He struggled to find the right words. Why was it so hard with her when it had always been so easy with other women?

Because it mattered with her.

"I suppose years of dating has taught me a few things." *Shit. I shouldn't have said that.*

CHAPTER 21

ALAYNA LOOKED AWAY. He had been nothing but honest about his life after her, but she didn't want to think about the other women he'd been with.

Everything she told him had widened the distance between them again. She could feel it. She came around the coffee table to sit down. "Thank you for standing guard while I took my bath."

He ran a hand beneath her hair. "I've had tougher duties, but not by much. I was tempted to leave my post and come join you."

She searched his face. She was so pathetically desperate to believe him. "Even after everything I told you?"

He tugged her closer and caught her lips. The way he tempted her into a response, leaving her breathless and hot.

When he drew back, she said, "I don't want you to see me as a victim, Bowie."

"I don't. I see you as brave and strong. And watching you clean your weapon made me hard." He flashed those devastating dimples.

She laughed and caressed his beard-stubbled cheek. "Since the policeman has disappeared, can we lodge something under the doorknob until we get a deadbolt on the front door?"

"Yeah, we can do that." He tucked a long strand of hair behind her ear. "You're safe with me, Alayna."

From everyone but him. He held her heart in his hands already. Always had.

He rose and helped her to her feet. "I'll take care of the chair, you check the girls."

The suggestion made her panties wet with excitement. They were going to sleep together like a real couple.

"How's the neck?" he asked when he joined her in the bedroom.

"Much better now."

Bowie held her close. "What have you got on under this?" He ran his fingers beneath the lapel of her robe.

"Something I bought two years ago on a whim but have never worn. It was in a box in the closet and must have gotten buried, because it somehow escaped the destruction." She ran her hands up his broad chest to unbutton his shirt. As she parted the garment, she leaned forward to press a kiss over his heart.

She felt the sharp rise of his chest before he shook free of his shirt and let it drop to the floor.

He searched her face. "Are you sure you feel up to…"

"This is what I need, Bowie."

Bowie folded back the silky fabric of her robe, and she shrugged it away.

She'd never dressed to seduce a man before and felt self-conscious in the red lace camisole and satin tap pants. The bruises weren't exactly the right accessory.

"You look sexy as hell." His voice was husky.

His pupils overwhelmed the golden rim around them as desire darkened his gaze. His kiss was as possessive as his touch when he cupped her breast and kneaded it. Her flesh seemed to swell beneath the caress, the nipple distending.

Alayna traced the muscular width of his shoulders with her fingertips and stretched upward to loop her arms around his neck and press against him as close as she could get.

Bowie cupped her ass, lifting her, and she wrapped her legs around his waist. He carried her the two steps to the bed, lowered her to the mattress, and followed her down in a controlled move that took her breath as his erection rubbed against her in just the right spot.

While his mouth did crazy, erotic things to hers, her hands and fingers explored the textures of his hair, the smooth skin of his shoulders, and the coarser hair on his chest. She dragged her teeth against the taut muscle between his neck and shoulder and he shuddered, his hips thrusting against her.

She flipped him over and sucked his earlobe into her mouth as she straddled him. He murmured her name on a sigh, driving her arousal with his voice, the restless caresses of his hands, his feverish kisses.

She unbuckled his belt, unfastened his pants, and helped him wiggle free of them. His erection sprang free, and she folded her fingers around it, and lowered to run her tongue over the tip, then took him in. She sucked, changing the pressure from light to tight and back again, until he groaned her name. When his erection swelled, she knew he was on the verge. She reached for the nightstand drawer and took out a box of a condoms she'd bought as soon as they'd returned from Big Bear, ripped it open, and fumbled for one of small packets. She tore open the package and sheathed him.

Bowie sat up, reached for the lacy camisole, and pulled it up and off. She wiggled free of her tap pants, then went back to straddle him again. Leaning forward and bracing her hands on either side of his head, she gazed at his face. His cheeks were flushed and his breathing uneven.

She kissed him as she lowered herself over him, and paused to enjoy the sensation of penetration and the fullness when he was seated deep inside her. He caught her breasts in his hands, then guided the peaks to his mouth. A fresh wave of heated arousal raced through her, and she began to move, chasing the release his answering thrusts promised.

The pulse of Bowie's orgasm triggered her own, and pleasure swamped her, leaving her fingers and toes tingling.

HE HAD NEVER felt content after sex. As soon as he got his rocks off he was usually ready to move on. But with Alayna's head on his shoulder, her body curled against his side, and her knee bent across his thigh, he was content. And he had a strong sense of déjà vu, like they had never been apart.

His heart raced like he'd just done a sprint. This was too easy.

He had to be straight up with her in case the guys gave him shit in front of her.

"My team thinks I'm some kind of Casanova."

"They do?"

"I've dated a lot, and they think dating and…other things…automatically go together in ways they don't a lot of the time." He ran a hand up and down her bare back, letting the warm, satiny smoothness of her skin to soothe him for a moment. His pulse started to slow.

When she remained silent, he glanced down to find her studying him. "Women have always been drawn to you, Bowie. But you were never a player when we were in high school, though you could have been."

"Well, the first few years in the teams, I was. I was cocky, arrogant, and when women find out you're a SEAL, they want a notch on their belt, and you just want to do something besides the training … After the first two or three years, which were more like six months each, it didn't hold as much appeal."

She raised herself up on an elbow. "What's changed?"

"More and more deployments. Eight so far, and a recent promotion."

"Eight—" She moistened her lips with the tip of her tongue.

He wanted to kiss her again, but the conversation wasn't exactly conducive to that. "The partying just got to be too much work."

"Why did you do it?"

To dull the pain and fill the loneliness. Is that why she married a man she didn't love? "I had to have something outside of work. But the work makes it hard for you to have anything normal. And the kind of women I was dating were more out for a good time than looking for…more."

Her arm tightened across his abdomen. "I understand."

Did she?

"I'm telling you this, because when you meet some of the other guys, they may give me some shit. They won't say anything to you, but…"

"They'll be curious about why you're with me."

"Yeah."

Shit. If he wanted to do right by her, he'd forget about all this. "You and the girls need someone who can be there for you twenty-four-seven, Alayna."

She flipped the heavy waves of hair over her shoulder. "We all do, Bowie. But it's a pipe dream."

He hadn't expected that. "What do you mean?"

"How often does anyone have that? The young lawyer who works eighty hours a week to build his client list so he can make partner? The doctor who sees a hundred patients a day? The businessman or woman who travels for a living and only sees their family on weekends? The woman who has to work eighty-hour weeks to climb the corporate ladder? Or the single mother who has to work as many hours just to put food on the table?

"How many of those families all sit down at a table and eat dinner every night?"

None on a regular basis, he'd bet.

"Everyone follows their own passions and dreams, because if they didn't, they'd never truly be happy. But it means you can't have that cookie-cutter life everyone talks about, but no one ever gets.

"I think love is about respecting the drives and needs of the person you're with. And letting them know you truly care about them, that you want to share in their accomplishments while you still give them room to succeed. But it's also about letting them know they're not alone."

His throat felt tight. They'd both been alone for a long time. But at least he had his team. Who did Alayna have besides her girls?

"What's your passion, Alayna? What would you do, if you could?"

"I'd finish my degree and join the firm I work for now. When I get the girls all in school, I'll apply for some grants and go back to finish. I want to make a stable life for my girls."

But who would she share her accomplishment with once she'd done that?

He couldn't say *share it with me*. As good as the sex was, and as drawn as he was to her and the girls, there was no guarantee he'd be around to share it. And he was wary of laying his heart out there for her to step on again. He looked up to find her watching him.

Alayna rolled over and got out of bed, and for a few seconds he was able to admire the generous swell of her breasts as she bent to pick up her camisole. She slid back into it with a little wiggle that definitely piqued his interest enough to make him hard again. When she stepped into the satin tap pants, there was a grace in her movements that reminded him of how much she'd loved to dance.

She straightened. "You've been locked up tight since we met again. You're so careful about the things you share. Everything is on the surface. I know I hurt you ten years ago. I hurt myself just as badly. I know you don't trust me, yet. But I trust you. I'm not asking for any promises, Bowie. Just a chance."

Jesus! She sounded so…calm. He'd seen that calm before, and it wasn't good. She was letting him off the hook. So why didn't he feel any relief?

She studied him for a moment longer. "One of the girls might get up and come to get in bed with me during the night…just a warning." She went into the bathroom.

He rose to get sleep pants and a sleeveless tee from the gym bag he'd tossed in the corner. He slipped into cotton sleep pants then sank down on the foot of the bed and twisted the sleeveless tee.

He recognized the emotional see-saw he was on. One minute desperately wanting to recapture what they had before, and the next afraid of suffering the same long-term effects of another breakup.

She'd made love to him, with him, and he just treated her like they'd fucked and he had one foot out the door, or close to it. He was reverting to the same behaviors he always did.

But Alayna wasn't just a date.

She was the one.

She'd always been the one, and he was blowing it. He needed to stop doing this mixed-signal thing and get down to it one way or the other.

When the bathroom door finally opened, he looked up and searched her face. She hadn't been crying, thank Christ, but she didn't look happy, and her jaw was set. Before she could speak he said, "I need to tell you more about what to expect if you really want to give this thing a chance."

She strode forward and sat down, but left a two-foot span between them. She rested her clenched hands on her knees. The signals she was putting out weren't lost on him.

Her gaze held a challenge. "The question is, do you want to?"

An ache of regret and guilt settled in the pit of his stomach. "Yeah, I do." He ran his hands over his face. "So fucking bad."

She searched his face. "I'm listening."

"What we had before wasn't just a crush, or puppy love. It was the real deal."

Her composure started to crumble, but he saw her kick it back. "Yeah, it was."

"I've never gotten over it."

Her voice fell to a hoarse whisper. "I haven't either."

"I've made you feel like shit twice now, right after we made love. It won't happen again."

"Good, 'cause I'll kick you out next time."

He knew if he smiled, even though it was because of her moxie, she'd probably follow through with that promise now. "I'd deserve it."

Her hands unclenched and clasped each other in her lap, but she remained where she was.

He untwisted his T-shirt and slipped it on. "You need to

know what it's really like to be a SEAL, and a SEAL's girlfriend, so you'll get the whole picture."

Her shoulders fell and her jaw relaxed. "Are you trying to scare me off?"

"Hell, no. But you need to be prepared."

She moved closer, and he slipped an arm around her, nestling her against him.

She rested her head in the bowl of his sholder and pressed a hand against his chest. "I can do hard, Bowie, as long as I know I'm not alone."

He tried to swallow but couldn't. "I don't know how many women I've been with, Alayna. Too many. But there's never been anyone for me but you."

Her arms tightened around him, and her breathing hitched with a sob. He pressed his lips to her forehead, then tipped her face up to press a kiss to her lips. Her tears tasted salty, but the kiss was sweet. While he dried her face with the tail of his T-shirt, he said, "You're not alone."

Then proceeded to prove it to her.

CHAPTER 22

A SMALL KNEE gouged Alana in the hip, and then a tiny, clumsy hand used her breast to brace against, and she flinched from the pain, coming completely awake. Rosa climbed into bed beside her and wiggled beneath the covers. Dull sunlight brightened the room to a pale grayish hue.

Alayna glanced at the illumined face of the clock on the nightstand. Five o'clock. She stifled a groan. She and Bowie had been up until two making love and talking. How long had it been since she'd done that?

She smiled at the quick thought of the funny, non-secret stuff he shared about being a SEAL, instead of the reality he said he was going to enlighten her about. His best friend, Zach O'Connor…he called him Doc…was featured in most of his stories. She couldn't wait to meet him.

"Boy sleeping," Rosa whispered. Putting a tiny finger against her lips she made a hissing sound between her teeth.

"Yes, Bowie's sleeping." Alayna's shifted to look over her shoulder to take in Bowie's sleep-rumpled appearance. Rich, deep brown hair spiked atop his head. Dark lashes lay against his cheeks. Heavy beard stubble shadowed his jaw. While asleep, his completely male features, relaxed from their usual intensity, looked younger. Tenderness and love welled inside her like a bubble, making her chest feel full.

She cuddled Rosa close and breathed in the baby lotion smell that still clung to her. Her hair was growing longer, nearly brushing her shoulders, and hung in soft, wispy ringlets.

"Boo-boos." Rosa said, her fingers tracing the finger marks that stood out against Alayna's skin.

Alayna hoped she was young enough that she wouldn't remember anything about her injuries. "They'll go away soon."

But the sight of their father trying to strangle their mother was going to remain with Emilia and Addie forever. She should have done more to protect them from Aaron. She should have taped his messages long ago and gone to the police. She was going to make certain he never saw them or touched them, or her, ever again.

"Go back to sleep, Sugar Pop. It's too early to get up," she whispered.

Rosa yawned, burrowed against her, and tucked her head beneath Alayna's chin.

Bowie's hand cupped her elbow and she glanced over her shoulder. A smile curved his lips, and he wiggled in behind her to hold her, including Rosa in his embrace.

Feeling secure, Alayna fell asleep.

"YOU SPENT THE night last night, Mr. Rivera?" Gloria asked, looking around the apartment.

"Yes." He didn't see any reason for her to know where he'd slept. The only one of the girls who knew was Rosa, and she wasn't talking. "They pulled the police officer off duty, and I didn't feel comfortable leaving Alayna and the girls alone. I also wedged a chair under the doorknob, and I'll be installing a deadbolt when I get back if the super hasn't already done it." He continued to meet her gaze for several moments.

Finally she looked away. "I hope you secure that weapon while you're here."

"Of course, Mrs. Harper. I'm very careful."

Alayna came out of the girls' bedroom. "They're playing school. Emilia is teaching Rosa her alphabet, and Addie's being the helper. They're allowed to draw on the chalkboard on the wall, but they're responsible for cleaning up after they're through. I let them use the little handheld vacuum cleaner, and I think it's Addison's turn. There's a sheet in the linen closet where I store it."

Gloria's features went still. "They'll be fine."

"After we go to court, I have a meeting with my lawyer, but we should be back by three o'clock."

Warren laid the TV remote on the coffee table. "We'd like to take the girls to the park after lunch, if that's okay."

Alayna's expression grew anxious. "I know the girls would like that, but I'd really rather that you stay here. I know it's an inconvenience, but after everything that's happened lately…"

"It's okay. We understand, Alayna," Warren rushed to reassure her.

"Thank you. I appreciate you both looking after them for me."

"They're our grandchildren. Of course, we want to look after them," Gloria sniped.

Bowie caught the subtle shift in Alayna's expression. She didn't reply, but went to get her purse from the kitchen table. "I don't want to be late, so we need to go."

He waited until they were halfway down the hall to the elevators before speaking. "You must have the patience of Job, Alayna. I don't know how you can resist punching her out."

She looked fierce as they walked down the hall to the elevator, "I will not sink to her level. I will not be a bitch. I will kill her with kindness."

Bowie grinned. They stepped into the elevator.

"And next time I'll take them to daycare. They'd have more fun there anyway."

He laughed.

Court dragged on for two hours, leaving Bowie to wonder how Alayna had managed to deal with all the bullshit associated with fighting her ex in court. They were running late by the time they left the building and got in the car to go to Williard Kappes' office.

Alayna apologized for their tardiness as Kappes showed them into his office. After one glimpse of the man they'd been scheduled to see, Bowie's radar went on high alert. He recognized the guy from the news. He'd been in and out of court fighting one lawsuit after another, and his name had been connected with several shady deals along the way. It was said he had connections with the Russian mob.

What the hell had Kappes been thinking when he set up this meeting?

After completing the introductions, and some hesitant hand-shaking, the lawyer invited Alayna and him to sit on the couch. Bowie focused on the man across from them.

Karrick Gilman was an imposing man. His thick, silver-gray hair waved back from a broad forehead. His pale blue eyes were startling in a face that looked top-heavy with his large nose and thin-lipped mouth. Dressed in a suit that probably cost more than Bowie made in a month, he looked like a thug trying to pass as a businessman.

"I'd like to speak to Mrs. Harper alone." His voice was sur-prisingly cultured.

"No," Bowie spoke before even thinking about it. He wasn't leaving Alayna alone with this asshole.

ALAYNA'S GAZE SHIFTED from Gilman to Bowie. Though he looked relaxed, there was an air about him that suggested action held in check. Was this how he was when he went into battle? Everything he told her last night continued to rattle around in her head. One minute she was on an emotional high of highs, and the next anxious for no reason other than she was terrified this tentative chance for them to be together again would be stolen away from her.

She dragged her attention back to the moment and took the bull by the horns. "I'll answer your questions as truthfully with them in the room as I would without them, Mr. Gilman."

He studied her silently.

"I have nothing to do with Aaron's business. I never have. If I knew where your money was, I'd tell you. First because it would be the right thing to do, and second because it would keep Aaron from having it."

"You're a single mother with three children to raise. It can't be easy financially and otherwise." His eyes never wavered from her face, and prickles of alarm raced up the back of her neck.

"It isn't easy, but just because I lived with Aaron for four years as his wife doesn't mean we share the same moral character. That was the reason we parted ways three years ago."

"Is he responsible for those bruises on your neck?"

Though they were still tender, she ignored them. "Yes, he is. He broke into my apartment and attacked me yesterday. The police were there, supposedly staking the place out, but he escaped."

"Why did he do it?"

"Because he hates me. And because I refuse to help him."

His eyes darkened. "That's a lot of rage for a short marriage."

"Yes, it is."

"Were you unfaithful?"

"No. He was."

Gilman's brows rose. "Why?"

"Because he wasn't the center of my universe, my children were, and he couldn't compete."

Gilman smiled. There was something predatory in his expression that had her heart skipping a beat. "What one thing would he desire more than the money he's stolen?"

Looking into his face was like watching a cobra—mesmerizing and terrifying. Chill bumps raced up her arms. "To end me."

"If we could create the opportunity, would it draw him out?"

Bowie tensed to move. Alayna placed a hand on his arm. "I think I know where Mr. Gilman is going with this." Would Aaron have to see her, if she were dead, just to give her a last "fuck you" before she was buried? What did that say about their relationship?

"I would like nothing better than to agree with this, Mr. Gilman. But I can't. In order for it to work, it would have to be maintained as real. It would have to be real for my girls, and I'm the only stable person in their lives. I can't do that to them."

"I understand." He fell silent for a moment.

"I can suggest something else, though. Aaron's parents are here, visiting the girls, waiting for word about their son. I'm almost certain his mother is in contact with him."

"There might be a way for us to use the connection he has with his mother. Your mother-in law's phone would have to have spyware installed on it so her calls can be monitored, recorded, and traced."

"That will require a warrant," Kappes said, "Otherwise it's illegal, and a federal crime. And you'd have to have proof that she's receiving calls from her son."

Bowie shifted in his seat. "If Detectives Gray and Stansberry are still on the case, that could be a problem."

"How so?" Williard Kappes asked.

Bowie exchanged a look with her. "They've been very aggressive with their investigation. I think someone is offering them an incentive to find Harper."

"I have no issue with that." Gilman said. "It will give them a stronger motivation to capture him."

"They might not want to share the arrest with anyone else."

"I don't care who arrests him. But I'd like a few minutes alone with Harper before he's placed under arrest."

"You and everyone else he's stolen from," Kappes said, earning a frown.

Alayna broke in before an argument could start. "Even if you capture him, if he's lost the information he needs to access the accounts he's funneled the money into, how do you think you'll get your money back? If he used his office or home computer, the police have already had enough time to analyze them and would have been in touch with you, wouldn't they?"

"According to the police, he had someone in the accounting department cooking the books. So if he sold a thirty million-dollar piece of property, he got a six hundred thousand-dollar commission instead of the three hundred thousand he would have been paid normally. The extra three hundred thousand was funneled to offshore accounts."

So his clients got screwed twice. Twenty percent commission was highway robbery. Alayna turned to look at Bowie. "The man burned in Aaron's car could be the accountant."

"Could be. Gray and Stansberry won't be calling to tell us. They haven't even mentioned there was anyone else missing from his office."

How could she marry a man capable of murdering someone and burning his body?

Bowie gripped her arm just above the elbow and gave it a reassuring squeeze. "We can't be sure, Alayna."

"Alayna," Gilman spoke her name.

She needed time to think, to figure out how to process this latest development. Reluctantly she looked up.

"Do you think you can gain access to Aaron's mother's phone and find out if she's been in touch with him?"

"Probably. But why aren't the police coming to me with this idea?" Her question seemed to catch and hold everyone's attention.

"They may be monitoring both his parents' phones and yours already, Alayna," Kappes said.

"They haven't had access to my cell phone, and doesn't spyware have to be installed hands-on? I don't know about Aaron's parent's phones. They can check mine all they want. I haven't tried to call him." She never wanted to see or speak to him again.

"He'd be smart enough to pick up a burner phone since they're harder to trace," Bowie suggested. "They could ping his location if they can get the number and the phone is active."

Alayna cast a look in his direction.

He shrugged one wide shoulder. "We sometimes use burner phones on ops." He turned his attention to Gilman. "Before

Alayna goes into...spy mode...you might want to call Sherwood and find out whether he's already monitoring everyone's cell. Or if he's open to this."

Gilman stared at Bowie a long moment, his expression stony, and his gaze flat. "I'll get right on that." He removed a smart phone from an interior pocket of his suit jacket, wandered over to the window, and turned his back to them to make the call.

Alana reached for Bowie's hand and linked their fingers. His protectiveness eased her anxiety, but she was still shaking.

He brushed warm lips against her forehead. "You do know who this guy is?"

She leaned forward closer to his ear and gave his hand a squeeze. "I know. I'm glad you're here with me."

"Don't make a deal with the devil, Alayna."

"I don't intend to, but as long as Aaron's out there, the people who are after him are a danger the girls and me...and to you as long as you stand between us and them. This has to end, Bowie."

Gilman strode back to them and took his seat. His jaw pulsed. "I'll give you a hundred thousand dollars if you check your mother-in-law's phone and forward the number to me if you find one, Ms. Wieland."

Shocked, Alayna stared at him. A hundred thousand dollars could be a nest egg that could stand between her and the girls and a disaster. But she'd be signing Aaron's death warrant if she accepted it. "Without the account numbers and location of the money, he'd have nothing to offer you, Mr. Gilman." Her mouth almost too dry to speak, she still managed to say, "I can't do it."

"He assaulted you. You owe him no loyalty."

"It isn't that. If I did what you want me to do and something happened to him, I'd be just as culpable as you."

"How do I know you don't have the information?"

She knew it was going to come down to this. She continued to look him in the face, though the desire to look anywhere but at him was strong. "I don't have the flash drive. The police have searched my apartment twice. There's nothing there. My girls and I just want to be left in peace. We don't have anything to do with any of this."

Gilman rose, and for a long moment continued to study her, his gaze so intent it was almost palpable. Her stomach muscles tightened painfully. He strode across the office, threw open the door, and left.

Alayna drew a deep breath. For several seconds everyone remained silent. "I hope he believed me," she managed.

Kappes cleared his throat, his expression unreadable. "I'm certain he did."

Bowie's silence stretched. He stood and offered her a hand. "Let's go."

Her body weak, her knees shook as she rose.

They reached the anteroom where Jeannine, Kappes's secretary worked. Bowie tugged her to a halt. "Wait for me here. I need to ask Kappes something."

BOWIE HAD SELDOM known true rage, but it blazed through his system now. He strode back into the office and closed the door. Kappes had moved from his seat behind his desk to stand at the window. Bowie sidled up to him, crowding his space. "How much did he pay you for this meeting?"

Kappes eyed him warily, leaning away. "Nothing."

Bowie kept the pressure on, the urge to snap this fucker's neck strong. "She trusted you. Completely. And you sold her down the river. For that hundred thou he offered her?" He knew he was right when Kappes broke eye contact.

"I know a killer when I see one. I've dealt with enough in places you'd piss down your leg just flying over. This man is like the Russian mob. Shit follows him wherever he goes. And you gave her to him." He tried to breathe through the adrenaline blasting through his system like molten lava. "If something happens to her or the girls, I'll come for you."

Kappes paled visibly.

"Give me that fucker's number."

Kappes removed his cell phone from his inner suit pocket, his hands shaking. He wrote the number down on a post-it and tore it off.

Bowie stuck it in his pocket. "You realize you're in bed with the devil now. He'll be back for more. He knows your price."

Kappes's Adam's apple bobbed.

Bowie closed the office door softly behind him. He nodded to the woman sitting at the desk outside and gripped Alayna's elbow. In the elevator on the way down, he drew her close against his side. "It's going to be okay."

Silence stretched between them in the car. Bowie couldn't think of a thing to cut it with. The need to get to the apartment and check on the kids overwhelmed everything else. When they turned into the street the apartment complex sat on, Bowie slowed. Everything looked quiet. He breathed a sigh of relief and pulled into a parking space. His phone rang, and Alayna startled.

He snatched the device from the cup holder and opened it. "It's Tess, Weaver," he announced before answering the call. "Hey."

"I'm sending you a list of clients. You need to be careful, Bowie. Harper was swimming among the sharks."

"I just met one of them."

"Who?"

"Gilman."

"Jesus! Whatever led him to believe he'd be able to fuck these guys? Gilman's completely out of his league."

She sounded so much like Brett, he smiled. "I don't know, but I'll keep you posted."

"Please do, and keep them safe."

"I'll do my best. I owe you, Tess."

"No you don't. You're part of Brett's family. Be careful."

"Will do."

As soon as she hung up, his phone dinged and a short message with the attachment appeared on the screen. He opened the document on his phone and read down the list. Some he recognized, others he didn't. There were enough he did know to light up his adrenaline again.

"Come on. I'll download this onto your computer, and we'll go from there."

On the way up on the elevator, he rested an arm around Alana's shoulders and she curled in against him, slipping her arms around his waist. Her heart hammered against his ribs.

"What is it?"

"Just a case of nerves. I'm glad you're here with me, Bowie."

"I am too."

Instead of using the bell, Bowie unlocked the apartment door with his key.

"Girls?"

Alayna's voice seemed absorbed by the quiet. She rushed to the bedroom door.

He knew they were gone before she said the words.

"I asked them not to take them out." Her face was pale but for two bright spots of color on her cheeks. "You don't think they've taken them to the airport?"

Jesus! He hoped not. "Call them." His muscles tightened, her tension and anxiety feeding his own.

She jerked her phone free of her purse.

His released a breath when she said, "Where are you?" Her features tightened and a frown crumpled her forehead. "We're on our way."

"What's going on?"

"They're at the park. Gloria says we need to come right away."

At the fear in her expression, he tried to offer comfort. "Take it easy, Alayna."

They took the stairs down and rushed to the car. Bowie whipped the vehicle around and headed west toward the park. Five minutes later they ran into bottleneck of police cars and an ambulance.

"Bowie—" Her voice sounded strangled.

His breathing blocked in his throat he swerved the SUV to the side and parallel parked in an empty slot. They bailed out of the vehicle, Bowie caught her hand, and they rushed down the street, past the police cars, until they reached a taped-off area. Three policemen stood at the perimeter. They fought their way through a crowd gathering behind the tape.

Alayna's breathing rasped as she bit out, "Where are my children?"

CHAPTER 23

S HE COULDN'T BREATHE. The need to scream was locked inside her chest, held there on the brink by the inability to get enough air into her lungs. Everything seemed gray. The grass, the trees, even the sky.

Rosa was gone. Taken by two men dressed in black ski masks. Were they the same men who'd tried to kidnap her? *Rosa. Are they hurting her? Please, God, don't let them hurt her. My baby.*

Numbness crept up her arms and legs. If she hadn't been sitting down on the bench seat of the picnic table, she'd have been on the ground. She clenched the fabric of her blouse over her breast with both hands and rocked with the pain.

"Are you all right, Ms. Wieland?" Captain Sherwood asked.

She couldn't look at him. If she did, she'd start screaming. He wasn't here to help her Rosa.

Bowie's voice cut across like a blade. "Fuck no, she's not okay. She's in shock."

She's only two. Don't let them hurt her.

Bowie came into her line of sight. He cupped her face in his hands and looked into her eyes. "You have to breathe, Alayna. Just breathe, baby. It's going to be okay. We're going to get her back. Whatever it takes, we'll get her back. Take a breath for me."

Where were Addison and Emilia? Were they okay? "Girls?"

"They're okay. They're sitting right over there with Gloria."

Bowie pointed to a picnic table forty feet away. Two policemen in uniform stood guard over the three. Seeing Emilia and Addison without their sidekick nearly brought her to her knees.

Alayna staggered to her feet and started toward them. Bowie slipped an arm around her and held her steady while they walked. The world suddenly came back into focus as she set her sights on her daughters. She had to be strong for them.

As soon as they saw her, they ran to her. She fell to her knees to hold them close. Their tears blended with hers as she rocked and comforted them.

"Rosa's gone, Momma. They grabbed her and punched Papaw. I tried to run after them, but they drove away too fast," Emilia's broken tone undid the momentary strength she'd dragged forward.

She cupped her daughter's face in her hands. "It isn't your fault, Emilia. You're a wonderful sister for trying to help Rosa. We're going to get her back. We're going to find her." *Please, God.* "We're going to do whatever we have to do to get her back."

Her face still wet, and the girls clinging to her, she pushed to her feet to face Gloria.

The woman seemed to have shrunken since that morning. Her hair was mussed, and her skin looked sallow.

"I'm sorry, Alayna. Warren tried to stop them, but they knocked him down They've taken him to the hospital."

Fuck Warren and *fuck* this bitch. "Give me your phone."

Gloria quickly withdrew her cell phone from her pocket and handed it to her.

Alayna's hands shook as she swiped the screen and went to the calls received. She looked for the ones that came in after they left last night. The single number had no name connected to it. She tilted the screen so Bowie could see it. She punched it and waited for it to ring.

"Mom? I told you not to call me." Aaron's voice came across irritated and impatient.

"They've taken, Rosa. Who's looking for you, Aaron? Give me the name." She was aware of Bowie standing close and typing the number into his phone.

"God!" There was silence for a moment, then he seemed to pull himself together. "I don't know. It could be Karrick Gilman, Martin Terban, or Mitchell Pickett. I think it's one of them. Are the police looking for her? What are they doing?" It was the closest to caring about Rosa he'd ever shown. But it was too late.

She ended the call without answering and turned her attention back to Gloria. "I told you not to leave the house. I told you it was dangerous. But you deliberately ignored my wishes. I know it was you who made that decision. Because you make all the decisions, and always get your way. And Warren went along because it's easier to do that than put up with your bullshit. This is your fault, Gloria. If something happens to her—"

A near sob interrupted her tirade, and her composure threatened to implode. Her voice thickened around the emotion gripping her. "It will be your fault. I want you to think about that every moment she's gone." She wanted to pummel the woman so badly she trembled with it. "You arrogant, stupid, bitch."

Gloria recoiled from her final blast.

Alayna slammed the expensive phone down on the picnic table, shattering the screen, then tossed it to the ground and ground her heel into it until it started falling apart. "Don't ever call or come to my apartment again. You're no longer welcome. You've seen your grandchildren for the last time."

She took Addison and Emilia's hands and walked back toward Captain Sherwood.

WITH A HAND on her arm, Bowie stopped her halfway there. "I need to make a call, Alayna."

Her eyes, on fire with emotion only moments ago, had dimmed again with worry. "Gilman?"

"Yeah. Gilman can get it done before the police can get a warrant."

Her eyes darkened, and her features took on a fierce determination. "Do it."

Bowie pulled the number from his pocket and dialed it.

"I thought I might be hearing from you, Lieutenant."

"Alayna's youngest daughter, Rosa, has been kidnapped. You have to move fast if you want to track Harper's number. He'll toss the phone soon."

"Where would you like the money sent?"

"I don't want your money. I know you had men out looking for Harper. I need the intel they gathered while hunting for him. I'm looking for three guys, each six-foot, between one-ninety to two-ten, dark hair. They may be brothers. They have to be some of Harper's victims. They attempted to kidnap Alayna at the bank, and now they've taken Rosa. She's only two. She doesn't talk much."

His emotions started to get away from him, and he closed his eyes against the tears that reared up. "She won't be able to identify anyone. If your guys identified anyone like them, I need to know about them."

Trusting this man was like trusting a lion not to attack if you walked up to pet it. But they didn't have much of a choice. They had nothing to offer the assholes who'd taken Rosa.

"Deal. Give me the number."

Bowie read off Harper's number from his phone.

"Don't call me again at this number. I'll get back to you on a different phone as soon as we have Harper in hand."

Bowie closed out the call. His throat ached with emotion as numerous memories, already captured and held, flooded his mind. Rosa with her fishy grin saying, "Good taco." Rosa clinging to her monkey while he held her until she fell asleep. Rosa calling him Boy because she couldn't say Bowie. If they lost her, Alayna would never be the same. And he wouldn't either.

He had to shut off his clamoring fears so he could do what needed to be done. He needed to make certain Rosa got home in one piece. If Gilman didn't double-cross them. If he wasn't the one holding Rosa hostage to begin with. And God help these assholes if anyone hurt Rosa. He'd scorch the earth to find them and end them.

He focused on Alayna and the girls as he rushed up the shallow knoll where they waited, gathering them all into his arms and holding them.

COULD TIME PASS any slower?

Alayna's eyes strayed to the clock for the hundredth time. Every minute seemed to last an hour. Her small, barren apartment had been crammed with tech people setting up the phone to route her calls through a base unit instead of her cell phone. Now they had cleared out, leaving behind a specialist in negotiation, a tech guy to man the phones, another agent whose duties she didn't know or understand, and a female officer to stay close to her and the girls.

Being trapped inside was somehow worse. The small rooms seemed claustrophobic. She wanted to rush out the door and go search for her child. But she was stuck here, waiting for her phone to ring.

She touched her eyes gingerly with her fingertips. They were raw and puffy from crying, and Emilia and Addie were still weepy. They'd take turns clinging to Bowie, then her, then back to Bowie again. Thank God she had them to distract her while they waited for word.

Finally she could take it no longer and took the two into her bedroom to lie down. She cuddled them until they drifted off, exhausted by their grief and trauma. As she watched them sleep, she was grateful they had found a respite from the emotional overload and fear, because she saw no way she could close her eyes or focus on anything but her missing daughter.

As a family, they would never get over this. It would stick with them the rest of their lives. They'd all have to go to counseling to deal with the aftermath. After Rosa came home. *Please, God, let her come home.*

FBI agents Ferguson, Cash, and Ellison sat in the kitchen at her small table, where they'd hooked up a recording device in case someone called to make demands.

Agent Ellison seemed more restless than the other two. He wandered the living room every hour and came back to fold his long, lanky six-three frame back into his chair.

Ferguson was the man in charge, mid-forties, his hair silvered at his temples, and his calm demeanor had a practiced discipline the other two hadn't attained yet.

Agent Cash was the youngest, newly out of training, but he had the same look and stance as the others as he lounged easily in his chair. All three had been quiet and respectful, their attitude calming. But she avoided being in the room with them. Their presence only underlined the fact they were all being held hostage by the monsters who took her baby.

Bowie beckoned for her to join him in the children's room.

A canister of Legos had been knocked over, and she bent to pick them up and put them away. Bowie gathered a set of cards with animals on them from Addie's bed and stacked them on the small, round table in the corner they used as an art center.

Bowie slumped onto the narrow twin bed Rosa slept in. He'd picked up her most beloved toy, her monkey. The fluffy stuffed animal was dressed in overalls and tennis shoes with a plastic banana in its hand.

Bowie's jaw muscles worked and his features were still. "Has she named him?" he asked, his voice husky.

"She says it's a she. Her name is Bebe. When she was younger she called her baby, but since it sounded like Bebe, the girls and I started calling her that, and it stuck."

He laid the toy carefully on the pillow at the head of the bed.

He was suffering just like the rest of them, though he'd been unwaveringly positive and encouraging, untiring in the comfort he gave them all.

But he couldn't entirely hide his feelings. He had grown attached to Rosa, and the feeling was mutual. Her baby needed him as much as the rest of them did. Alayna stepped between his legs to hold him, and Bowie turned his face against her breasts while she stroked his hair.

She heard the buzz of his phone set on vibrate, and he pulled back and answered the call while rubbing the heel of his hand over his tear-glazed eyes so he could read the screen. "A different number."

"Yeah." His expression morphed from grief to one of sharp focus instantly. "Good. I'll be waiting." He hung up and pulled her down on the bed beside him. He lowered his voice to a rumble. "Gilman has Aaron. He's dumped the phone, but they found him a few blocks away. And Gilman thinks he knows who has Rosa. He's putting out feelers. He's going to contact me as soon as he's got more intel."

She voiced a thought that had plagued her ever since he'd called. "What if he's stringing us along and he has her? Now he has Aaron and something to torture Aaron with to get the account numbers from him." Would threatening his daughter or hurting her mean anything to Aaron? How many times had he walked right past her when she was crying? How many times had he avoided picking her up? Her throat ached for her child.

"When we go into a mission, we have intel to help us know what we're getting into. Gilman is the only resource we have. The police won't share what they know with us. And now they're cut out of the investigation, and the FBI have come into this thing cold, I thought he was our only option at the time, Alayna. And even then, he was still willing to pay for Aaron's number. I told him I wanted intel instead of money, so we can deal with the people who have Rosa. I hope he'll come through."

Alayna clung to him for a moment. He read bad guys all the time. He read Gilman the moment they walked into Willard Kappes's office. She had to trust his instincts. The FBI would be investigating all the people on the list. They'd peg Gilman, just as Bowie had. She curled against him. "We're going to get her back."

"Yes, we are." He opened his phone again and handed it to her. "Tess sent me this list earlier today. Do you recognize any of these names?"

She scanned the list. "Gilman, Martin Turban and Mitchell

Pickett. Aaron said he thought one of those three was after him."

"While you were getting the girls down, I researched several on the list, just so we know what they're about. Gilman and Pickett are on a level of wealth and reputation far above the others."

She voiced an idea that had occurred to her. "But they wouldn't necessarily be as desperate as they'd need to be to kidnap a child. They have an Amber alert on Rosa. Her picture is everywhere. Capturing Aaron and beating the shit out of him until he hands over the information they need, yes, but I think they'd want to stay away from the high-profile crime of kidnapping."

Her fear was, if they were desperate enough to kidnap Rosa, they'd be willing to kill her if they didn't get what they wanted. Her heart thumped inside her ears. "It may be someone who's lost less, but they need the money more."

"I thought of that too. There are three families Aaron screwed out of money. One owns a computer solutions center that will probably go belly-up before the end of the year if they don't get an infusion of cash." He pointed a finger at a name at the bottom. "Terrance Asher was the father who passed away. He had his whole estate, worth a million, with the firm. He left it all to his sons, who listed it with Aaron.

"The next are the McGuires. The father and mother died within a month of each other. They left their entire estate to the kids, two boys and a girl. They're straighter than straight, so I don't really think it's them."

"The last are the Fredricks. They run a chain of dance studios for children that stretch across California from San Francisco to Los Angeles. It must be pretty lucrative, because each studio brought in about two hundred thousand last year."

"If someone calls, what should I tell them, Bowie? I don't have any information to offer them in exchange. And I don't know where Aaron is. What can I tell them so they won't hurt her?"

"Tell them she's only two and doesn't talk much, that she won't be able to identify them if they release her. Keep saying her name so they know she's a person. That she's loved. Tell them about her, that she likes tacos. That she loves music and loves to dance. That she does everything with her sisters, and that her sisters are missing her because she isn't here. That she needs her favorite toy to go to sleep. That she hums herself to sleep, but needs to be held.

"I have some savings, Alayna. About twenty thousand. Tell them to give you an account number, and I'll transfer it to them. Tell them whatever you have to keep them on the phone as long as you can, so the guys in the next room can ping their location."

A phone in the other room rang. Alayna shoved herself off the bed and ran toward the sound, dodged around the agent, and reached for the phone. "Hello."

Rosa's broken sobs came over the speaker like a knife to her heart. Bowie stepped around to face her, and his eyes locked on hers, offering her calm, sharing his strength. Rosa's sobs were suddenly cut off as a door closed.

A male voice scrambled by some kind of device came over the line. "She's going to do a lot more of that unless you do exactly what we tell you. We want five million dollars wired to an account in the Cayman Islands by tomorrow morning at ten o'clock, or you'll never see your little girl again. Once the money is in place, we'll call back with a location to pick her up. We'll text you the account number at nine-thirty tomorrow morning."

"Please, don't hurt her. Her name is Rosa. She's never been away from home before. She can't sleep without Bebe, her monkey. Please, she's just a baby. She doesn't talk much. She won't be able to identify you."

"I don't give a rat's ass what she can or can't do, Mrs. Harper."

"My ex-husband is on the run. All I have access to is twenty thousand dollars. Please. She's everything to me." She bit back a sob. "If I had the money I'd give it to you, but I don't have it."

"I guess you'd better start looking for your husband then, so you can pay the ransom. We can get twenty thousand for her on the open market. Maybe more if we do an auction online. She's beautiful, blonde. We can sell your little girl to the highest bidder."

The cruelty of what he said had visions of things happening to her baby she'd already imagined and desperately wanted to block from her brain.

"Tomorrow at ten or you'll never see her again." The line went dead.

Nausea rolled over Alayna, and she darted out of the kitchen to the hall bathroom, falling to her knees and heaving helplessly into the toilet.

CHAPTER 24

"I'M CALLING THE cybercrimes unit to get involved," Agent Cash said, and wandered into the living room to make the call.

The phone rang, and Agent Ferguson spoke briefly to someone.

Bowie's continued silence drew the agent's attention and he looked up. "They were able to ping the phone's location. It was in Old Town, and the phone was moving. He was either in a car or walking on the street. Then it went dead."

It was what Bowie expected. "Is there a way we can access the five million if we need to pay the ransom?"

"We don't suggest the families pay the ransoms, Lieutenant. Even if they can come up with it."

"So you'd let them kill her?"

"We try to negotiate with them first."

"I didn't hear any negotiating going on here tonight. I heard a man giving the child's mother an impossible ultimatum."

"Our team is good at what they do, Lieutenant. At the moment they're analyzing every person involved in Aaron Harper's crimes and putting the pieces together. They're already pulling camera footage off the street in Old Town to see if they find any familiar characters."

"And if you can't put the pieces together before nine tomorrow morning?"

Bowie waited for Ferguson to respond. When the agent remained silent, he continued.

"These men aren't going to negotiate. And they're not going to be satisfied with the twenty thousand dollars. And they won't sell Rosa. They can't afford to retain ties to her any longer than they have to." They'd kill her.

"We don't know that yet."

"You know what I do for a living?"

The Agent nodded.

"Then you know you can't bullshit me like you can Alayna to keep her calm." He'd seen how things could go south in a heartbeat too many times before.

"Does the FBI have access to an emergency fund to pay the ransom if you can't catch these fuckers soon enough?"

"No."

"Twenty thousand is all I have, Agent. Alayna has nothing. She has no family she can turn to, and neither do I."

When the Agent remained silent, Bowie stalked out of the kitchen and down the hall.

Alayna slumped on the bathroom floor holding a wet cloth to her forehead. The policewoman hovered over her, offering her comfort that would be as empty as he felt the FBI agents' negotiations would be.

A surge of protective concern struck him at the sight of her pasty face. She needed some hope to cling to. Otherwise she wasn't going to make it through this. He helped her climb to her feet, then lifted her, carried her into the children's room and placed her on Rosa's bed.

He climbed onto the narrow bed to hold her.

The policewoman peeked in then went back down the hall to the living room.

"I need you to do something for me, Alayna."

"Anything."

"I need you to close your eyes and rest. The girls need you. I need you to be strong for me, and them, and Rosa. She's going to need you when we bring her home."

"I can't sleep, Bowie. Every time I close my eyes I imagine what they might be doing to her."

"These guys only want the money, honey. That's all they're interested in." *Please, let it be so.*

"How are we going to get the money?"

For the first time he lied to her. "The FBI will come through."

"Do you think they will?"

If it offered her even a second of relief from what she was going through, the lie was worth it. "Yeah, I do." His throat felt tight. He pressed a kiss to her forehead. "Rest for me, Alayna. I'll wake you if I hear anything from Gilman."

She closed her eyes. Fifteen minutes passed before she finally relaxed, and her breathing leveled out into sleep.

His phone buzzed. He reached for it, glanced at the screen. Another strange number. Gilman was changing phones every time he called. Smart man. Bowie eased his arm from beneath Alayna's head and walked out into the hall to answer the call. "Yeah."

"We've found them," Gilman said. "They're the Asher brothers."

"Where?"

"Brian Asher left two hours ago. He caught a flight on a private plane under the name of Stewart Keith. The pilot filed a flight plan for Guatemala. He's probably going to Grand Cayman.

"The other two, Tim and Frank are here in town. They've been spending time at their warehouse. If they have the girl, it will be there."

"Give me the address." Bowie grabbed a crayon and one of the girls' drawings and wrote down the address. "They called thirty minutes ago, demanding five million, or they're going to sell Rosa to the highest bidder."

"They won't. They'll kill her and dump her body at sea. They own a yacht. I'm sorry I don't know what marina they have it docked at. You need to move quickly."

"I'm going now." He crammed the address into his pocket and paused only a second to look down at Alayna. Her beautiful face looked ravaged by grief and fear. He wouldn't add to that. He rushed out of the room, pausing by the female police officer. "Alayna's asleep. When she wakes, tell her I'll be back soon. I just have to get out of here for a few minutes. This waiting is killing me."

"I understand."

Instead of taking the elevator, he hit the door to the stairs and then jogged his way through the entrance to his car. He turned left out of the parking lot and gunned it into traffic.

He could call Doc or Lang and ask for their help, but if there was any blowback it might cost their careers. If it cost his, at least he'd know he'd done the right thing. He swung by his apartment to pick up some tools he might need, threw the items in a backpack, and rushed back out to the car.

Once in the vehicle, he keyed the address into the GPS app and hit go. His focus was on following the directions as he wove in and out of traffic. He hit an industrial section of town. As soon as he heard 'destination is on the right' he drove on past, checking out the tall fence that surrounded the facility, and the three cars and two vans in the parking lot.

If there were more than the two tangos on-site, things might get interesting. He drove around the block as he scanned the neighborhood for cops and security, and parked fifty feet east of the warehouse. They'd probably have motion-sensor lights and an alarm, along with security guards…things he didn't have to worry about in a war zone.

He grabbed the backpack then froze. Two men exited the building. One carried a duffel bag in his arms, not by the straps, but like a baby. The bag was easily big enough for Rosa to fit inside. They moved to a silver Jaguar parked in front of the building. One hit the key fob and opened the trunk. The other placed the duffel inside. Bowie's stomach clenched at the way the guy handled the bag gingerly. Would she have enough air in that bag?

The two climbed into the car, the driver revved the engine, then threw it into gear. Bowie started his SUV as the Jag's tires peeled off on the asphalt and turned east. He fell in behind the vehicle, leaving thirty feet of space between them. The desire to stop the car was strong, but he didn't know if the brothers were armed. He used his thumb to open his phone, found Alayna's number, and hit dial.

"Hello?" Her voice coming over the phone set his heart to thundering. He didn't want to upset her. "Are Agent Ferguson and Cash still there?"

"Yes."

"Are they listening?"

"Yes."

"Someone called my phone and said the Asher brothers are the ones responsible for Rosa's kidnapping. One flew out in a private plane thirty minutes after the kidnapping to Grand Cayman Island under the name of Keith. The other two have just left their warehouse, and I believe they're on their way to one of the marinas, where they have a yacht. They loaded a duffel bag in the trunk of the car."

"Where are you?" Agent Ferguson came over the line.

He merged onto the interstate a few cars behind the Jag. "I'm on the I-5 headed toward the bay. The caller said they have a yacht and mean to load Rosa onto the boat." He left the rest to the agent's imagination. "We're taking the South Rosecrans exit."

"Don't lose them. Agent Cash is directing police units to your location."

"No sirens. You don't want these guys making a run for it with Rosa in the trunk. But hurry." Was she already dead? Had they smothered her? Given her drugs? She hadn't been moving inside the bag, if she was even in there. But they were headed to Harbor drive. There was more than one marina on the road.

After five more minutes, when they passed the convention center, he was getting antsy. "Where the hell are you guys?"

"There's been an accident, and traffic is blocked. Two units have been held up. Four other units have been directed your way."

"Jesus Christ!"

The Jag whipped into the dock parking lot. Bowie swore, then raced to find a parking space at one of the local restaurants. He bailed out of the car and scanned the area behind him as he ran back the direction he had driven. In the distance, two men walked toward the gate leading onto the dock. One held a duffel bag. Bowie broke into a run.

He'd never get through security at the dock. He spoke into the phone, identifying the dock. "They're out of the car and almost to gate three. Tell your guys to double-time it." He shut off the phone and broke into a run. He crammed the phone into his back pocket, leaped onto the chain link fence enclosing the facility, and swung over the top. The shell surface along the fence nearly threw him into the water, but he gripped the wire and held on, then rushed down the property line as close as he could to the gate, eased into the water, and swam across the twenty-foot span between two fishing craft docked there.

The Asher brothers passed, and he heaved himself out of the water and onto the platform. Keeping low, he followed them down the dock to the last row of vessels. He slipped behind a sailboat as they untied the bow and aft lines and climbed onto their yacht. The two disappeared belowdecks but came up almost immediately and mounted the ladder to the flybridge cockpit.

Bowie dialed Alayna's number again and thanked the tech gods who created waterproof cell phones. Behind him, police cars pulled up, and eight officers approached the locked gate.

"The cops aren't going to make it in time." The engine on the yacht rumbled to life close by. "Call the Harbor Police and Coast Guard and tell them to head them off. I'm going onboard." He pocketed the phone.

Bowie slipped from behind the sailboat. The loud rev of the yacht's motor covered the pounding of his feet as he ran to the stern. He climbed the steps and ducked beneath the covered deck just as the vessel pulled out of its berth into the waterway.

He descended the five steps into the main cabin. The interior gleamed here and there, the rich wood trim in the space catching the light from the wide windows. He moved past white leather benches and a marble-topped table, through a galley as big as his kitchen at home, to a hall. The first door on the right proved to be a head with a shower, sink, and commode. The second door on the left was empty, the bed made neatly. He searched the attached bathroom and moved on to the first closet. It was empty, so he opened the second. Pants, shirts, dock shoes and, of all things, a tuxedo.

He slipped back into the hall to the second door on the right side. The duffel bag lay at the end of the bed. He rushed forward and jerked the zipper down. Inside lay several bottles of champagne cushioned by clothing.

His stomach hollowed as disappointment ricocheted through his system. Bowie bent at the waist and gripped his knees. Where was she? She had to be here. Unless they already killed her and dumped her body somewhere. Pain nearly shredded his battle-ready calm.

He moved to the closet closest to the exterior bulkhead, shoved aside two cinderblocks blocking the door, and opened the door. Several items hung inside but nothing else. He moved on to the other. It was empty except for a metal dog cage that sat in the bottom, covered with a towel. He tossed aside the heavy cloth, and his heart plummeted at the sight of the child who lay motionless inside. She looked small and pale, her clothing stained with what looked like vomit, her pants stained from other bodily fluids. Her hair, hanging in fine clumps, partially hid her face. "Dear God, let her be alive."

He fell to his knees next to the cage and smelled the sharp, pungent scent of urine. A small padlock held the door shut. *Why the fuck had he left the backpack behind? Fuck!* He shoved several fingers through the bars and touched her arm. She was warm, and he strained to see her small chest rise and fall with her breathing. Seeing the steady movement, his shoulders fell, and he rested his forehead against the bars until he got his emotions under control.

"Rosa." He gently pinched her small wrist. She didn't respond. She had to be drugged.

Bowie pulled out his phone, breathing a sigh of relief when a few bars showed on the screen. They were fast getting out of range. He dialed Alayna's number again. "Rosa's on board. You need to get the Harbor Police and Coast Guard out here."

"They're already on their way. Are the brothers armed, Lieutenant?" Ferguson asked.

The signal faded in and out as Bowie moved around the room, then out into the galley looking for a stronger connection. "I wasn't close enough to see. But I'd go with the premise that they are."

Bowie scanned the room for something to use to force the lock on Rosa's cage. He opened the widest drawer next to the sink and found the silverware. He reached for a fork. The loud report of a pistol filled the cabin and a chunk of wood from the cabinet closest to his face broke off to fly through the air and pepper his arm with splinters. Bowie dropped his phone and dove for cover as more bullets followed his progress behind one of the galley cabinets. His heart beat in his ears and he drew his Sig, waiting for calm.

The tall, dark-haired man at the door yelled. "Frank."

"Tim Asher." Bowie yelled over the man's panicked shouts. "I'm Lieutenant Daniel Rivera with the United States Navy. The FBI knows you have Rosa Harper." Bowie maneuvered to a squatting position to return fire. "If you let me take her, it solves one of your problems. Just get close enough inland to drop us off, then you can make a run for Mexico as soon as you hit open water."

"Fuck you. You're a dead man."

Shit. "Wrong answer."

Bowie bobbed up and opened fire on the shadow in the door. Asher fell backwards onto the deck, screaming. He gripped his leg and rolled on the ground. Off to one side, a hand grabbed Tim's arm and dragged him out of range.

"Frank Asher, the Harbor Police and Coast Guard are on their way. Save yourself and your brother, and turn around and take us back to the dock."

Silence stretched a beat then two. He peered around the corner of the cabinet. Nothing moved on the deck beyond the cabin door. A dull thud came from down the hall. Bowie crawled through the narrow space and glanced inside the stateroom. A hand swung a hammer working to break the triangular, waterproof window high up on the wall. The glass shattered and a hand pointed a Beretta at the closet where Rosa lay.

Bowie fired, and the hand and gun retreated hastily. A sound came from behind him. He rolled to face the threat, bringing his Sig to bear on the target. Frank Asher rushed down the hall, a nine-millimeter pistol gripped in his hand.

The simultaneous discharge of their weapons in the narrow space pierced Bowie's ears, at the same moment he gasped at the quick, agonizing punch to his shoulder.

Asher's head snapped back, and he dropped like his legs had been cut out from under him. He fell facedown and lay still. A large, red pool spread out on the carpet to one side of him. The smell of spent gunpowder hung in the air.

"Frank!" Tim shouted from the door.

"Frank's not able to talk right now. You need to turn this vessel around and take us back to the dock. Your brother needs medical attention."

He needed a little himself. Where the fuck were the Harbor Police and the Coast Guard?

Blood ran down one side of his chest and dripped onto the floor. He had to move. He was too easy a target in the narrow hallway. Bone shifted in his left shoulder, and he gritted his teeth against the pain. He crawled forward into the stateroom and struggled to sit next to the closet. Dragging in deep breaths to alleviate the nausea, he assessed his condition. Blood soaked his shirt front and back. He touched the back of his shoulder and found a hole almost at the top of his shoulder. The bullet had traveled through. He cut off thoughts about how much damage it might have done. Help would be here soon. He'd be fine. But he needed to get the bleeding stopped.

He grabbed the towel he'd thrown aside earlier and tried to tear it in half. Putting pressure on his left hand sharpened the pain in his shoulder. His vision washed to white. He waited for it to pass.

Stepping on the towel to hold it in place, he ripped it in half, folded it into a pad, and forced it under his shirt over the bullet wounds front and back. He pushed back against the edge of the door, holding the pad in place over the exit wound while he kept pressure on the entrance wound with his hand.

After five minutes, he wiped the blood from his right hand with the other half of the towel and turned his attention to Rosa. He reached through the bars to touch her, wanting to check her pulse. If the sound of gunfire wasn't waking her…

What if they gave her too much? She needed medical assistance. *Now.*

Taking a deep breath, he prepared to stand.

CHAPTER 25

A S DARKNESS FELL, Alayna's nerves stretched to the breaking point. She tried to distract herself by preparing a meal for the girls and the FBI agents still waiting for news. Her stomach pitched and nearly heaved again at just the idea of food, and after setting out plates for the men and the female officer Tanner, she wandered into the living room and paced the small space.

She returned to the kitchen and approached Agent Ferguson. "We can't just sit here and wait for a phone call. We have to do something."

She'd had enough of waiting. Her heart was still pounding from the sound of gunfire ending Bowie's conversation with them. He was in trouble. Her baby was in trouble. "Can't the police there commandeer a boat from the marina and follow them?"

"I promise you, everything that can be done is being done, Ms. Wieland. The San Diego Harbor Police, the US Coast Guard, and our hostage rescue team have been deployed, plus Lieutenant Rivera is a SEAL, and he knows how to handle himself in situations like this."

Alayna shook her head. His attempt to sooth her fears didn't work. "Bowie doesn't have his team with him. He doesn't have body armor." She nearly lost her composure. "Two of the most important people in this world to me are there, and they're in trouble, possibly hurt. I want to be there when they bring them both off the boat."

"They won't be there, Ms. Wieland. They'll be airlifted immediately to a local hospital to be checked out. I promise you, as soon as we receive word they're at the hospital, we'll take you to see them both."

Alayna tugged at her hair and pulled it back from her face. She was going to go crazy.

Addie looped her arm around her leg. "Bowie will bring her back," she said, with such conviction Alayna had to fight back the sobs.

"Yes, he will." He'd give his life to make it happen. And that's what she was grateful for and terrified of. She'd done without him for ten years. She didn't want to ever have to do it again.

ROSA WAS SAFER in the cage, but he didn't trust Tim Asher not to come back and try to shoot her through the window again. He wrestled the cage out of the closet one-handed, dragged it across the hall to the other stateroom, and shoved it into the closet there. He stopped to search Frank Asher's body for the key to the padlock. Aside from his wallet, his pockets were empty.

Night was falling in earnest, and the interior of the galley kitchen was shadowed. His foot hit his phone and it slid across the floor and under the edge of a walnut-stained cabinet, where he retrieved it. He called Alayna's phone again, but only got the busy signal of being out of range. With his gun in one hand and his other hand tucked into his belt to keep from moving his shoulder, he cautiously climbed the steps and peered out to the deck above.

Tim Asher had turned on the yacht's running lights. A blood trail smeared the wood where his brother had dragged him clear. The ladder leading to the flybridge was smeared with blood.

The whomp-whomp-whomp of a helicopter came from the darkness overhead, its large searchlight scanning the water and coming in fast.

With the coast guard close by, Bowie went back to searching the galley for something to beat the lock off the dog cage. Finding an aluminum meat tenderizer, he hurried back into the stateroom. His left arm and shoulder knifed with pain every time he moved them.

He laid his Sig on the floor and used his right hand to grip the hammer-like instrument and beat at the lock until it sprung and released. Shoving back the cage door, he touched Rosa's neck and found a pulse. It seemed strong and even. Anger rebounded from his relief, and he picked up the lock and threw it across the room. He wanted Tim Asher to pay for every moment of terror Rosa had experienced.

Bowie closed the cage door and picked up his Sig. Should Rosa wake, he needed to know where she was in case they needed to bug out in a hurry when rescue found them. He shoved to his feet and had to grab onto the edge of the closet to regain his balance. The bleeding had stopped, but he'd lost enough blood to cause him some concern. The mission wasn't finished yet.

He left the stateroom, and, keeping low, dodged through the galley and cabin to the steps leading up on deck again.

Lights flashed through the windows as a coast guard vessel pulled alongside the yacht and kept pace with it. "Tim and Frank Asher, this is the United States Coast Guard. Cut power to the engine and prepare to be boarded."

The sound of gunfire came from outside. Bowie kept low as fire was returned.

Bowie holstered his weapon and climbed the stairs to the deck, only to hear a bullhorn announce:

"To all who are on board, you need to abandon ship now. You are headed to shore at thirty knots. You are only a hundred yards from shore."

A surge of adrenaline hit Bowie's system and he took the steps in a leap and rushed to the stateroom. He bent to open the cage and eased Rosa free. Her small body lay limp in his arms. If they hit the water too hard, he'd lose his grip on her and she'd drown. Or if he lost consciousness, he'd lose her.

He scanned the cabin for something to tie her to him. The drapes were tied back with decorative rope with tassels. He yanked two of them free. Laying her on one of the couches, he tied the rope around her upper body then created a loop to put around his neck. She hung like a rag doll against his chest, facing out. The other two ropes he tied around his body and secured her against him as tightly as he could.

He exited the cabin and raised a hand to signal to the coast guard vessel and the helicopter above as their lights came to bear on him and Rosa. One of the Asher brothers had deployed the swim platform and he climbed out on it.

The yacht rolled in the wake of the forty-seven-foot MLB keeping pace with them, throwing Bowie off-balance. He gripped the bulkhead to keep from going in headfirst. He put his hand over Rosa's mouth and nose, turned his back to the water, and jumped.

The water, a cold bitch, stung like hell and took his breath. Rosa woke with a squeal and began to cry.

It was the most beautiful sound he'd ever heard.

One of the powerful spotlights on the MLB focused in on them as they throttled back and turned to come back to them.

He rolled onto his back to hold her as far out of the water as he could, and rested his injured arm over her. "Bowie's got you, Little Bit."

The helicopter bugged out, following the yacht's course. A sound like a scream vibrated across the water as the yacht struck the rocks along the coast and ran upon the beach. The engines continued to run for a few seconds, then died.

One minute passed, but seemed to last at least five in the cold pacific waters. Two coast guard crewmembers in wet suits swam toward him. "Lieutenant Rivera?"

"Yeah." His teeth chattered, spiking his concern for Rosa. She was shivering, and she'd gone quiet again.

"How you doing, sir?"

"I've been better, and Rosa has, too. You need to get her aboard now."

"We're going to take care of that right now, sir. How badly are you injured?"

"I've been shot in the shoulder. It's a through and through, but it's shattered my collarbone, and I can't move that arm." The cold water had ramped up the injury to a screaming ache.

"I'm going to tow you to the MLB. We're going to get you and the little lady warmed up and transported to the hospital ASAP. Just relax, sir, and let me do the work."

That was a damn fine idea.

"THEY'VE TRANSPORTED LIEUTENANT Rivera and Rosa to the trauma unit of UC San Diego," Agent Ferguson said as he closed out the call. "They'll transfer him to the military medical center as soon as they're certain he's stable. He was shot in the shoulder, has lost some blood, and has some bone damage that will require surgery. Rosa was sedated the entire time she was in the Asher brothers' custody, but they said she's awake now, stable, and doing well."

Lightheaded, Alayna braced a hand on the kitchen counter to maintain her balance. "I want to go to them right now."

"Of course. But there's just one other thing."

"What is it?"

"Even though the Asher brothers were responsible for Rosa's kidnapping and possibly your attempted kidnapping, Ms. Wieland, they haven't been linked to Mrs. Harper's death. In fact, it would have been impossible for them to attack you at the bank and kill her at the same time."

Alayna had thought one probably followed the other. If the Asher brothers hadn't killed Bliss, who had?

That idea had her stomach cramping with worry and guilt. Had she handed her ex-husband over to a killer? She took a deep breath. She'd done what she had to, to save Rosa. Bowie wouldn't have been aboard their yacht to rescue her if Gilman hadn't come through with valuable information.

"It's important you stay close to us until we tie up the last few loose ends."

"Okay."

The three Agents rose as a unit.

Alayna rushed into the girls' bedroom. She couldn't believe how wonderfully behaved they'd been throughout this ordeal. She was going to do something special for all three of her babies as soon as Rosa was home. "Bowie found Rosa, and we're going to see her. Get your shoes on, girls."

The two squealed with joy and jumped up and down, then rushed to put their shoes on. Alayna went to the closet and got jackets for them.

In the car, Addie leaned against her and hugged her arm. "I knew Bowie would find her."

Knowing he was out there trying to free Rosa and bring her home had been the only thing that made it possible for her to hold it together. But would his arm and shoulder be okay? If he'd sacrificed his career for them, after everything else…

The SUV pulled up at the front door of the medical center. Agents Ellison and Cash exited the vehicle and acted as barriers between her, the girls, and the press, as they rushed to the emergency entrance and inside.

It was wonderful to have someone fight through the paper-work and take the lead. All she wanted to do was see her Rosa and Bowie. Once on the eighth floor, Alayna felt the urge to run, but followed behind Agent Cash at a steady pace. When they finally reached Rosa's room, she pushed past him and dashed over to her child.

"Momma!" Rosa reached for her despite the stiff immobilizer that kept her from bending her elbow. An IV trailed from her small arm. Her eyes looked puffy, as though she'd slept for a long time, and her hair stuck up in wisps and curls.

Alayna hurried to lower the railing on one side of the bed and, mindful of the IV, gathered her close. She'd already shed so many tears, she didn't think she had any left, but they came in a sudden rush. She held Rosa's small body close and pressed her lips to her forehead, her cheeks, and smoothed her fine hair. "How's my Sugar Pop?"

"Momma sad?" Rosa patted her cheek. The hospital gown she wore fell back to reveal a few finger-shaped bruises.

Alayna kissed her hand. "No, baby. Momma's crying because she's so happy to see you."

Emilia and Addie pressed close to touch their sister. Addie climbed up on the hospital bed like a monkey to cuddle close to Rosa. "I missed you, Rosa." She began to cry.

Emilia's cheeks glistened with tears, and Alayna slipped off the bed, set Rosa down, and lifted Emilia onto the bed so she could be closer. The girls clung to their sister.

Alayna held them all. "Everything will be fine."

"Where Boy?" Rosa asked.

"I don't know." Alayna looked to Agent Ferguson. "Has Bowie been transferred to the Naval Med Center yet?"

"I can check for you."

"Please do. We want to see him." She couldn't leave Rosa now she'd been found, but the need to see him and be reassured he was all right warred with her need to be with her child.

Ferguson left to check with the staff. "He's still on the premises in a room down the hall. They brought them both to the trauma unit because Rosa was dehydrated and suffering minor hypothermia. The doctor will be in to speak with you in just a moment."

Even as he spoke a tall, gray-haired woman came into the room. She smiled. "You must be Rosa's mom."

"Yes."

"She's doing very well. We've put the IV in because she was a little dehydrated, and we wanted to flush the sedative out of her system. Once we'd done that, she bounced back almost immediately. She's a little raw from wearing a pull-up too long, and we had to cut her clothes off and bathe her, but she shows no signs of any kind of trauma or abuse other than a few bruises, sustained, I'm sure, when she was grabbed."

Alayna drew a sharp breath. None of the nightmare scenarios

that had played through her mind had happened. She closed her eyes against another wave of emotion. "When can she go home?"

"We'd like to keep her overnight. Just in case."

"That sounds good." Now one worry had been relieved, she needed to make certain Bowie was truly okay. "All three of the girls and I would like to see Bowie before he's transferred."

"He's resting comfortably. I see no reason why they can't, but children aren't normally allowed on this floor because of the nature of the injuries we treat. Rosa will be transferred to pediatrics in a short while."

"I understand."

"Agent Ferguson knows the Lieutenant's room number."

"Thank you. And thank you so much for taking care of my baby."

The doctor rested a hand on her arm. "I'm glad she's back with you and safe."

BOWIE OPENED HIS eyes at the soft sound of the door swinging inward. Alayna carried Rosa on her hip while Agent Ellison pushed an IV pole behind her. The five of them crept into the room, probably in case he was sleeping.

"How are my girls?" he asked, his voice a little gravelly.

"Bowie." Addison broke ranks and ran to his bedside. She eyed the bandage that immobilized his left arm, then stated the obvious. "You're hurt."

"Just a little."

She lay her face down on the bed and sobbed.

His heart turned in his chest. No one had ever cried over him before. He stroked her hair. "The doctors are going to fix me. I'm going to be just fine."

Emilia leaned in close to Addie and rested her hand on her sister's shoulder to comfort her. Bowie gave her arm a gentle squeeze.

Her gaze, solemn and intent, rested on his face. "You brought

Rosa back."

"I had a little help from some other guys. I couldn't have done it without them."

She nodded.

"Girls, Bowie is going to be leaving in a few minutes. I'd like to speak to him alone." She handed Addison a tissue. "Tell Bowie 'bye, and we'll see him tomorrow."

Addie was still a little tearful as she wiped her face and nose inexpertly and bid him goodbye. Emilia got up on tiptoe to kiss his cheek.

"Come with me, girls. I'll walk you back to Rosa's room," Agent Ellison said from the door.

Alayna nodded at the two. "I'll be right there."

The door closed, and she set Rosa down on the bed beside Bowie and smiled when he automatically hooked his good arm around Rosa to hold her in place. Rosa wiggled around to lie beside him and patted his cheek. "Boy."

He kissed her gummy hand.

Alayna leaned down and kissed him. "What you did for Rosa—for me, and the girls…" She kissed him again.

"I did it for me, too, Alayna. I couldn't lose her either."

She rested her forehead on his shoulder. "I love you, Bowie. I've loved you since I was fifteen. I never stopped loving you. I don't think I ever will."

"Good, because I need you. I need you and the girls." Saying the L word was harder for him, but he'd get there.

The door opened, and a nurse walked into the room. "The ambulance is here to transport Lieutenant Rivera to the Naval Medical Center."

"Rosa will be released in the morning. I'll be there as soon as I can."

She bent to kiss him again. He returned the fervent pressure of the kiss, then slipped his arm around her, holding her there, murmuring, "If they ask you about the phone calls to or from Gilman, you don't know anything. Okay?"

Alayna studied his face, then nodded. "Okay."

CHAPTER 26

FINDING SOMEONE WILLING to babysit her children after what had happened to Rosa was impossible, even with a police guard outside the door. Separating the girls in any way right now didn't seem a good idea, either.

She didn't want to call the hospital and tell Bowie she couldn't be there while he was in surgery. The tug of war between her need to be there for Bowie and her responsibility to her children tore at her.

A knock at the door concerned her. What next could happen? She opened it to find one of the policemen standing there with Langley and Trish Marks. After a second of surprise, Alayna said, "It's okay. They're friends." She beckoned the couple in. "I thought you guys were due to stay the entire week in Big Bear."

"We are." Trish explained. "We had some friends come down to stay with our kids and decided you might need a hand with yours while you stay with Bowie at the hospital during his surgery."

"Did he call you?"

"No." Langley answered. "My CO called and said Bowie was shot and explained the details. We watched the television updates all evening about the kidnapping and Rosa's rescue. My CO thought you'd feel a little more secure if someone from Bowie's team could come over to the apartment to stay with your girls so you can be there when he wakes up."

"He did?" A breathless feeling expanded her chest.

"Yeah. We drove back last night so we'd be here in time to babysit the girls."

"I was going to take them with me back to the hospital. Rosa was released at seven this morning, and the girls were restless all night after everything that happened. They've all gone back to sleep now, and I can't begin to tell you how much I appreciate this."

"We'll stay as long as you need us," Langley said.

"Thank you." She bit her lip. "I hope it won't take long."

"It is likely to be three or four hours at least," Langley commented. "It's a hospital."

"Give me your number, and I'll call you and keep you posted about everything that's going on while I'm there." It took only a moment to key in Trish's number. She quickly texted her own in return.

"If the girls are any trouble, just call me."

"We'll be fine," Trish assured her.

"I need to go now, so I can be there before they take him to surgery." She threw on her jacket, grabbed her purse, and tucked her cell phone into the front pocket.

When she hesitated at the door, Trish laid a hand on her arm. "Don't worry. We'll take good care of them."

Impulsively, Alayna hugged them both. "Thank you."

The police officer at the door keyed in his radio as she left the apartment. "There's a car waiting downstairs at the door for you, Ms. Wieland."

"Thank you."

She rushed to the elevator and rode it to the lobby.

When it stopped at the foyer, another policeman waited there to walk her out. A tall man stood outside and turned to face her as she exited the building. Her stomach jittered at sight of Detective Gray and his partner Detective Stansberry. "What are you doing here?"

"We heard what happened to your little girl and Lieutenant

Rivera. We're off duty today and volunteered for protection detail. We'd like to make it up to you for the way things went, Ms. Wieland."

"I don't need for you to make anything up to me for anything, Detective. I just need you both to go away." She started toward her own car parked in the lot.

"Wait, Ms. Wieland." The police officer at the door grabbed her arm. "If you walk off without your detail, they'll pull the officers upstairs. It's a show of disregard for the danger you and the children could be in."

Putting her children, or Trish and Langley, in danger was the last thing she wanted. "How can I trust them when they put the lives of my children at risk because they were more interested in chasing the money than my ex-husband and the Asher brothers?"

"We had no evidence, Ms. Wieland," Stansberry said. "There were no prints, no DNA. Nothing. If we had anything at all, we'd have brought them in."

She studied both men's expressions, searching for any subterfuge.

"I'd never have risked a child, Ms. Wieland. I have a son. I'd move mountains for him if I had to." Gray's sincerity when he talked about his boy shone through. As hard as she tried to hold onto her distrust, it wavered.

Her gaze swung to the other police officer. "We're going to the military hospital. Lieutenant Rivera is having surgery."

"Yes, ma'am, we were notified."

He opened the rear passenger door for her, and she slid in. Detective Gray walked around and got into the driver's seat while Detective Stansberry took the front passenger seat.

Silence hung in the car, thick with tension. "How is Rosa doing?" Gray asked.

"She has some bruises from being manhandled, and she's a little clingy. All the girls are."

"It will take them some time to get over what they've been through. You may want to take them to see someone."

"I'm going to. We're going as a family."

"That's a good idea." Stansberry looked over his shoulder at her.

"They drugged her and locked her in a dog kennel. They planned to throw her overboard to drown." She'd never get past the pain. "I'm so grateful she was asleep and didn't know what was happening. What's worse is she would never have been able to identify them. She doesn't talk much."

"Jesus!" Stansberry murmured.

They fell silent the rest of the way to the hospital.

"Walk her up, Stans. I'll park the car," Gray said as he pulled up to the front of the Medical Center. "I'll find you."

With the military presence around the hospital, Alayna experienced none of her new normal of jumpiness while being out in the open as they walked through the main entrance and approached the desk for directions.

Once she reached Bowie's room, her stomach did jig.

"I'll wait for you here. He doesn't need to be upset before he goes under."

She'd never have thought Stansberry or his partner were capable of sensitivity. They certainly hadn't shown her any during their investigation. "Thank you."

She gave the door a tap and eased it open. The bank of windows behind Bowie's bed threw light across the entire room and reflected off the tile floor. It was a typical hospital room, with two beds and curtains available to pull between them. Bowie saw her right away and smiled.

"Come in."

Her attention shifted to the woman who rose from a chair positioned in front of the windows. Though she hadn't seen Bowie's sister Carmelita in ten years, she recognized her immediately. With her perfectly-shaped lips, luscious, dark hair, and oval face, she was still as beautiful as she was as a middle school student when Alayna and Bowie graduated.

Her muscles felt stiff and her stomach cramped with nerves. There would probably be some words exchanged. Bowie didn't need that right now. She hoped they could maintain civility until he was taken to surgery.

She moved forward to stand on the opposite side of the bed. Her eyes fell on a man sitting in a wheelchair next to Carmelita. Her mind blanked with shock. Why was Ciro in a wheelchair?

"Why is she here?" Carmelita asked.

"Because I want her here, Carmelita," Bowie said in a measured tone. "And because, after ten years, we're exactly where we should have always been—together."

"Why?"

"Because neither of us has ever cared about anyone else the way we care about each other. We need each other."

Alana reached for Bowie's good hand, careful not to disturb the IV. She wanted to say, 'Because I never stopped loving your brother," but words would never make a dent in Carmelita or Ciro. She was a Wieland, the enemy. She remained silent.

Carmelita's gaze shifted from her to Bowie, then back again. "Her brother put Ciro in that wheelchair."

"And your mother accepted money in exchange for not producing a witness to the beating. Matt could have gone to prison for what he did, and he deserved to, but she said she needed money for Ciro to have an operation. And my father gave it to her."

"You're lying!" Carmelita started around the bed.

Ciro gripped her arm. "It's true."

Carmelita's mouth flew open. "It's not."

"She used the money for her booze, and to pay off all her tabs. How do you think she paid for new clothes and that used car she bought right after?"

"But she didn't have money to pay for your operation or your therapy," Carmelita said in a voice just above a whisper, her expression flat with pain.

How could a mother forsake her child's needs for her own? Her brother's beating had put Ciro in the wheelchair. His mother's greed had kept him there. She read the realization on Carmelita's face and on Bowie's.

"You still send her money, Ciro. Why do you do that?" Carmelita cried.

"To keep her out of my life, same as you and Bowie." He sounded tired.

Which was easier, walking away completely and ending things, or having a mother you had to pay off each month to keep her out of your life? Either way caused pain. They had all suffered for the past, Ciro more than anyone.

Bowie broke the silence. "Alayna hasn't seen her parents in ten years. She walked away from her family after Matt was convicted and went to prison for beating her severely. You can't blame her for something her brother or father did. It would be like Mom's exes blaming us for all the shit she put them through."

"I never blamed Alayna," Ciro said. "When Matt went to prison, I felt I'd received some justice. And at least I didn't have to endure being called a whore in court like you did to get it." His face, so much like his brother's, creased in anger. "Your brother and father are pieces of shit."

"Yes, they are."

Though Bowie's expression was grim, he lifted her hand to his cheek, his unshaven jaw prickly against her palm. She leaned down and brushed his rich brown hair off his forehead. "How are you feeling? Are you in any pain?"

"No. They've given me something that's making my thinking slow as molasses, but it kills the pain pretty good."

"When are they taking you to surgery?"

"Twenty minutes," Carmelita said.

"You said last night they'll be able to fix this."

"They will, but there's a little more to it than just repositioning the bone," Ciro said as he wheeled around the end of the bed. "They're going to have to graft bone to fill in a space on his collarbone. The bullet shattered it, and they'll need to pick out the splintered pieces, fill in the gap with the graft, and put in a plate and some screws to hold the whole thing together."

Chilled, she asked, "Where is the graft coming from?"

"From his pelvis."

Nausea turned her stomach to rubber.

"It's going to be okay, Alayna," Bowie murmured.

She nodded because her throat felt too tight to speak.

"The guy who shot me couldn't shoot for shit. I'm still here, and he's not."

Carmelita shook her head. "The FBI were just leaving when we got here. They questioned him before they gave him the pain meds so he wouldn't be under the influence."

Alayna tried to look at Carmelita's willingness to share information as a step in the right direction.

"They'd already reconstructed what went down from the scene. They just had to hear my version to see how it fit with the evidence." Bowie's speech sounded a little slurred. "They shook my hand as they left, so it must have been okay."

Prickles raced up the nape of her neck. There was more to the whole thing. Things they couldn't share with the FBI. The phone calls would make them seem like accessories to Aaron's kidnapping and possibly assault. Or had they killed him? She was surprised at how little emotion the idea inspired. She was done in every way with her ex-husband. If he wasn't dead, he'd go to prison, and she'd petition the court to make sure he could never see the girls again. It felt like a two-hundred-pound weight had been lifted from her shoulders.

"I told them about our meeting with Gilman in your lawyer's office, and that I called him and told him not to bother you again."

The other times Gilman contacted them where on burner phones, so there were no ties to Gilman. Maybe they'd be able to bluff their way through this.

Alayna caressed his cheek. "I don't believe he'll contact me again. I don't have anything he needs."

But as much as she wanted those phone calls to be the end of it, it would never end until the money was found and Bliss's killer was identified.

She noticed Bowie's lids drooping. "We'll all be here waiting for you when you get out of surgery. Just think, you'll have a whole household of females to wait on you hand and foot when you come home."

"Little Bit okay this morning?" he asked, his words coming slow.

"She's fine. Trish and Langley are with them."

He stuck up a thumb, but his eyes remained closed.

When two orderlies showed up to take him to surgery, she kissed Bowie's forehead and murmured, "I love you." Into his ear. Then stood back for his brother and sister to do the same.

The orderlies repositioned the IV and wheeled the whole bed out. "They have a waiting room for family down the hall. You're welcome to join us," Ciro said.

She was amazed by him, and grateful. He seemed not to harbor any bitterness toward her for the terrible thing her brother had done to him. "Thank you, Ciro. I'd like that."

Detective Gray and Stansberry stood outside the door as she exited the room. "We're going to stay in a waiting room down the hall," she notified them. The two detectives tagged along behind them and took seats against the wall across from where she, Ciro, and Carmelita sat, where they could see everyone entering the room.

"Who are those guys?" Ciro asked.

"They're part of the protection detail the FBI has set up until they find the money my ex-husband stole, and find out who killed his wife."

"What happens if they never find either?" Carmelita asked.

A good question. She wished she knew the answer. "I'm praying they'll find both."

CHAPTER 27

H E DIDN'T KNOW how they weren't all dead. The explosion had practically been on top of them. Automatic fire sounded in the distance. The air hung thick with concrete dust.

He tasted grit, spat, and wished he had a bandana to cover his nose and mouth. He could only guess where Hawk and Brett were. Rubble and the cloud of dirt had changed the landscape of the street. He picked his way toward the fallen wall where Hawk had been positioned before everything went to hell.

He nearly tripped over LT, who was rolling on the ground, holding his knee. "Check Brett," he snapped, and pointed to where their teammate lay sprawled. He knelt and felt for a pulse. It was there, but seemed too damn faint.

Where the hell was Doc? "We need Doc. I think I can find him. Stay still, LT. I'll be right back." Night vision was fucked because of all the dust. He shuffled toward where he'd last seen Doc taking cover. He found him lying flat on his back, probably thrown by the explosives concussion. He grabbed his arm and dragged him to his feet. "Brett's hurt bad. Get a move on."

"Bowie, you need to wake up now."

What the fuck? He was awake. They needed to bug out of here. The place would be crawling with tangos any minute.

"Bowie, open your eyes."

His eyes were open.

"Wheels up, Bowie. Get your gear." Hawk's voice carried through the dust-clogged air. Relief crashed over him. The chopper would be here to pick them up any moment. His started to heave to his feet, but the pain took his breath. His eyes snapped open. His hand gripped Hawk's arm tight. His gut felt like it had been ripped open.

"Shit." He clutched a hand against his abdomen and encountered a bandage.

Hawk's face came into sharp focus as he pushed him back against the pillow.

"Relax. Otherwise you may tear loose those staples. And I may need my arm back."

Bowie released him. "Sorry. Wow, I was dreaming."

"Yeah, I got that," Hawk said.

Derrick Armstrong was about to be released from prison in the next few weeks. He understood why he'd been dreaming about the mission again and again, but dammit, he needed to move on.

"Who were you pulling around?"

"Doc. He was dragging his feet."

Hawk shook his head. "I stopped by to see how you're doing."

This was the third time someone woke him up, but he felt more alert now. He scanned the room for Alayna, and saw her purse and jacket lying on the chair next to the bed. She'd probably just gone to stretch her legs. Ciro and Carmelita left right after he woke up from surgery.

"I'm still groggy, but I'm good…as long as I don't try to do any sit-ups or play tennis with this left arm."

"An Agent Ferguson from the FBI came by the office to apprise me of the situation and your part in the baby's rescue."

Shit! He searched Hawk's face to read his reaction. The Lieutenant could play on his Native American ancestry and do a stone-faced Navaho chief imitation his forefathers would be proud of. Bowie couldn't read a damn thing from his expression.

"Ferguson made it clear that if you hadn't gone on board, Rosa Harper would be dead. He also went over the findings they made studying the crime scene. But I'd like to hear the story from you."

Bowie ran a hand over his face, trying to shake off the last, lingering effects of his medication. He went through each of the steps he'd taken to track the Asher brothers to the Marina and notify the police of their movements. He stressed how delays in the officers' arrival left him no choice but to go onboard.

He switched his thoughts away from the emotionally charged moments when he realized the two brothers had decided to kill a helpless two-year-old by throwing the cage they'd put her in overboard. He still got queasy thinking about it.

He focused on the moment when shots were first fired and when he returned fire. He'd identified himself, tried to talk them into going back to the dock. He relived the moment he fired to keep the gun aimed at the closet Rosa was in from discharging, then rolled to face Frank Asher. He hadn't known the guy, like all the tangos he'd taken out, but Asher was just as determined to kill him. Two inches to the right and he'd have managed it.

He and Rosa both would have been swimming with the fishes.

"You do realize they found four bullets surrounding where you were lying on the floor? The one that hit you and passed through and three more."

He went to shrug and flinched. "Finger of God, LT, or Asher was a lousy shot."

Hawk shook his head. "As far as the Navy is concerned, they'd just as soon our guys avoided getting into gun battles with civilian kidnappers." He paused, and Bowie tensed. "From me and HQ, the good press we're getting outweighs those factors, and it doesn't hurt that the FBI is singing your praises. The Coast Guard is getting some good press, too." Hawk offered his hand. Bowie took it and they shook.

"It's been ruled a good shoot. All in self-defense."

"Thanks, LT." Bowie felt he'd dodged a career bullet along with the other three that missed him. The FBI would be looking at his cell phone records to try and trace the calls and see who called him about the Ashers. How had Gilman known they would be leaving at that very moment, and that they'd be going out on the boat to drown Rosa? He got an itchy feeling every time he lingered on those questions. Had he been used as an assassin to cover up something even worse?

"How long does the doc say you'll be out of commission?"

Bowie dragged his thoughts back and drew a deep breath. "Fourteen weeks." His chances of leading his own team were probably fucked. It would be longer than that before he could build range of motion back up and get in top shape.

"You can come back and work for me until you're back physically and ready to lead a team, then we'll go from there. I have some projects in mind HQ has agreed are worth exploring."

His interest instantly piqued, Bowie nodded. "If it's something I can take care of with only one shoulder, I can start as soon as the doc removes my dressings. My hands still work."

"It's a desk job, but you'd be out of the office a lot. Gotta warn you, though, there will be paperwork."

"I can handle it, Hawk."

"I know you can, otherwise I wouldn't have mentioned it. I'll give you more info once you're ambulatory and able to come in."

"Ten to fourteen days is when the dressings come off."

"Call the office when the doc gives you the okay for light duty."

A tap came at the door. Alayna slipped into the room.

"Hawk, I want you to meet Alayna."

"You're Bowie's CO." She ignored the hand Hawk extended and moved in to hug him. "Thank you so much for calling Langley and Trish and asking them to stay with my girls." She backed away. "I really appreciate it."

"I'm sorry for what your little girl had to go through. How's she doing?"

"She slept through most of it. I'm hoping that will spare her from a lot of the trauma. Physically she's okay, thanks to Bowie." She moved to the bed. "I didn't want to interrupt your visit, but I feel guilty leaving Trish and Langley looking after the girls so long.

I thought I'd better get back." She leaned in to brush a kiss against his cheek. "You two go ahead and finish your visit. I'll just slip out."

"See if you can bring the kids this evening," Bowie slipped his good arm around her hip, holding her in place.

"I'll have to check what their rules are about children on the floor." She brushed his hair back with her fingertips in a possessively feminine gesture he was beginning to enjoy more and more. "Call me if you need anything, and I'll bring it over."

She gathered her jacket and purse and flashed Hawk a smile. "It's nice to meet you."

"You, too."

As soon as she left the room, Hawk turned back to him, his expression one of intent inquiry. "The kids?"

"There's three, all girls. Cute as they can be, smart, and well-behaved. And I'm as crazy about them as I am about Alayna. Well, almost. Little Bit can't say Bowie yet, so she calls me Boy."

Hawk pondered that for a moment. "I'm happy for you, Bowie."

Hawk's understated response made him a little wary. His SEAL buddies were notorious for giving each other a hard time. He remembered doing bodyguard duty with Brett Weaver. Brett had warned him when he finally fell it would be like having a tank dropped on his head.

It was more like having his heart mended and filled. Not just by Alayna, but her girls as well. His heart just hadn't been open enough to accept another woman. It had taken Alayna and her three girls to pry it open again.

"How long have you known her?" Hawk asked.

"We dated in high school. We were going to go to college together, get married, and have a family after we established our careers. She wanted to be a lawyer."

The look in Hawk's eyes sharpened. "What happened?"

"It's a long story."

Hawk took the seat next the bed. "I've got time."

Bowie laughed, then gasped and pressed a hand to his abdomen. His teammates were nosy as hell, too. And though Hawk had moved on to bigger things…

DETECTIVE STANSBERRY EXITED the hospital, and Alayna followed close behind.

"How's he doing?" he asked while they stood at the curb to wait for Detective Gray to pick them up.

"He's doing well. It's going to take some time, but he'll heal." And be able to go back to his SEAL team. She was beginning to realize it wasn't just about a team. It was about family. Trish and Langley making a three-hour drive to babysit for them. His CO coming to the hospital to see him after surgery. Those were things family did, not just people who shared a working relationship.

She texted Trish's number to let her know she was leaving the hospital and would be home in a few minutes.

Detective Gray pulled up, and Detective Stansberry opened the back passenger door for her. Alayna slid in, and he shut the door. Stansberry reached for the door handle, but it was locked. Detective Gray stomped on the gas and pulled away.

"What are you doing?" Alayna shrieked.

Gray gunned it around a corner. Alayna turned to look behind them to see Stansberry running after the car. Gray sped up and left him behind.

This can't be happening. It can't be. "Where are you taking me?"

"My boy is sick, Ms. Wieland. You have to tell me where that flash drive is."

"I don't know, Detective. I swear to you I don't." Her fingers flew as she dialed 911 and left the phone open on the seat. "You need to take me home, Detective Gray. It's your duty to take me home."

His silence had her stomach tumbling.

"Tell me where the flash drive is."

"If I knew, don't you think I'd have given it to the Asher brothers for Rosa? They wanted five million dollars. I didn't have the money. They were going to kill my daughter!"

"You had your watchdog hunt them down so you didn't have to pay them. He's a professional killer. A military-trained killer. But he isn't here now to protect you. You have access to millions, and all I need is a cut to see my boy gets well."

With her heart lodged in her throat, she couldn't catch her breath. "What's wrong with your son, Detective Gray?"

"He has lymphoblastic leukemia. We've mortgaged our house. Used up our retirement funds. The medical coverage just isn't enough. His treatment is sixty-four thousand dollars a month, and the insurance doesn't cover it all."

"Dear God. Please, Detective. If I knew where the flash drive was, I'd give it to you. But I don't. Every inch of my apartment has been searched by you and Detective Stansberry, plus half a dozen other people. The last person who knew where it was was Bliss, and she's dead. Have you gone to their house and searched it?"

"Yeah, I've searched it. Where's your husband?"

"I don't know." She didn't know where Gilman had him, or even if he was still alive.

Cars slammed on their breaks as Gray cut across traffic into the parking lot of a strip mall and whipped behind the buildings. As soon as the car stopped, Alayna jerked hard on the door handle and shoved against it, but it remained locked. She cursed child-proof locks.

Her heart thundered as Detective Gray hit the key fob, un-locking the doors. She slid across the seat to the opposite side, wrenched up on the handle, and had it partially open when he dove across the back seat and grabbed the back of her jacket. She slithered out of it and dove out of the door, landing hard on her knees on the asphalt, her slacks only partially protecting her skin. She was up and running in a second, past dumpsters and stacks of broken-down boxes. If she could just make it to the corner— other people would be there.

His running steps pounded behind her, getting louder as he gained on her. Desperation gave her a burst of speed. His fingers tangled in her hair, and he hauled her back so hard she fell. He tripped over her, caught his balance, then straddled her. His chest heaved from exertion, his teeth bared in rage. She threw up an arm to block the blow she sensed was coming.

He knocked her arm away, found her throat instead, and squeezed. "Where is he?"

She shook her head, doubled her fist and punched him in the Adam's apple as hard as she could.

He coughed and grabbed his throat as he held hers. He drew back and backhanded her so hard it snapped her head sideways, hard, wrenching her neck. Her entire face burned from the blow, and for a moment she wanted to curl up and wail with the pain. Instead she screamed and grabbed his ears, hauled herself up, and butted him in face. He yelped and reared back and slapped her again. Her ears rang, and the world went gray.

Light wove back into her senses when he flipped her on her stomach, bent her arm behind her, and slapped handcuffs on one wrist, then the other. She tasted blood where her teeth had cut into her cheek. She remained limp.

He gripped the back of her neck so hard his fingers dug in hard enough that her eyes stung and her nose ran.

Drops of blood dripped past her face to land on the asphalt. At least she'd drawn blood.

"Where is he?" he hissed in her ear.

"Gilman has him. He's probably already dead."

"You'd better hope he isn't." He lifted her by the arms hard enough that she was afraid they might pop out of their sockets. She scrambled to get her feet under her, and he marched her back to the car, opened the trunk, thrust her inside, and slammed the lid.

Her jaw and neck hurt, and her cheek felt numb. In the intense darkness of the trunk, claustrophobia hit her. What did he plan to do with her?

CHAPTER 28

H AWK WANDERED OUT, destined for a quick visit with Zoe, his wife. He said something about a cup of coffee or a soft drink if he could catch her during a break.

Zoe'd know who he was going to get for physical therapy as soon as the docs said he was ready for it. She'd take good care of him.

Bowie turned on the television and muted it. After only a few minutes, hard as he fought it, he couldn't keep his eyes open. When someone entered the room, he kept his eyes closed, hoping they'd go away.

When a familiar male voice said, "Lieutenant Rivera." His eyes flew open. Detective Stansberry's hair, dark with sweat, stood on end. Wide-eyed and shaking, he looked shell-shocked. "My partner has taken Ms. Wieland."

Bowie started to sit up and swore. "What the hell? What you mean he took her?"

"He's desperate. His son is dying. They've drained every resource, and the cost of the treatment is beyond reason, beyond anything anyone could pay. He still believes she knows where the flash drive is."

Bowie breathed through a mind-numbing rush of emotion that threw his heart into overdrive. "She doesn't. Alayna lives for her children. If she knew, she'd have forked it over to the Ashers when they had Rosa. You didn't see her when Rosa was gone. She was inconsolable, desperate."

"That's what my partner is, Lieutenant. His out of his mind."

"Have you called it in?"

"Yeah." He wiped his sweating face with his jacket sleeve. "There are units looking for the car—for him. He's disabled the GPS tracker on the vehicle. Does Ms. Wieland have any information he might follow up on as to where the drive might be?"

Bowie tried to shake away the fog of emotion clouding his thoughts. "Her ex thought Gilman was after him, had people out to get him. If Gilman's found him… He might try to follow up on that. Would he go to Gilman's? Does he even know where Gilman lives?"

"Yeah, we know."

Bowie threw the blankets aside, and, holding his abdomen eased his legs over the side of the hospital bed. "Get my clothes out of that cabinet over there." He started to point with his bound arm and flinched. "Shit!"

"You just had major surgery. You can't leave the hospital."

"Watch me. The woman I love is in trouble, and I'm not going to lie here and wait for news. You're taking me with you." When Stansberry started to say something, he cut him off. "Or I'll call some of my buddies to come get me, and we'll all show up."

"All right, all right," Stansberry went to the cabinet and got the bag of clothes.

IT HAD TO be a shotgun digging into her hip. What if it was loaded? Could it accidentally discharge if she wiggled around too much? Surely a policeman wouldn't store a loaded weapon in the trunk of his car. She turned on her side and pushed against the object to shift it, but she was lying on top of something else, some kind of cloth, stiff enough to prevent her from being able to reach the shotgun. Exhausted, her face throbbing, her shoulders aching, she couldn't hold back the tears.

What would happen to her children if she died?

They'd end up with Gloria and Warren.

Dear God. No way was she going to let that happen. She was going to fight Gray until she had nothing left.

The car came to a stop. Though the sound was muffled, she heard Gray talking to someone. The car moved forward for a short time, then came to a stop and the engine was turned off. A door opened and closed. When the trunk was opened, light lanced into her eyes, and she squinted and blinked. Gray's nose looked twice its normal size, and a crust of blood darkened his nostrils. He reached for her and dragged her out of the trunk. The rim of the opening scraped along her thigh, and she gritted her teeth. He set her on her feet none too gently. She shot him a glare.

The large, two-story brick mansion sprawled across an acre of lawn bordered by a wall. They approached the front double doors while above them a mounted camera moved to follow their approach. Gray pushed the button on the intercom next to the door.

Gray drew his weapon, racked the slide, and placed it against her temple. "Hurry up. Otherwise I'll put a bullet in her brain and leave her body on his doorstep."

For the first time the idea that Gray had killed Bliss solidified in Alayna's mind. Her stomach tumbled, and she swallowed, hoping to hold the nausea at bay. How many people would he be willing to sacrifice for his son?

How many would she, if it was one of her girls? She didn't want to dwell on that.

After what seemed like an hour, the door on the right opened. A large, bald man dressed all in black stood at the door. Gray shoved her forward while the barrel of the pistol hit the back of her head. The man in black sidled away, his hands held out in a universal message of non-aggression.

"Mr. Gilman is in his office." He turned to lead the way.

The pistol resting in the small of his back was just out of her reach, and with Gray's Glock 22 pressed to her head, Alayna's need to pee became urgent. If he tripped or lost control... She had no other choice but to put one foot in front of the other.

"Where is the rest of your staff?" Gray asked.

The man spoke over his shoulder. "They know to stay out of this area when we have visitors."

He guided them across the foyer to a set of double doors within sight of the main entrance, opened them, and stepped through. He sauntered over to stand next to Gilman's desk.

As they crossed the threshold, Gilman leaned back in his desk chair. His pale blue eyes swept over her, then settled on Detective Gray. "What can I do for you Detective?"

"I want to see Aaron Harper."

Gilman raised a brow. "Go get our guest, Ray."

The big man sauntered back out of the door.

"Please take a seat, Ms. Wieland," Gilman said.

Gray's fingers dug into her sore shoulder. "She's fine where she is."

"You're the only one with a weapon at the moment, Detective."

"I'd like to go to the bathroom," Alayna announced.

"You can go right here," Gray said.

He had become a monster, high on power and beyond reasoning, and she'd become an easy target, just like she'd been for her husband, her father, and her brother.

Time to put a stop to this bullshit.

Alayna looked at Gilman, but she spoke to Gray. "My father is a white supremacist." Gilman's brows shot up. "I've been ashamed of that my whole life. For the most part he left me and my sisters alone. But he wanted my brother to follow in his footsteps, and he did. He taught my brother how to be a brutal monster. A weapon to do all the things he was too much of a coward to do himself.

"As soon as I graduated from high school, I cut ties with my family and went off to college. I had grants and scholarships. My father sent Matt to beat some sense into me, and my brother ended up serving eight years for that assault." Alayna turned to look up at Gray, and the barrel of the pistol brushed her ear, then her battered cheek. Her stomach threatened to heave. "Your son may survive, Detective, but you won't be in his life if you allow the monster to win."

She saw the shift in his expression. He released her shoulder to reach into his pocket and remove the handcuff key. He tossed it onto Gillman's desk. "Uncuff her."

Alayna moved around Gillman's desk and turned her back. He unlocked the cuffs and placed them on his desk.

"The bathroom is through that door, Ms. Wieland." Gilman gestured to a door to the left. "I'll have Ray fix you an ice pack when he returns."

Alayna nodded. Conscious of the gun still locked in Gray's hand and aimed at her, she moved slowly as she walked to the bathroom, opened the door, and went in. The door represented temporary safety, and with the release of tension, her legs wobbled, and she leaned against the vanity to draw several slow, deep breaths while she waited for her strength to return.

She used the restroom, then went to the sink and washed her hands, the medicinal smell of the soap strong. Next she braved a look at her reflection in the mirror. One side of her face was grotesquely swollen, her eye a slit. She cupped water in her hand and rinsed her mouth to rid it of the taste of blood. The cut inside her cheek smarted at even that.

She wanted very badly to stay inside the bathroom, away from Gray, away from Gillman, who put on such a civilized front but was as much or more of a monster beneath the surface.

How had he known what the Ashers were doing and when they were going to do it? Had he been pulling their strings along with hers and Bowie's? And would he lead Gray down a path too?

The detective was as desperate as Aaron had been when he attacked her. Both obsessed with money. Both willing to kill for it. The FBI would eventually find the stolen funds without the flash drive. The problem was, each one of these men didn't just want *their* money, they wanted the whole bank.

She gripped the doorknob, but instead of opening it, leaned her forehead against the wood and closed her eyes. If she could will herself away from this place, she'd do it.

They'd come in to get her if she stayed much longer. She ached all over. Maybe Ray could get her some Ibuprofen to go along with that ice pack. Taking a deep breath, she opened the door.

FROM BEHIND THE heavy metal gates that barred their way, Bowie studied the topography of the house and the land around it. It was a beautiful place. The house was huge, two stories, and built like a fortress. He bet even the windows were bulletproof. The lawn looked like a carpet, every blade of grass trimmed to the same height.

They hadn't a clue what room Alayna and Gray could be in. Without recon, they'd never know. "Why can't you just knock on the door and go in? He's your fucking partner."

"He's not rational. His son is dying despite the chemo, and he doesn't want to accept it. They've already given up everything they have trying to keep him alive."

"Killing Alayna or her ex won't get him any closer to what he wants."

"I'm more concerned he might kill himself, Lieutenant."

Suicidal fuckers with guns always wanted to take someone with them. That's what was worrying him more than anything. *Dear God, let her be okay.* If he lost her again… He'd lose the girls too. He couldn't do it. The four of them were the family he needed, wanted.

So far Stansberry hadn't called in any backup, only gotten a car delivered to the hospital by a patrol unit. "You haven't told anyone he's gone off the rails, have you? There never was anyone looking for him."

The detective continued to focus on the house. "He's got over twenty years on the force. If he loses this job, he'll lose everything else along with it. He's already spent his pension on chemo."

"Jesus." Pressure built behind Bowie's eyes as his temper rose.

"He could have already killed Alayna."

"He hasn't. He won't."

"You better hope it's true, Detective." Bowie could only pray Stansberry knew this guy as well as he thought he did. "You have to call for backup. They're in there alone, and you don't know what Gilman is capable of."

He turned to look over. "How do you know this guy?"

"He requested, through Alyana's boss, to speak to her. Gilman offered her a hundred thousand dollars to access her mother-in-law's phone and get Aaron's number from it so he could track him down. She turned him down because she was worried he'd kill him. Right after the meeting, her daughter was kidnapped."

"By the Ashers."

"Two hours after their meeting. So you have to wonder if the Asher brothers were really acting alone?"

"We won't know that until the FBI talks to the third one, Brian…when they find him."

"My bet is he's already dead. He went to Grand Cayman to pick up the money as soon as it was transferred, but it never arrived. You'll find his body a few months from now when it washes up on a beach somewhere. Gilman was bound to have someone following him just in case it came through."

"How do you know all this?"

He couldn't very well admit to his and Alayna's part in all of this. "I've hunted men like him for the last seven years. Men worse than him. I know how they think."

Stansberry paused a beat. "You wouldn't know how to short circuit that gate, would you? So we can get it open if we need to."

"That might be considered breaking and entering, Detective."

"I'll take full responsibility."

Bowie studied him for a moment. "Do you have a screwdriver, pair of pliers, and something to cut wires with?"

"There's always a tool kit in the back of the cars. I'll get it."

"I hope your bladder's full."

"Why?"

"Because sometimes it takes a little water to short things out."

HOW MANY TIMES had she wished someone would beat the crap out of Aaron Harper for what he had done to her? And even more for what he hadn't done for his daughters? She had hoped to find him battered and broken. Though he appeared thinner, and his head was shaved, she saw no bruises, no outward sign of stress other than his staggering progress ahead of Ray as he pushed him into the room and shoved him down in a seat.

Gilman, rested his elbows on his chair arms and steepled his fingers. The predatory gleam she had seen briefly in her boss's office shone through despite his attempts to feign indifference. "If you think you can get the information out of him, Detective, be our guest. We have been unsuccessful thus far." He studied the ceiling. "I can arrange for my computer expert to access the accounts once we have the information."

Gun still in hand, Gray approached Aaron. He gripped him by the jaw and raised his head to look down into his eyes. "Has he been drugged?"

"No, but it has been several days since he's slept."

Wasn't that how they broke prisoners of war? No sleep, no food, constant noise.

Alayna shifted the ice pack lower on her jaw. The Ibuprofen Ray gave her, without her even asking, dulled the headache pounding at her temples to a bearable level. She probably had a concussion.

Gray slapped Aaron so hard he yelped and rocked sideways, only the chair arms saving him from falling to the floor. Having been on the receiving end of a similar blow, Alayna flinched.

Gray got in his face. "Where is the flash drive, Aaron?"

Aaron threw an arm up to protect his face. "I don't know. I don't know. Bliss hid it, and she's dead. I've looked everywhere."

"Maybe whoever killed Bliss took it," Alayna suggested. Silence stretched several beats.

"You have to have it, Alayna. Give it to them."

She shook her head. "You cowardly, sniveling, whiney, asshole. You *know* I don't have it. You destroyed my house looking for it. You even destroyed your children's toys and clothing looking for it. Who are you going to throw under the bus next? Your mother?"

He lunged toward her, and would have attacked her had Gray not knocked him back. "Leave her the fuck out of this."

"Then leave me the fuck out of it. I've tried for three years to get you to leave me the hell alone. To leave me out of your life completely." She rose from her seat and stalked closer until Ray grasped her arm and pushed her toward a chair. "If I had the flash drive I'd hammer it into tiny pieces so none of you could have it. You're all insane. Nothing is important enough to merit all this."

"Where did your wife say she put it?" Gray asked.

"She put it inside one of the children's baby dolls. But I tore them all apart looking for it, and it wasn't in any of them. It must have dropped out somewhere. They carry them around with them everywhere."

Gray looked at her. "You have to have some idea of where they could have lost it."

"They're not allowed to bring their toys to daycare or school. Aaron's house, my apartment, my car, Big Bear. Anything they've had in Bowie's car has either been bought new or something already searched. Those are all the places they've been with toys. You've searched all those places, haven't you? It's gone, lost. Or been thrown out with all of the belongings Aaron saw fit to destroy."

Defeat shadowed Gray's face. He grabbed Aaron and dragged him to his feet.

"What are you doing, Detective?" Gilman asked getting to his feet.

"I'm taking him to the station. He has no information, but he still has to face charges for embezzlement."

"I'm afraid I can't allow you to do that." He motioned toward Ray, and the man drew his weapon. "No one steals from me and gets away with it."

Detective Gray raised his gun. "You don't want to do this. I'll tell them you turned him over to me, and your part in all this goes away. Go, Alayna."

She hesitated a second, then ran toward the entryway. She turned to look behind her to see Aaron crouching behind the detective, using him as a shield as they crossed the expensive oriental rug to the door. Detective Gray's aim never wavered from Ray.

A shot rang out from the desk and Gray staggered. He raised his weapon and fired twice. He lurched back as another bullet hit him mid-chest and toppled out into the hall. Blood blossomed on his blue shirt and spread like a river.

Aaron sped to the front door, jerked it open, and ran out.

Chickenshit cockroach. Alayna grabbed the detective's Glock 20 and took cover.

BOWIE STIFFENED TO attention at the muffled sound of gunfire from the house. The front door flew open and a bald guy ran out like the place was on fire.

Stansberry drew his weapon and darted through the gate they'd just sprung. "Call it in. I'm going up. Tell them Gray and I are on-site." He ran up the hill.

Bowie's need to follow him was almost impossible to control, but he was injured. He wouldn't be any help.

Bowie snatched open the car door and reached for the radio. After identifying himself, he said, "Officer needs assistance, shots fired, shots fired. We need an ambulance at Karrick Gilman's residence." He read off the address on the computer GPS.

The guy who'd run out of the house squeezed through the gap in the fence and started toward the car. Despite the man's shaved head, Bowie recognized Aaron Harper.

"Are there wounded?" the dispatcher asked. Bowie laid aside the radio. "There's about to be." He waited for Harper to reach the car and shoved the car door open full force. Harper bounced off the door with a wompf and landed hard on the asphalt.

Bowie climbed gingerly out of the vehicle to stand over him. He wasn't in any shape to tussle with the guy if he put up a fight, but he'd damn sure give it a shot. He reached down, grabbed Harper's wrist and dragged him to his feet. He shoved him toward the back of the vehicle and opened the back door. "Get your ass in the car."

Without a word or struggle, Harper climbed in and lay down on the seat.

Another shot sounded from atop the hill, and Bowie's head shot up. *Alayna! Oh, God, please let her be alive.*

GRAY'S LABORED, RATTLING breaths filled the foyer. She looked toward the open front door, then back at Gray. They'd kill him. He was wounded and helpless, and she shuddered as thoughts of her girls rushed through her mind.

She gripped Gray's wrist with one hand and strained to pull him to one side, out of the line of fire. He was incredibly heavy, but she didn't dare put the pistol down. She managed to move him a couple of feet, and then Ray darted toward the open door. She pressed back against the wall, out of his line of fire.

"You should have run, lady. I didn't want to shoot you."

She remained silent, but slid down the wall to make herself as small a target as possible while gripping the pistol the way she'd practiced a thousand times. Her entire body trembled, and her breathing came in shaky gasps.

Ray swung out and she fired twice in quick succession. He stumbled forward, tripped over Gray's legs, and sprawled facedown. She crawled forward to take his gun out of his hand and slide it out of reach.

"OhGodohGod." She looked up as she sensed movement at the office door. Gilman, bleeding from the shoulder, gun in hand, stood over her. She tensed, waiting for the weapon to go off, the bullets to pierce her body, and flinched as a booming percussion echoed through the hall. Gilman dropped to his knees, then toppled onto his side.

She turned to look toward the front door.

Stansberry ran to her. "Are they all down?"

"Yes."

He took the pistol from her, then went to check Ray and Gilman, leaving their weapons where they were.

Alayna checked Gray's pulse, but there wasn't one, and he wasn't breathing. Stansberry knelt beside his partner. How long had it been since Gray stopped breathing?

"There are towels in the bathroom. I'll get them. You start CPR."

She rushed through the study and into the bathroom, opened the vanity and yanked out two towels. Stansberry's shoulders were bowed when she returned, and he wiped his jacket sleeve over his eyes. He'd ripped open Gray's shirt, exposing the three bullet holes in his chest. "He's gone."

Alayna dropped the towels on the floor and knelt beside him. "He tried to protect me at the end, Detective. He told me to run. But when he was shot and fell, he was still breathing. I couldn't leave him."

"Did he do that to your face?" he asked.

She looked away. She didn't want to add to his pain. The sounds of approaching sirens screamed in the distance.

"I'm sorry. I should have told Sherwood what was going on."

Alayna touched his arm.

"I'll need a statement, but Bowie's waiting for you at the bottom of the driveway, and he's probably going crazy. Go to him, let him know you're okay before the others get here."

She didn't have to be told twice. She couldn't stand to be in this grand foyer saturated with the smells of death and spent gunpowder any longer.

As soon as she reached the front door, she broke into a run. Bowie stood waiting for her at the open gate, the bandages across the top of his chest snow white against his skin, and his arm hung in the sling. He raised his good hand when he saw her.

The way he shoved his fingers through his hair and bent his

head, his shoulders heaving, caught her by the throat, and she put on some more speed.

She was out of breath when she reached the bottom of the drive. He held out his one good arm, and she rushed in close, wrapped her arms around him, and held on tight.

"Every minute was an hour, Alayna."

"I know. It was for me yesterday."

"You're hurt." He touched her cheek and jaw gently.

"I'm okay. We're okay."

"I love you," Bowie's voice cracked. "I couldn't say it before, but standing out here, waiting a lifetime to know if you were alive, I was kicking myself for not saying it."

She tipped her face up to him. "You could say it again, just so I can be sure I heard you right."

He laughed, then caught his breath and pressed a hand to his side. "I love you." A police car, siren screaming, swung into the drive, drowning out anything else he might have added. But his kiss said it all.

16 Hours Later

BOWIE WOKE TO the smell of frying bacon and coffee. The prescription pain medication made him drowsy and wiped out his appetite, but for the first time since his surgery the morning before, he felt hungry.

Holding his side, he swung his legs over the side of the bed, struggled to his feet, and shuffled into the bathroom. The call of nature taken care of and his teeth brushed, he felt almost human, and wandered down the hall to the kitchen.

Alayna stood at the stove arranging cooked strips of bacon on a paper towel-lined plate.

Rosa greeted him with a smile and raised the strip of bacon she was eating toward him. "Boy eat, too."

He buffed her forehead with a kiss. "Mama will give me some in a minute." He went to Alana and brushed a kiss against her cheek. "Where are Emilia and Addie?"

"They wanted to go back to school, so Rosa and I took them. I had a talk with their teachers, and I'm keeping the phone close in case there's an issue."

"Being with their friends will keep them distracted, and their normal routine should help them feel secure."

"That's what I thought, too." Alana broke eggs in the hot grease.

Bowie wandered over to the silverware drawer to set the table.

"Mama wash, Bebe," Rosa said poking the stuffed monkey propped up against the orange juice pitcher on the table. Stripped of her overalls and tennis shoes Bebe looked a little forlorn.

He smiled at Rosa as he relocated the toy farther away from her greasy hands. "Bebe smells better and looks better this morning."

"Bebe got boo-boo."

Rosa was certainly being a little chatterbox this morning.

Alayna set a plate in front of him with four rashers of bacon, two fried eggs, and two pieces of toast. She bent to kiss the top of Rosa's head. "Mama's going to fix the boo-boo as soon as we finish eating, baby." After filling both their coffee cups, she got her own plate from the counter and sat down next to him.

When she used her fingertip to slide something over the vinyl tablecloth toward him, he paused, fork in hand. Bowie stared at a flash drive about the size of a dime. "Holy fu—" He caught the swear word half-uttered, glancing at Rosa, then Alayna.

They ate their meal, neither saying another word, the flash drive lying between them like a live grenade.

While he sipped his coffee, Alayna cleared the table, wiped Rosa's hands clean, and he held her on his thigh while they watched Alayna stitch up the tiny slit in the inside seam of Bebe's leg. "Bebe's clothes and shoes will be dry in just a few minutes. I'll bring them to you, and you can dress her. I've set out the puzzle you like on the coffee table. Why don't you and Bebe go put it together?"

"Okay." Rosa wiggled, and Alayna lifted her down.

Unable to contain his curiosity any longer, Bowie asked,

"What do you want to do with it?"

"The FBI will recover the money eventually without it, won't they?"

"Yeah. I'd say they'll be able to trace the transfers eventually."

"If I bring it to them now, they'll think I knew where it was all along."

"Possibly."

She remained silent for a moment. "If I mail it to them, they might be able to trace it back to me somehow."

"Without fingerprints on the drive or envelope, possibly not."

"But it wouldn't be worth the worry, would it?"

"No, I don't think so."

"That's what I thought too." She scooped up the drive and went to a cabinet to retrieve a plastic cutting board. From a bottom drawer next to the sink she pulled out a hammer. She beat the tiny drive into powder on the cutting board, then raked the pieces down the garbage disposal, turned on the water, and flipped the disposal on.

When she returned to the table, Bowie snagged her around the hip with his good arm and tugged her close. "You are the most remarkable woman I've ever met, Alayna."

Her brows rose and a gleam lit her eyes. She kissed him. "I'm glad you think so. It was an easy decision to make. There's not enough money in the world worth risking you or my girls."

Bowie rested his head against her breast. "I feel the same way, honey."

EPILOGUE

Three Weeks Later

AFTER HAVING SEATED her and Bowie, Sherwood leaned back in his chair with a sigh. "I know after everything you've been through, this is probably the last place you want to be, Ms. Wieland. But I think you owe you something for everything that happened. You could have raked us through the coals in your interview with the press, but you didn't, and we appreciate it."

Alayna bit her lip. "I thought Detective Stansberry and Detective's Gray's family had been through enough with his death. I didn't want to heap any more pain on them."

Sherwood paused, his gaze directed through the glass walls of his office and the desks bunched together outside it. "It's appreciated by everyone in the squad. You may have forgotten, Ms. Wieland, but you dialed 911 while he drove away. The entire conversation you had with Detective Gray was taped. We were still trying to get a fix on your location when Lieutenant Rivera's call came in."

He cleared his throat. "None of what I'm going to tell you can be repeated since it's an ongoing investigation, and I could lose my job for sharing this information. But the two of you more than earned the right to know some of it."

"The FBI have connected the Asher brothers with Gilman. We believe he set up the entire kidnapping in an attempt to force you to give up the flash drive or contact your husband for him to do so. He directed the brothers to get rid of your daughter."

Hearing it straight out gave her goose bumps, and she rubbed her arms. Bowie reached across to grip her hand, his features like stone.

"He must have had a change of heart, though." He shifted his attention to Bowie. "We believe he was responsible for the phone call that directed you to their yacht. Had you not gone in when you did…"

He cleared his throat. "Brian Asher has been found. He's been on the run from Gilman's people since he flew to Grand Cayman, and he turned himself in to escape them. He spilled everything as soon as he was in custody.

"The bullets we recovered from the wall in the Harpers' kitchen, and the one that killed Bliss Harper, have been matched to the gun used by Raymond Bandoni, Karrick Gilman's body-guard. It seems it was a two-prong strike set up by Gilman. Bandoni was visiting Bliss at the same time the Ashers were attempting to kidnap you, Ms. Wieland."

She thought it was Detective Gray until he tried to protect her. And Bandoni's reluctance to shoot her saved her life. Perhaps Bliss's death had been an accident and he didn't have a taste for killing women. Who knew? In any case, he was a murderer, just like his boss. Maybe if she reminded herself of that often enough, she'd stop having nightmares about the shooting.

"It took a great deal of courage for you to stand your ground with him, Ms. Wieland."

"Detective Gray was still breathing, and I knew he'd shoot him again. I couldn't leave him."

"After what he did to you, it was very courageous—and gen-erous—of you."

"He once told me he'd move mountains for his son. I'd have robbed a bank to get my baby back. Bowie had to do the hardest thing to save her. I know what it's like now. I know what it cost him. I'd carry that burden for him if I could."

Bowie's voice was gravelly with emotion when he said, "I'm

okay, Alayna."

She squeezed his hand. "I wish I could have saved Detective Gray's life. It would make it seem more right somehow."

"I understand," Captain Sherwood said.

"How is his boy doing?"

"He's responding to treatment. Because of the press, people have donated enough money to fund his treatment for a few months. And the pharmaceutical company has offered to cut the cost to extend that time."

"It's a shame Gray had to lose his life for that to happen."

"Yeah, it is."

"How's Detective Stansberry?" Bowie asked.

"He's taken a short leave. He and Gray were partners for a long time."

Alayna nodded, then rose. "Thank you for sharing this with us, Captain."

She offered her hand, and Sherwood shook it, then Bowie's. "You didn't ask about your ex-husband."

The Cockroach. "That part of my life is over. I've filed for sole custody and am building a case to show just cause for having his parental rights revoked."

"If you need any help with that, I'm sure several of our officers who've had to deal with him would be happy to testify on your behalf."

Alayna laughed. "I'll keep that in mind."

Sherwood smiled for the first time.

BOWIE SUCKED IN a deep breath as they left the station and headed for the car. His side was still a little tender as he walked across the parking lot, but it was healing. And though he still had to wear the sling for his arm, the bone was knitting as it should.

"I have the rest of the day off," he said.

"You have?"

"And I bet if you called into the office, since it's past noon, they might give you the rest of the day off, too."

When they reached the SUV, Bowie leaned back against it and cuddled her against him. "And the kids aren't due to be picked up until five. That means we have four whole hours to ourselves for that date we've never had."

Alayna leaned into him and nestled close enough to bring his semi-erect penis to immediate attention. "What did you have in mind?"

For a moment his mind was blank, because all his attention was directed south.

"I haven't eaten, have you?"

"No," he croaked while she toyed with the buttons on his shirt.

Her green gaze focused on his face. "We're both on the mend, and it's been two weeks and five days, Bowie."

If she'd been keeping track... He'd been under strict doctor's orders to take it easy and let his hip heal. The doctor had already removed the staples and the incision had nearly healed, though it still looked ugly. "We could visit a drive-through for some Chinese right now and take it home."

"That sounds nice."

He walked around to open the door for her, got her settled, then hustled around to the driver's side. "Don't you need to call?"

"No. I told them before I left that I wouldn't be back for the rest of the day."

Bowie grinned, fastened his seatbelt, and put the car in gear.

The aroma of General Tso's chicken, pepper steak, egg rolls, and fried rice filled the elevator as it rose to Alayna's floor, but Bowie had never been less hungry for food. He wanted Alayna's lips, the touch of her hands, the taste of her when he went down on her, and the way she moved beneath him when he was inside her.

What made her different from all the other women he'd been with? He was still mulling over that one when they placed the bags of food on the kitchen counter.

"You've gone quiet. What are you thinking about so intently?"

"You." He took her hand and drew her out of the kitchen and into her bedroom. She'd used some of the insurance money for a new comforter and pillows, and new lamps, giving the space a unisex feel instead of the totally feminine vibe of before. Had she done that for him? Probably. She was thoughtful like that.

He removed the sling from around his neck. His collarbone was knitting, but he still had some pain. As long as he didn't make any sudden movements or put too much pressure on the arm, he was good.

He cupped her face in his hands. The bruise on her right cheek had faded, and the swelling was gone, again revealing the lovely symmetry of her features. He traced the curve of her cheekbones with his thumbs, then bent to kiss each cheek, brushed the tip of her nose, then caught her mouth with his. Her lips parted for him, and he teased her, tracing the seam with his tongue, then drawing back.

Alayna murmured his name, her voice breathy and weak, her wistful tone making him so hard it was almost painful. He urged her closer as he tangled his tongue with hers.

She rose on tiptoe and stretched high to mold herself against him. He cupped her ass to hold her tight while the kiss went on and on. They were both breathless when he raised his head.

After he snagged her zipper and pulled it down, she leaned forward to let the top fall down her arms, baring her cleavage in a pale green lace bra that cupped her breasts like seashells. He ran his fingers beneath one silky strap.

"Did you buy this for me?" he asked.

She laughed. "I bought this with you in mind." She stepped out of the dress and tossed it over the back of a small chair wedged in the corner of the room.

He realized what he'd said and laughed, then turned serious again when he saw the matching panties, more a thong with a shell-shaped patch that covered so little, he thought he might come just looking at her.

"If I'd known what you had on under that dress this morning, you'd never have made it out of the house."

"I'll have to flash you next time, so you'll know." She pulled the comforter off the bed and tossed it on the floor. When she crawled up on the mattress, he nearly swallowed his tongue. Her, bare, round, shapely ass drove him crazy.

He stripped off his clothes and slid in beside her. She turned against him and draped a knee over his hip, her fingers following the freshly healed incision along his collarbone before she pressed her lips to it. When she looked up, he knew in a heartbeat what made her different from all the other women who had passed through his life. The blend of tenderness and love he read in her face reached deep inside him and filled the emptiness he'd lived with for too long.

"I love you, Alayna." He had never meant the words more or needed to say them so badly.

"I'm so grateful you were there at the bank that day. I think I'd have searched for you my whole life if you hadn't been."

He kissed her with all the pent-up emotion he couldn't express in words. He couldn't touch her enough, hold her close enough. For every caress he gave her, she replied with one of her own.

When he peeled away her delectable undies, he did it with a reverence he'd never shown another woman. Because she wasn't any other woman, she was the one.

Bracing his weight on his good right arm, he thrust inside her, fitting their bodies tightly together, and he reveled in the pleasure and rightness of claiming her, of belonging to her. They moved together slowly, taking their time, stretching out their pleasure.

Alayna had never felt so close to him, so overwhelmed by the act of making love. Every time he drew back and pressed forward to fill her, she ached with need, yet felt complete. The pleasure built until she rose beneath him sealing their bodies together as the orgasm crested and took her. With two more thrusts, Bowie followed, and the sensation lifted her up again in a gentler wave.

For a long moment neither of them moved. When he did, he was quick to pull her against him, skin to skin.

"I think we need a bigger place."

Alayna laughed. Out of all the things she expected him to say, that was the last.

"The girls need more space. They're going to want their own rooms, and your closet isn't big enough for both our stuff, and my place is only one bedroom. I have that twenty thousand as a down payment. We could find a house."

She cupped his cheek and turned his head to look him in the face. "Don't you think you might be rushing into things?"

He swept her features with a look that stole her breath. "We've wasted ten years, Alayna. How much longer do you want to wait?"

Her eyes misty, she blinked back the tears and said, her lips nearly touching his, her warm breath stirring him again, "Not one more minute."

THE END

BOOKS BY
TERESA J. REASOR

MILITARY ROMANTIC SUSPENSE
BREAKING FREE (Book 1 of the SEAL Team Heartbreakers)
BREAKING THROUGH (Book 2 of the SEAL Team Heartbreakers)
BREAKING AWAY (Book 3 of the SEAL Team Heartbreakers)
BREAKING TIES (A SEAL Team Heartbreakers Novella)
BUILDING TIES (Book 4 of the SEAL Team Heartbreakers)
BREAKING BOUNDARIES
(Book 5 of the SEAL Team Heartbreakers)
BREAKING OUT (BOOK 6 of the SEAL Team Heartbreakers)
BREAKING POINT (A SEAL Team Heartbreakers Novella)
BREAKING HEARTS (Book 7 of the SEAL Team Heartbreakers)

PARANORMAL ROMANCE
TIMELESS
DEEP WITHIN THE SHADOWS (Book 1 of the Superstition Series)
DEEP WITHIN THE STONE (Book 2 of the Superstition Series)
WHISPER IN MY EAR
HAVE WAND, WILL TRAVEL
(A Magic and Mayhem Novella)
HAVE WAND, WILL TRAVEL: ONCE BITTEN, TWICE SHY
(A Magic and Mayhem Novel)
HAVE WAND, WILL TRAVEL: ADVENTURES OF A WITCHY
WALLFLOWER
(A Magic and Mayhem Novel)
(Coming June 20, 2018)

HISTORICAL ROMANCE
CAPTIVE HEARTS
HIGHLAND MOONLIGHT
TO CAPTURE A HIGHLANDER'S HEART: THE TRILOGY

The Highland Moonlight Spinoff Trilogy in parts
TO CAPTURE A HIGHLANDER'S HEART: THE BEGINNING
TO CAPTURE A HIGHLANDER'S HEART: THE COURTSHIP
TO CAPTURE A HIGHLANDER'S HEART:
THE WEDDING NIGHT

SHORT STORIES
AN AUTOMATED DEATH: A STEAMPUNK SHORT STORY
CAUGHT IN THE ACT: A HUMOROUS SHORT STORY

CHILDREN'S BOOK
WILLY C. SPARKS: THE DRAGON WHO LOST HIS FIRE